By JANET EVANOVICH

THE FOX AND O'HARE NOVELS
with Lee Goldberg
The Heist

THE STEPHANIE PLUM NOVELS
One for the Money
Two for the Dough
Three to Get Deadly
Four to Score
High Five
Hot Six
Seven Up
Hard Eight
To the Nines
Ten Big Ones
Eleven on Top
Twelve Sharp
Lean Mean Thirteen
Fearless Fourteen
Finger Lickin' Fifteen
Sizzling Sixteen
Smokin' Seventeen
Explosive Eighteen
Notorious Nineteen

THE BETWEEN THE NUMBERS NOVELS
Visions of Sugar Plums
Plum Lovin'
Plum Lucky
Plum Spooky

THE LIZZY AND DIESEL NOVELS
Wicked Appetite
Wicked Business

THE BARNABY AND HOOKER NOVELS
Metro Girl
Motor Mouth
Trouble Maker (graphic novel)

NONFICTION
How I Write

NOTORIOUS
NINETEEN

NOTORIOUS NINETEEN

A STEPHANIE PLUM NOVEL

Janet Evanovich

BANTAM BOOKS • NEW YORK

Notorious Nineteen is a work of fiction. Names, places, characters, and incidents are the products of the author's imagination or are used fictitiously. Any resemblance to actual events, locales, or persons, living or dead, is entirely coincidental.

2013 Bantam Books Mass Market Edition

Copyright © 2012 by Evanovich, Inc.

Excerpt from *Takedown Twenty* by Janet Evanovich copyright © 2013 by Evanovich, Inc.

Published in the United States by Bantam Books, an imprint of The Random House Publishing Group, a division of Random House LLC, a Penguin Random House Company, New York.

BANTAM BOOKS and the HOUSE colophon are registered trademarks of Random House LLC.

Originally published in hardcover in the United States by Bantam Books, an imprint of The Random House Publishing Group, a division of Random House LLC, in 2012.

This book contains an excerpt from the novel *Takedown Twenty* by Janet Evanovich. This excerpt has been set for this edition only and may not reflect the final content of the forthcoming book.

ISBN 978-0-345-52776-9
eBook ISBN 978-0-345-52775-2

Cover design by Phil Pascuzzo

Printed in the United States of America

www.bantamdell.com

9 8 7 6 5 4 3 2 1

Bantam Books mass market edition: November 2013

NOTORIOUS NINETEEN

ONE

"I DON'T KNOW WHY we gotta sit here baking in your car in the middle of the day, in the middle of the summer, in the middle of this crummy neighborhood," Lula said. "It must be two hundred degrees in here. Why don't we have the air conditioning on?"

"It's broken," I told her.

"Well, why don't you have your window open?"

"It's stuck closed."

"Then why didn't we take *my* car? My car's got everything."

"Your car is red and flashy. People notice it and remember it. This is the stealth car," I said.

Lula shifted in her seat. "Stealth car, my big toe. This thing is a hunk of junk."

This was true, but it was *my* hunk of junk, and due to a professional dry spell it was all I could afford. Lula and I work for my cousin Vinnie's bail bonds office in Trenton, New Jersey. I'm a fugitive apprehension agent, and Lula is my sometimes partner.

We were currently parked on Stark Street, doing surveillance on a rooming house, hoping to catch Melvin Barrel coming or going. He'd been accused of possession with intent to sell, Vinnie bonded him out of jail, and Barrel hadn't shown for his court date. Lula makes a wage as the office file clerk, but I only make money if I catch skips, so I was motivated to tough it out in my hellishly hot car, hoping for a shot at snagging Barrel.

"I worked this street when I was a 'ho," Lula said, "but I was in a better section. This here block is for losers. No high-class 'ho would work this block. Darlene Gootch worked this block but it turned out she was killing people as a hobby."

Lula was fanning herself with a crumpled fast food bag she'd found on the floor in the back of my car, and the smell of stale French fries and ketchup wafted out at me.

"You keep waving that bag around and we're going to smell like we work the fry station at Cluck-in-a-Bucket," I said to her.

"I hear you," Lula said. "It's making me hungry, and much as I like the aroma of food grease, I don't want it stuck in my hair, on account of I just had my hair done. I picked out the piña colada conditioner so I'd smell like a tropical island."

Lula's hair was fire-engine red today and straightened to the texture of boar bristle. Her brown skin was slick with sweat. Her extra-voluptuous plus-size body was squeezed into a size 2 petite poison-green spandex skirt, and the acres of flesh that constituted her chest overflowed a brilliant yellow spaghetti-strap tank top. At 5'5" she's a couple inches shorter than me. We're about the same age, which puts us in the proximity of thirtysomething. And we're both single.

My name is Stephanie Plum and I haven't got Lula's body volume or the attitude that goes with it. My attitude goes more toward survival mode. I have shoulder-length curly brown hair, blue eyes almost always enhanced by a swipe of black mascara, decent teeth, a cute nose in the middle of my face, and I can almost always button the top button on my jeans.

"Look at this fool coming at us, walking down the middle of the street," Lula said. "What the heck is he doing?"

The fool was a skinny guy dressed in homie clothes. Baggy pants, wifebeater T-shirt, $700 basketball shoes. He was jogging more than walking, and every couple steps he'd look over his shoulder and scan the street. He spotted Lula and me, made a course correction, and ran straight for us. He reached my car, grabbed the driver's side door handle and yanked, but nothing happened.

"What's with that?" Lula asked.

"My door's stuck," I said. "It happens when it gets hot."

The skinny guy had his face pressed to my window, and he was yelling at us.

"What's he saying?" Lula asked. "I can't make it out, and I'm gonna go blind from the sun reflecting on his gold tooth with the diamond chip in it."

"I think he's saying if I don't open the door, he'll kill me."

"That don't sound appealing," Lula said. "Maybe this is a good time to go get lunch."

I turned the key in the ignition, and the engine cranked over and died. I turned it again and there was silence. I looked back at the skinny guy and realized he had a gun pointed at me. Not just any old gun either. This gun was *big*.

"Open your door," he yelled. "Open your damn door."

Lula had her purse on her lap and was fumbling around in it. "I got a gun in here somewhere," she said. "Keep him busy while I find my gun."

I fidgeted with the door handle on my side so it would look like I was trying to open it. "Here's the plan," I said to Lula. "When you find your gun you let me know so I can duck down and you can shoot him."

"That would be a good plan," Lula said, "but I might not have my gun with me. I might have left it home when I changed from my red purse to my yellow purse. You know how I am about the right accessories."

The guy was really agitated now. He had the gun

against my window and his forehead was glued to the gun, like he was sighting for the kill.

"Maybe you should open the door and see what he wants," Lula said. "Maybe he just feels like going for a ride. In which case he could have this piece of dog doodie car, and I'd be happy to take a bus home."

"Hold on," I yelled at the guy. "I'm going to open the door."

"What?" he yelled back.

"Hold on!"

I hauled back and rammed the door full force with my shoulder. The door flew open, catching the guy by surprise, the gun discharged, and he went down to the ground and didn't move.

We got out of the car and stared down at the guy. He was statue-still and bleeding from his forehead.

"You killed him," Lula said. "You hit him with the door, and he shot hisself."

"It was an accident."

"Don't matter. You killed him all the same." Lula toed him, but he still didn't move. "Yep," she said. "He's dead."

I looked at my car and realized a bullet was embedded in the roof, just over the window. I bent down and took a closer look at the skinny guy.

"He's not shot," I said. "He got hit in the head when the gun kicked back. He's just knocked out."

"Hunh," Lula said. "That would have been my second theory."

We dragged him to the gutter so he wouldn't get run over and we got back into my car. I tried the key, but there was no response.

"I bet your battery's no good," Lula said. "That's my professional opinion. You're gonna have to call someone to juice up your battery. And in the meantime I'm going across the street to that sad-ass grocery store to get a soda. I'm all dehydrated."

I crossed the street with Lula, we got sodas, and we stood in front of the store chugging them down. A black Cadillac Escalade rolled down the street and stopped by my car. Two idiots wearing gang colors got out, scooped the skinny guy up, and threw him into the Escalade. A yellow Hummer careened around the corner, jerked to a stop half a block in front of the Escalade, and two guys in the Hummer leaned out the window and opened fire. The Escalade returned fire. A guy wearing a crooked ball cap popped his head out of the sunroof on the Hummer, aimed a rocket launcher at the Escalade, and *phoonf!* the rocket went wide of the Escalade and blew up my car. There was a moment of silence, then both cars roared away.

Lula and I stared wide-eyed and openmouthed at the fireball consuming my car.

"Jeez Louise," I said.

"Yeah, but you gotta look on the positive side," Lula said. "You don't have to worry about charging up the battery."

Lula's comment might have seemed casual considering the gravity of the situation, but truth is this wasn't the first time someone had exploded my car.

My cellphone rang, and I knew from the ringtone it was Ranger.

"You're off the grid," Ranger said when I answered.

"Someone blew up my car."

There was a moment of silence. "And?"

"I guess I could use a ride."

"Babe," Ranger said. And he disconnected.

"He coming for us?" Lula asked.

"Yep."

Ranger is Latino and former Special Forces turned semi-legitimate businessman. He's part owner of a security firm located in an inconspicuous seven-story building in the center of the city. I work for him on occasion, I've had one or two romantic skirmishes with him, and he has the sometimes annoying, sometimes convenient habit of installing tracking devices on my vehicles. His hair is dark brown and currently cut short. His eyes are mostly black. His body is perfect from the tip of his toes to the top of his head. He plays by his own rules, and his attitude is uncompromising. He only wears black, and he only drives black cars. He's smart. He's strong in every possible way. And being in his crosshairs is flat out scary.

No one came out of the little grocery store to look at the fire. No police cars or fire trucks screeched to the scene. It was as if this was business as usual and best ignored.

I looked down the street at the rooming house, wondering if Melvin Barrel was in there melting down in a pool of sweat. No air conditioners sticking out of any of the windows in the rooming house. For sure no central air.

"I bet that skinny guy you almost killed was running away from someone, and that's why he wanted your car," Lula said.

I leaned against the building. "It was a bad choice of cars."

"Yeah, but he didn't know that. All's he saw was two women sitting in a car like a couple dummies. He probably figured if we was stupid enough to be sitting in the car, we was stupid enough to give it over to him."

"He was wrong."

"Not by much," Lula said.

Fifteen minutes later Ranger eased his black Porsche Cayenne to a stop in front of Lula and me. I got into the front passenger seat, and Lula got into the back.

Ranger glanced at the charred cadaver of twisted metal and smoldering tires that used to be my car. "Yours?" he asked me.

"Yep," I said.

"Do I need to know how this happened?"

"Nope."

• • •

Ranger idled in front of the bonds office and Lula got out. I moved to follow Lula, and Ranger wrapped his hand around my wrist. "Stay. I want to talk to you."

I'm not currently in a physical relationship with Ranger. Ranger has clear priorities and matrimony isn't high on the list. In fact, it isn't on the list *at all*. Until recently marriage hasn't been high on my priorities list either, but my mother feels otherwise, and as much as I hate to admit it my mother is wearing me down.

"I need a date," Ranger said.

My voice ratcheted up an octave. "You want me to get you a date?"

"No. I want you to *be* my date. I have to attend a black tie event, and I need someone watching my back."

"Me?" I wasn't exactly The Terminator.

"People would talk if I brought Tank."

Tank is appropriately named. He's Ranger's shadow and second in command at Rangeman. And Ranger was right. Tank would make a controversial date.

"When is this?" I asked Ranger.

"Tomorrow night."

"Tomorrow? I can't just drop everything and do this tomorrow. You should have asked me sooner.

I'm seeing Morelli. It's Friday date night. We're going to the movies and then . . . "

"I can give you a better *and then*," Ranger said.

I went breathless for a beat at the thought of Ranger's *and then*. Morelli was an amazing lover, but Ranger was magic. I pulled myself together and narrowed my eyes at Ranger, hoping I looked determined.

"You and I are done doing *and then* with each other," I said. "There is absolutely no more *and then*. Morelli and I have an understanding."

"Which is?"

"It's vague."

"Babe."

"I'm serious this time. I might be ready to have a committed adult relationship."

Joe Morelli is a Trenton cop working plainclothes, crimes against persons. I've known him forever and our relationship has progressed from downright hostile, to deliciously hot, to *maybe we could actually live with each other without complete mayhem*. He's six feet of hard muscle and Italian libido. His hair is black and wavy. His eyes are brown and assessing. His style is casual. He wears jeans, untucked shirts, and a Glock 19, and he has a big shaggy dog named Bob.

"I'll pay you," Ranger said.

"Excuse me?"

"I'll hire you for the night. You can be my bodyguard."

At the risk of sounding mercenary, this got my attention. I was a month behind on my rent, and I wasn't having great luck with the fugitive apprehension stuff. Vinnie had mostly low bond skips this month, and I was barely making pizza money, much less rent money. And I was pretty sure I could muster enough self-control to keep from ripping Ranger's clothes off.

"What exactly would bodyguarding entail?" I asked him.

"The usual. You take a bullet for me if necessary, and you manage the small talk."

"You can't manage your own small talk?"

"Making polite conversation isn't at the top of my skill set."

"I've noticed." Okay, so this doesn't sound so bad, plus I'd get dinner, right? "What time will you pick me up?"

"Six o'clock. This event is in Atlantic City. Dinner is at eight."

TWO

I LEFT RANGER AND joined Lula in the bonds office. The building was brand-new and light-years better than the old office. It had been built on the same footprint as the old office but the walls were freshly painted, the tile on the floor was unscuffed, the furniture was inexpensive but comfortable and free from food and coffee stains.

Lula had claimed her usual spot on the faux leather couch, and Connie, the office manager, was at her desk. Connie is a couple years older than me, a much better shot, and better connected. Connie's family is old school Italian mob and far more professional than Trenton's gangsta morons when it comes to crime-related skills such as whacking, hijacking, and money laundering. Connie looks a lot like Betty Boop with big hair and a mustache. Today she was wearing a short black pencil skirt, a wide black patent-leather belt, and a tight red sweater with a low scoop neck that showed a lot of her Betty Boopness.

I looked over at the closed door behind Connie that led to my cousin Vinnie's private office. "Is Vinnie in?" I asked her.

Connie looked up from her computer. "No. He's downtown bonding out Jimmy Palowski. Palowski's neighbor caught him watering her flowers without a watering can, if you get what I mean. He got arrested for drunk and disorderly, and indecent exposure."

I sunk into the molded plastic office chair in front of Connie's desk. "My car got blown up."

"I heard. Same old, same old."

"I need money. Anything good come in?"

"Do you remember Geoffrey Cubbin?"

"Yeah. He was arrested last month for embezzling five million dollars from Cranberry Manor."

Connie handed me a file. "The judge set a really high bond, and Vinnie signed on the dotted line. Cubbin didn't seem like much of a risk. No prior arrests, and he was claiming he was innocent. Plus he had a wife and a cat. Men with cats are usually good risks. Very stable."

"And?"

"He's gone. Disappeared off the face of the earth, along with the five million. There's an article in the paper this morning. He was at home awaiting his trial, he woke up in the middle of the night with pain and fever and went to the ER, and four hours later he was minus his appendix. That was three days ago. When his wife arrived at the hospital yesterday to take him home, he was gone. Vanished. No one saw him leave."

"Is this our problem?"

"It'll officially be our problem on Monday. If he doesn't show up for court we'll forfeit the bond. Personally, I think it sounds like he skipped. His court date was right around the corner, and he panicked. If he'd gotten convicted, he'd be looking at a good chunk of prison time. You might want to poke around before the trail gets cold."

I took the file and leafed through it. Geoffrey Cubbin was forty-two years old. Wharton business school graduate. Managed the Cranberry Manor assisted-living facility. I studied his photo. Pleasant-looking guy. Brown hair. Glasses. No tattoos or piercings noted. His height was listed at 5'10". Average weight plus a few extra pounds. He had a wife and a cat. No kids.

The hospital was the logical place to start. It was also the closest. Cubbin lived in Hamilton Township, and Cranberry Manor was a thirty-five- to forty-minute drive when traffic was heavy in downtown Trenton.

"No," Lula said.

"No what?" I asked her.

"No, I'm not goin' to the hospital with you. I saw that look on your face, and I know you figured you'd start by goin' to the hospital. And I'm not goin' on account of I don't like hospitals. They smell funny, and they're filled with sick people.

Last time I was in a hospital it was depressin'. And I think I might have picked up a fungus. Lucky for me I got a high resistance to that sort of thing, and it was one of them twenty-four-hour funguses."

St. Francis Hospital is about a half mile down Hamilton Avenue from the bonds office. It's on the opposite side of the street from the bonds office, so it's officially in the Burg. The Burg is a close-knit, blue-collar, residential chunk of South Trenton that runs on gossip, good Catholic guilt, and pot roast at six o'clock. It's bordered by Chambers Street, Hamilton Avenue, Broad Street, and Liberty Street. I grew up in the Burg and my parents still live there, in a small two-family house on High Street.

"Not a problem," I said. "I can walk to St. Francis."

"He wasn't at St. Francis," Connie said. "He went to Central Hospital on Joy Street."

"You never gonna walk there," Lula said. "That's way off Greenwood."

"Drive me to the hospital," I said to Lula. "You can wait in the lobby."

"I'll drive you to the hospital," Lula said, "but I'm not waiting in no lobby. I'll wait in my car."

• • •

Central Hospital had been built in the forties and looked more like a factory than a hospital. Dark red brick. Five floors of grim little rooms where patients were warehoused. A small drive court for the ER. A double door in the front of the building. The double door opened onto a lobby with a standard issue information desk, brown leather couches, and two fake trees. I'd never been in the OR, but I imagined it as being medieval. The hospital didn't have a wonderful reputation.

"Hunh," Lula said, pulling into the parking garage. "I suppose I'm gonna have to go with you. If you don't have me watching out for shit, you're liable to not come out. That's how hospitals get you. You go in to visit and before you know it they got a camera stuck up your butt and they're lookin' to find poloponies."

"Do you mean polyps?"

"Yeah. Isn't that what I said? Anyway my Uncle Andy had that done, and they said he had them polyps, and next thing they took his intestines out and he had to poop in a bag. So I'm here to tell you there's no way I'm poopin' in a bag."

"I'm not crazy about this conversation," I said. "Could we move on to something else?"

Lula parked her red Firebird on the second level and cut the engine. "I'm just sayin'."

We entered the hospital through the front door and I approached the woman at the desk.

"I'm investigating the Cubbin disappearance," I said to the woman. "I'd like to speak to your head of security."

"Do you have ID?" she asked.

Here's the deal about doing fugitive apprehension for a bail bondsman. I have all sorts of rights to apprehend because the bondee has signed them over, but I'm not a police officer. Fortunately most people aren't clear on the technicalities. And most people don't look too closely at my ID. Truth is, I bought my badge and my laminated ID on the Internet. Seven dollars and ninety-five cents plus postage. They look pretty genuine. Not that I'm lying or anything. They say Bond Enforcement Agent, and they have my name on them. Not my problem if people confuse me with a cop, right?

I flashed her my badge and my ID, her phone rang, and she moved me along.

"First floor," she said. "Room 117. Down the corridor to the right. If no one's there you can page him on the intercom at the door."

I mouthed *thank you* and Lula and I went in search of Room 117.

"I've only been here a minute, and already I can feel myself getting hospital cooties," Lula said. "I itch all over. I got the hospital heebie-jeebies."

The door to Room 117 was closed. I knocked and someone inside grunted acknowledgment. I opened the door and was surprised to find Randy Briggs in a tan and blue security guard uniform.

I've crossed paths with Randy Briggs on several occasions, and some have been more pleasant than others. Briggs is single, in his early forties, has a small amount of sandy blond hair and a narrow face with close-set eyes. He's three feet tall, and he has the personality of a rabid raccoon.

"Whoa," I said. "What's with the uniform?"

"What's it look like?" Briggs said. "I'm head of security."

"You were always a tech guy," I said. "What happened to the computer programming?"

"No jobs. The shit's made in China and the tech support comes from Sri Lanka. The only reason I got *this* job is because they were afraid I'd pull a dwarf discrimination suit."

"They let you have a gun?" Lula asked.

"Yeah," Briggs said. "I'm real good at shooting guys in the nuts, being they're at eye level."

It was a small office furnished with a desk and some uncomfortable-looking chairs. There was a dinosaur computer, a phone, a stack of files in manila folders, and a couple walkie-talkies. There were a bunch of handwritten notes and several photographs tacked to a bulletin board behind the desk. It looked to me like one of the photographs was of Geoffrey Cubbin.

"Are those the ones who got away?" I asked Briggs.

"That's what they tell me. I haven't been on the job that long. I've only had one go south on my watch."

"Geoffrey Cubbin."

"Yep. The night nurse checked him at two A.M. and reported him sleeping. The next entry on his chart was at six A.M. and he was gone, along with his clothes and personal effects."

"Is that what his chart says?" I asked Briggs.

"No. That's what the paper said. Jesus, don't you read the paper?"

"So how's this dude manage to walk out of here if he just had his appendix yanked out?" Lula asked. "That gotta hurt. Maybe it was that he died and got rolled down to the meat locker and no one thought to look there. Oh no, wait a minute, he wouldn't have gotten dressed to die."

"Cubbin was looking at about ten years of eating prison food and stamping out license plates," Briggs said. "You could get past a little pain to walk away from that."

"I'd like to talk to his doctor and the night nurse," I said to Briggs. "Do you have their names?"

"No. And I'm not getting them for you either. I'm here to uphold hospital confidentiality. I'm the top cop."

"Looks to me like you're the bottom half of the top cop," Lula said.

Briggs cut his eyes to Lula. "Looks to me like you're fat enough to be a whole police force."

"You watch your mouth," Lula said. "I could sit on you and squash you like a bug. Be nothing left of you but a grease spot on the floor."

"There'll be no squashing," I said to Lula. "And *you*," I said to Briggs, pointing my finger at him. "You need to get a grip."

I whirled around and swished out of Briggs's office with Lula close on my heels. I returned to the lobby and called Connie.

"Do we know who operated on Cubbin?" I asked her. "I want to talk to the doctor."

"Hang tight. I'll make some phone calls."

Lula and I browsed through the gift shop, took a turn around the lobby, and Connie called back.

"The doctor's name is Craig Fish," Connie said. "I got his name from your grandmother. She's plugged into the Metamucil Medicare Gossip Hotline. He's a general surgeon in private practice, with privileges at St. Francis and Central. His office is in the Medical Arts Building two blocks from Central. He's married with two kids in college. One in California and the other in Texas. No litigation against him. No derogatory information on file."

We drove to the Medical Arts Building, and Lula dropped me off at the door.

"There's a Dunkin' Donuts shop in that gas station on the corner," she said. "I might have to get some donuts on account of I feel weak after being in the hospital and getting the cooties and all."

"I thought you were trying to lose weight."

"Yeah, but this could be an emergency situation. The cooties might have eaten up all my sugar, and I need to shovel some more in."

"That's so lame," I said to her. "Why don't you just admit you want donuts and you have no willpower?"

"Yeah, but that don't sound as good. You want any donuts?"

"Get me a Boston Kreme."

I took the elevator to the fourth floor and found Fish's office. There were two people in the waiting room. A man and a woman. Neither of them looked happy. Probably contemplating having something essential removed from their bodies in the near future. I flashed my credentials at the receptionist and told her I'd like to have a moment with the doctor.

"Of course," she said. "He's with a patient right now, but I'll let him know you're here."

Ten minutes and three dog-eared magazines later I was ushered into Fish's small, cluttered office.

"I only have a few minutes," he said. "How can I help you?"

Craig Fish was a bland man in his mid-fifties. He had steel gray hair, a round cherubic face, and his blue and white striped dress shirt was stretched tight across his belly. He wasn't fat, but he wasn't fit either. He had some family photos on his desk. His two kids on a beach somewhere, smiling at the camera. And a picture of himself getting cozy with a blond woman who looked on the short side of thirty. She was spilling out of her slinky dress, and she had a diamond the size of Rhode Island on her finger. I assumed this was his latest wife.

"Did Geoffrey Cubbin give any indication he intended to leave early?" I asked him.

"No. He didn't seem unusually anxious. The operation was routine, and his post-op was normal."

"Do you have any idea where he might be?"

"Usually when patients leave prior to discharge they go home."

"Apparently that wasn't the case this time. Does this happen a lot?"

"Not a lot, but more often than you'd think. People get homesick, dissatisfied with care, worried about expenses, and sometimes it's the result of a drug reaction and the patient isn't thinking clearly."

"Has Cubbin made an appointment for a recheck?"

"You'd have to ask my receptionist about that. I only see my patient list for the current day."

His intercom buzzed and his receptionist reminded him Mrs. Weinstein was in Examining Room 3.

I stopped at the desk on the way out and asked if Geoffrey Cubbin had scheduled a post-op appointment. I was told he had not.

Lula was idling at the curb when I left the medical building. I buckled myself in next to her and looked into the Dunkin' Donuts box on the floor. It was empty.

"Where's my donut?" I asked her.

"Oops. I guess I ate it."

Lucky me. Better on Lula's thighs than on mine. Especially since I was going to have to squeeze into a cocktail dress tomorrow night.

"Now what?" Lula asked. "Are we done for the day? I'm not feeling so good after all those donuts. I was only going to eat two, but then I lost track of what I was doing and next thing there weren't any more donuts. It was like I blacked out and someone came and ate the donuts."

"You have powdered sugar and jelly stains on your tank top."

"Hunh," Lula said, looking down at herself. "Guess I was the one ate them."

"It would be great if you could drive me to my parents' house so I can borrow Big Blue."

Big Blue is a '53 powder blue and white Buick that got deposited in my father's garage when my Great Uncle Sandor checked himself in to Happy Hills Nursing Home. It drives like a refrigerator on wheels, and it does nothing for my image. Only Jay Leno could look good driving this car. In its favor, it's free.

THREE

MY PARENTS LIVE IN a small mustard yellow and brown two-story house that shares a wall with an identical house that is painted lime green. I suppose the two-family house seemed like an economical idea forty years ago at the time of construction. And there are many of them in the Burg. Siamese twins conjoined at the living room downstairs and master bedroom upstairs, with separate brains. The house has a postage stamp front yard, a small front porch, and a long, narrow backyard. The floor plan is shotgun. Living room, dining room, kitchen. Three small bedrooms and a bathroom upstairs.

My Grandma Mazur lives with my parents. She moved in when my Grandpa Mazur's arteries totally clogged with pork fat and he got a one-way ticket to God's big pig roast in the sky. Grandma was at the front door when Lula eased the Firebird to a stop at the curb. I used to think Grandma had a telepathic way of knowing when I approached, but I now realize Grandma just stands at the door watching the cars roll by, like the street is a reality show. Her face lit, and she waved as we drove up.

"I like your granny," Lula said. "She always looks like she's happy to see us. That's not something happens every day. Half the time we knock on a door and people shoot at us."

"Yes, but that's only half the time. Sometimes they just run away. See you tomorrow."

"Tomorrow, Kemo Sabe."

"How's business?" Grandma asked when I got to the door. "Did you catch anyone today? Where's your car?"

"My car got blown up."

"Again? How many does that make this month?"

"It's the only one this month. I was hoping I could borrow Big Blue."

"Sure, you can borrow it whenever you want. I don't drive it on account of it don't make me look hot."

I suppose everything's relative, but I thought it would take more than a fast car to make Grandma look hot. Gravity hasn't been kind to Grandma. She also doesn't have a license, due to a heavy foot on the accelerator. Still, I suspected lack of license wouldn't stop her if she had access to a Ferrari.

I heard a car door slam and turned to see Lula coming toward us.

"I smell fried chicken," Lula said.

Grandma waved her in. "Stephanie's mother is

frying some up for dinner. And we got a chocolate cake for dessert. We got plenty if you want to stay."

A half hour later Lula and I were at the dining room table, eating the fried chicken with my mom, dad, and Grandma Mazur.

"Stephanie blew up another car," Grandma Mazur announced, spooning out mashed potatoes.

"Technically some gang guy blew it up," Lula said. "And the car wasn't worth much. The battery was dead."

My mother made the sign of the cross and belted back half a glass of what looked like ice tea but smelled a lot like Jim Beam. My father kept his head down and gnawed on a chicken leg.

"I wasn't in it," I said. "It was an accident."

"I don't understand how you have all these accidents," my mother said. "I don't know of a single other person who's had his car blown up." She looked down the table at my father. "Frank, do you know of anyone else who's ever had their car blown up? *Frank! Are you listening to me?*"

My father picked his head up and a piece of chicken fell out of his mouth. "What?"

"It's our job," Lula said. "It's one of them occupational hazards. Like another hazard is getting hospital cooties. We had to do some investigating in a hospital today, and I might have got the cooties."

"I bet you were tracking down Geoffrey Cubbin," Grandma said. "Connie called me asking about his doctor. I know something about it on account of Lorraine Moochy has a relative in Cranberry Manor, and Lorraine said Cubbin is gonna need a *lot* of doctors if those people get their hands on him."

"What else did Lorraine say about him?" I asked Grandma.

"She said he seemed like a real nice man and then next thing he stole all the money. Cranberry Manor's one of them places you buy into, and it isn't cheap. Cranberry Manor's top of the line considering it's in Jersey. Lorraine says it could close down, and her relative would have her keester tossed out onto the street."

"Sounds like she's boned," Lula said.

"Boned?" my mother asked.

Grandma selected another piece of chicken. "That's a polite way of using the *f* word."

My mother cut her eyes to the kitchen, and I knew she was thinking about refilling her "ice tea." Grandma and I are a trial to her. My mother tries hard to be a good Christian woman and a model of decorum, but Grandma and I not so much. It isn't that we don't *want* to be decorous Christian women. It's just that it doesn't always go that way.

"Vinnie bonded Geoffrey Cubbin out," Lula said. "And now we gotta find him."

"It's a real interesting case," Grandma said. "He just up and got dressed in the middle of the night and walked out. If you ask me it's fishy. And I know his doctor is named Fish, but I don't mean that way. Cubbin had stitches and everything. You don't go jogging down the hall and hailing a cab two days after you get your appendix cut out. You creep around hunched over, doing a lot of moaning and complaining."

"So what do you think happened to him?" Lula asked.

"I don't know, but seems to me he had to have help," Grandma said.

"That's what I think too. And why didn't anyone see him standing waiting for the elevator?" Lula asked.

"Budget cuts," Grandma said. "They hardly got any nurses working. And used to be they had cameras in the elevators, but I hear they go on the fritz all the time. I tell you, hospitals aren't what they used to be. Myra and I go to Central for lunch once a week, but the food's gotten terrible lately and people are turning surly."

"You must know a lot of sick people," Lula said.

"We don't go to visit sick people," Grandma said. "We just go for lunch. They always have a big buffet in the cafeteria, and it's cheap because that's where the people who work at the hospital eat. Everybody's wearing those scrub clothes. It's just like being in *Grey's Anatomy*. All the seniors eat there, and sometimes you can score a date. I met a real hottie there last month, but he had an aneurysm and died before I could haul him in. And then after lunch we go to the Costco and get desserts from the free-sample ladies."

"I love those ladies," Lula said.

"At the end of the month if Myra and me run out of Social Security we skip the hospital and just have lunch from the free-sample ladies," Grandma said.

"Honestly," my mother said. "You make it sound like I don't feed you. There's always good food here for lunch."

"I like to eat out once in a while," Grandma said. "Gives me a reason to put lipstick on. And there's always a lot of drama at the hospital. I got the dirt on all the nurses. You just gotta sit by the right people and keep your ears open."

"We should put you on the case," Lula said to Grandma. "We went to the hospital, and we couldn't find out nothing."

"You tell me what you're looking for, and I'll find it," Grandma said. "I'm real nosy, and I've been thinking about turning professional."

"That would be an excellent plan," Lula said. "We wouldn't have to go back to Central if you were there. We could spend our time doing other important stuff that's not in a hospital."

"It's not an excellent plan," my mother said. "It's an awful plan. Isn't it enough she causes havoc in every funeral home in a twenty-mile radius?"

"Not always," Grandma said. "I just don't like when they have a closed casket. I think it's a gyp. How do you know if there's anyone in there?"

My mother shook her fork at me. "I'm holding you responsible. If your grandmother gets arrested for disturbing the peace in that hospital you can kiss chocolate cake goodbye for the rest of your life. Pineapple upside-down cake too."

"Boy, that's hardball," Lula said.

"I wouldn't want you to do without pineapple upside-down cake," Grandma said. "I guess I shouldn't snoop for you. I gotta go to the hairdresser anyway. There's going to be a big viewing tomorrow night for Stanley Kuberski, and I want to look good. The paper said the Elks will be holding a ceremony for him, and there's a couple hot Elks I got my eye on."

"You should go with your grandmother," my mother said. "Loretta Gross's boy, Cameron, is an Elk. I bet he'll be there, and he just got a divorce."

"Is he hot?" Grandma asked. "I might be interested in him."

"He's too young for you," my mother said.

My father shoveled in potatoes. "*Everyone* is too young for her."

"I'm aiming for young," Grandma said. "When I go out with someone old they die before I can reel them in. Besides, I've been told I don't look my age."

It's true that Grandma doesn't look her age. She looks about ninety.

• • •

It was a little after eight o'clock when Lula and I left my parents' house. Lula drove off in her red Firebird, and I drove off in Big Blue. I had a bag of leftovers on the seat beside me, and I was at a crossroads. I could take the leftovers home, or I could drive the short distance to Morelli's house and share. Sharing seemed like the way to go since I was going to beg off our Friday night date.

Joe Morelli inherited a house from his Aunt Rose. It's just outside the Burg boundary, on a quiet street in a blue-collar neighborhood much like the Burg. It's a small two-story row house that is a comfortable mix of Morelli and his aunt. Her old-fashioned curtains still hang on the windows, but most of the furniture belongs to Morelli and his shaggy red-haired dog Bob. Bob is part Golden Retriever and part Wookiee. He eats everything, loves everyone, and mellows out Morelli.

I parked in front of Morelli's house, went to the door, and let myself in. "Hey!" I yelled. "I've got food. Anybody home?"

Bob gave a *woof* from the kitchen at the back of the house and I heard him gallop toward me. He came at me full speed, put his front paws on my chest, and knocked me flat on my back. He ripped the food bag out of my hand and galloped off.

Morelli sauntered over from the living room and helped me up. "Are you okay?"

"I was bringing you fried chicken, but Bob knocked me down and took the bag of food."

"Damn," Morelli said. "He can't have chicken bones. He hacks them up in the middle of the night."

Morelli left me to track down Bob, there was a lot of yelling and growling from the vicinity of the kitchen, and Morelli returned to the living room with the bag of food, a fork, and two beers. He wrapped an arm around my neck, pulled me into him, and kissed me.

"The Mets are up by two runs," he said. "What's going on with you?"

I sat next to him on the couch and took a beer. "I had to borrow Big Blue, so I had dinner with my parents."

"Something wrong with your car?"

"It accidentally got blown up."

Morelli turned and focused on me. "Car bomb?"

"Hand-held rocket."

The line of his mouth tightened a little, and his eyes narrowed ever so slightly. "It was an *accident*?"

"I was on Stark Street."

"That explains it," Morelli said, his attention back to the bag of food.

He ate the chocolate cake first. He gave some potatoes to Bob. And he put the rest in the fridge for later.

"This is a nice surprise," he said, settling back into the couch. "Do you want to take your clothes off?"

"Whatever happened to romance? What about foreplay?"

"Foreplay goes faster without clothes."

"Fast is important?"

Morelli flicked his eyes back to the television. "They're changing the pitcher. We probably have ten minutes."

"I need more than ten minutes."

Morelli grinned at me, and his eyes got soft and dark. "I know."

"And I get distracted by television."

He remoted the television off. "Yeah, I know that too."

"What happens after ten minutes and the new pitcher's ready to go?"

"Fireworks. And then you tell me I'm amazing."

"Suppose there aren't fireworks after ten minutes?"

"I'm no quitter," Morelli said.

I knew this to be true. "I think I'm getting in the mood," I said to him. "And I can see you're already a couple steps ahead of me."

"You noticed."

"Hard not to."

He nuzzled my neck, popped the snap at the top of my jeans, and slid the zipper down. "Let me help you catch up."

FOUR

MORELLI IS ALWAYS FULLY awake at the crack of dawn, ready to go out and enforce the law or, if I'm in his bed, to grab a quickie while I'm still half asleep. I opened an eye and saw that he was moving around in the dimly lit room. He was clean-shaven, his hair was still damp from his shower, and he was dressed in slacks and a blue dress shirt.

"Is this dress-up Friday?" I asked him.

"I have court." He took his watch off the nightstand and slipped it on. "I'll probably be there most of the morning."

I looked under the covers. I was naked. "Did we have sex this morning?"

"Yeah. You thanked me after and said it was great."

"You're fibbing. I never thank you."

I got out of bed and dropped one of Morelli's T-shirts over my head. I shuffled after him, down the stairs and into the kitchen.

Morelli's kitchen is small but cozy. He's laid new

tile on the floor, put in a new countertop, and re-painted the cabinets and walls. His appliances aren't new but they're newer than mine. His refrig-erator is usually filled with food. His cereal doesn't have bugs in it. And he has a toaster. This all puts him light-years ahead of me in the domestic god-dess race.

A door opens off the kitchen onto Morelli's nar-row backyard. He's had it fenced in for Bob, and Bob was impatiently waiting to get let out to tinkle. Morelli opened the door, and Bob bolted out into the darkness.

"You never get up this early," Morelli said, clos-ing the door, pushing the BREW button on the cof-feemaker. "What's going on?"

"I was hoping you knew something about Geof-frey Cubbin."

"The guy who disappeared from Central Hospi-tal? I don't know much. It's not my case."

"How could someone just walk away in the mid-dle of the night without anyone seeing him?"

"I'm told it happens," Morelli said. "And he had good reason to want to walk away. He didn't have a promising future."

"Who has the case?"

"Lenny Schmidt."

"Did he check to see if Cubbin called a cab?"

Morelli did a palms-up. He didn't know. "I as-sume you're looking for Cubbin because Vinnie wrote the bond."

I dropped two slices of bread into the toaster. "It's a high bond, and I could use the money. I need a new car."

"You always need a new car. What you really need is a new job."

I got two mugs out of his over-the-counter cabinet and put them on the little kitchen dining table. "Which brings me to the other issue. I'm going to have to cancel our date tonight. I told Ranger I'd do security for him at a party. He needed a woman."

"I bet," Morelli said.

"It's *security* at a *party*."

"I don't like you working with him. He's not normal. And he looks at you like you're lunch."

"You look at me like that too."

"Cupcake, you *are* my lunch." Morelli filled the mugs with coffee and spread strawberry jelly on his piece of toast. "Call me if you get done with the party early. If I run into Schmidt I'll ask about the cab, but I doubt Schmidt's done much to find Cubbin. Schmidt's got a full caseload, and at this point Cubbin is more your problem than his." He looked at the black T-shirt I was wearing. It hung about six inches below my doo-dah. "Do you have anything under that shirt?"

"You could peek and find out."

"Tempting, but I'm late for my morning meeting."

"Then I guess you'll never know."

Morelli lifted the hem of the shirt, looked under, and smiled. "I'm in love."

"What about your meeting?"

"I might make some of it if I use my flashers and run the lights."

• • •

Connie and Lula were already at the office when I rolled in. The door to Vinnie's lair was open, and I could smell cigar smoke.

"Is that her?" Vinnie yelled.

There was the sound of a chair scraping back, and Vinnie charged out, the cigar clamped between his teeth. Vinnie is slightly taller than me and looks like a weasel. His dark hair is slicked back, his eyes are crafty, his pants are too tight, and his shoes are too pointy. He has an affinity for pain inflicted by women wielding cuffs and paddles, and he's been rumored to enjoy intimate relationships with barnyard animals. He's married to a perfectly nice woman named Lucille, who for reasons I'll never understand has chosen to endure the marriage. And last but not least, probably because he's such a loser himself, Vincent Plum has a good understanding of the criminal mind, and that makes him an excellent bail bondsman.

"Where is he?" Vinnie asked me.

"Where's who?"

"That asshole Cubbin. Who else? You got him nailed down, right?"

"Not exactly."

Vinnie had his hands in the air. "What not exactly? What does that mean?"

"It means I don't know where he is."

"You're killing me," Vinnie said. "If this agency tanks, it's all your fault. It's on your head. Fatso over there will have to go back to the streets. And Connie'll be doing wet work."

"Excuse me?" Lula said. "Fatso? Did I hear you call me Fatso? Because you better tell me I heard wrong on account of I might have to beat the crap out of you if I heard right."

Vinnie clamped down tighter on his cigar and growled. "Just *find* him," he said to me. And he retreated into his office and slammed the door shut.

"Get a grip," I yelled at him. "He's not even officially FTA until Monday."

"We've got donuts," Connie said, pointing to a box on her desk. "Help yourself."

"I'm going to talk to Cubbin's wife," I said to Connie. "And then I'm going to take a look at the nursing home. Maybe you could make some phone calls for me and find out if he took a cab somewhere when he checked out of the hospital."

Lula was on her feet, her head swiveled around trying to check out her ass. "That's the second person told me I was fat this week. I don't feel fat. I just feel like I got a lot of all the good stuff. What do you think?" she asked Connie and me. "Do you think I'm fat?"

"Well, you're not *thin*," Connie said.

"Some of me's thin," Lula said. "I got thin legs. I got Angelina Jolie ankles."

Connie and I looked at her ankles. Not fat. Possibly Angelina quality.

"It's just between my armpits and my hoo-ha that I'm better than most ladies," Lula said. "I got stuff a man could hang on to. That's one of the reasons I was so good as a 'ho."

"As long as you're healthy," I said to her. "You're healthy, right?"

"Yeah, I feel great. And one of these days I'm gonna go get myself checked out to take a look at my cholesterol, my sugar, and my blood pressure."

Connie took the box of donuts off her desk and threw it into her wastebasket.

"So now what?" Lula asked. "We going to see Mrs. Cubbin?"

I had Cubbin's file open to his bond sheet. He looked worried in the photo, or maybe he was squinting in the sun.

"He lives in Hamilton Township, by the high school," I said.

"We could sneak around and look in his windows and see if he's hanging out in his undies, watching television and popping painkillers," Lula said.

Twenty minutes later Lula and I pulled up to

Cubbin's house. It was a modest white ranch with black shutters and a forest green front door. A white Camry was parked in the driveway leading to the attached garage. Very Middle America.

"Which one of us is going to do the sneaking around, and which one the doorbell ringing?" Lula asked.

"I'm ringing the doorbell," I told her. "You can do whatever you want."

I walked to the small front porch, rang the bell, and Lula skirted the side of the house. The front door opened, and a woman looked out at me.

"What?" she said.

She had fried blond hair, an extra forty pounds on her small frame, a cigarette hanging out of the corner of her mouth, and a spray tan that had turned a toxic shade of orange.

"Mrs. Susan Cubbin?"

"Unfortunately."

"You don't like being Mrs. Cubbin?"

"For eight years I've been married to a man with a two-inch penis and one nut. The loser finally grows balls and steals five million dollars, and I can't get my hands on it." She took a long pull on her cigarette and squinted at me through the smoke haze. "And?"

I introduced myself, showed her my semi-fake badge, and gave her my card.

"Bounty hunter," she said. "So I'm going to help you why?"

"For starters, this house was put up as insurance against the bond."

"Like I care. It's got mold in the basement, the roof's falling apart, and the water heater is leaking. The mortgage is killing me, and the bank won't take it back. I can't even get this disaster foreclosed. I don't want the house. I want the friggin' money. I want to get my stomach stapled."

"Have you seen your husband or heard from him since he left the hospital?"

"No. He didn't even have the decency to tell me not to come pick him up to go home."

"Has anyone heard from him?"

"Not that I know about."

"Did he withdraw any money from your bank account?"

"Do I look like someone who has money in the bank?"

"Most people who skip at least take clothes, but your husband disappeared with just the clothes he wore when he checked in to the hospital."

"He's got five million dollars stashed somewhere. The jerk can buy new clothes."

"Do you have any idea where he might have gone?"

"If I knew where he went, I'd be there, and I'd choke him until he coughed up the money."

"Cranberry Manor would be grateful."

"I don't give a fig about Cranberry Manor,"

Susan said. "Those people are old. They're gonna die. *I* want the money."

A police car angled to a stop behind Lula's Fire-bird and two guys got out. One was sort of a friend of mine, Carl Costanza. We'd done Communion together, among other things. Costanza and his partner stood, hands on their gun belts, looking at Lula's Firebird, then looking at me, sizing up the situation. I gave them a little wave and they walked over.

"We got a report from a neighbor that a woman was acting suspiciously, creeping around this house," Carl said.

"That might be Lula," I told him.

"Who's Lula?" Susan Cubbin asked.

"She's my partner," I said.

"And why is she creeping around my house?"

"She thought she saw a cat. And she's a real cat lover."

"Oh jeez," Susan said, "don't tell me my cat got out again."

"It could always be some other cat," I said.

"I gotta make sure. What color was it? Where's your partner?"

"Hey, Lula!" I yelled.

Lula poked her head around the side of the house. "You call me?"

"What color cat did you see?"

"Say what?"

"You know, the cat you went to find . . . when

you were walking around the house just now. What color was it?"

"White," Lula said.

"Thank goodness," Susan said. "My Fluffy is orange."

"Case closed," Carl said.

"I'd appreciate it if you'd let me know if you hear from your husband," I said to Susan.

"Yeah," Susan said. "Likewise."

We followed Carl and his partner to the curb.

"Was he in there?" Carl asked Lula.

"Not that I could see," Lula said. "You're talking about the white cat, right?"

"Right," Carl said.

We all got into our cars and drove away.

"Now what?" Lula wanted to know.

"Now we visit Cranberry Manor. Did you see anything unusual when you were snooping?"

"I didn't see any sign of Geoffrey Cubbin, but someone had been packing a suitcase."

"Men's clothes or women's clothes?"

"Looked like women's clothes."

My cellphone rang, and Grandma's number came up.

"I'm at the beauty parlor, and I need a ride," Grandma said.

"Where are you going?"

"To the hospital, of course. I'm on the job. I just made that baloney up about the beauty parlor to get out of the house. I figured if your mother knew

I was going to the hospital she'd head for the liquor cabinet."

"We'll be in big trouble if she finds out I took you to the hospital."

"She won't find out. I'm wearing a disguise, and I have a fake ID. As far as anyone knows I'm Selma Whizzer today."

"What's going on?" Lula wanted to know.

"It's Grandma. She's at the beauty parlor, and she needs a ride to the hospital so she can snoop for us. She said she's in disguise."

"I gotta see this. Is she at the beauty parlor on Hamilton by the bridal shop?"

"Yes."

"I'm on it. Tell her we're fifteen minutes out."

FIVE

LULA ALMOST JUMPED THE curb when she saw Grandma in front of the hair salon. Grandma was wearing a blond Marilyn Monroe wig, a hot pink tank top, black Pilates pants, and black kitten heels. She looked like the senior version of an inflatable sex toy doll that needed more air.

"Your granny's real fashion forward with the retro wig, and I love the little pink tank top," Lula said, "but we gotta fatten her up. I don't like to be critical, only she's got too much skin. You could fit a whole other person in that skin."

Grandma tottered over on her little heels. "What do you think?" Grandma said, climbing into the backseat. "I bet you didn't know who it was standing there until I waved at you."

"It's a good disguise," Lula said, "but you might be cold in that tank top when you get into the hospital."

"I got a sweater in my purse," Grandma said.

"I'm all prepared. I could take care of any situation. I'm packing heat more ways than one."

Lula pulled out into traffic. "You telling me you got a gun?"

"Of course I got a gun. I got a big one too. A person's gotta be prepared. You never know when you might have to stop a bank robbery."

"That's true," Lula said. "Good thinking."

"It's *not* good thinking!" I said.

Grandma clicked her seat belt into place. "You sound like your mother."

"Sometimes she's right." Truth is, she was almost always right. And my life would probably be improved if I listened to her more often.

"What are you girls doing today?" Grandma asked.

"We're going to check out Cranberry Manor," Lula said. "It's one of them exploratory trips."

"Maybe I could go with you," Grandma said. "I always wanted to see Cranberry Manor. I heard a lot about it. And then you could drop me off at the hospital on the way back."

"That's not a bad idea," Lula said. "Granny could be our decoy. We could go incognito."

Grandma sat forward. "I could say I'm interested in moving there on account of my son-in-law is a horse's patoot."

"And your mother wouldn't get so mad at you if she found out you took Granny to see about moving into the old people's home," Lula said.

A half hour later we parked in the visitors' lot and entered Cranberry Manor through the front door. It was a typical senior living complex, with a pleasant reception area and two wings for residents.

"This is real pretty," Grandma said. "They have flowers growing outside and everything looks fresh painted."

"That's not going to last long being that they're broke," Lula said.

We stopped at the small informal reception desk in the lobby and told the woman we'd like a tour.

"I'm interested in living here," Grandma said. "I want to see everything."

"Wonderful," the woman said, taking in Grandma's hair and tank top, trying to maintain a friendly smile. "I'll ring Carol. She's our salesperson."

Carol appeared immediately, undoubtedly excited at the thought of extracting money from someone who might not have heard Cranberry Manor was filing for bankruptcy.

"Just down the hall is the dining room," Carol said, leading the way.

"I like the sound of that," Grandma said. "Do they serve cocktails?"

"Not cocktails, but residents can have wine with dinner."

Grandma peeked inside the dining room. "Just like being at a fancy restaurant with tablecloths and everything. Can I have oatmeal and eggs and bacon at breakfast?"

"Yes."

"And coffee cake?"

"Yes."

"Sign me up," Grandma said.

"We have more to see," I told her.

"Yeah, don't get carried away with the oatmeal," Lula said.

"We have two identical wings," Carol said. "They each have their own social center."

The social center we visited looked like a big living room. Large-screen television, three game tables, couches and chairs arranged in conversational groups. Four women were playing bridge at one of the game tables. Two men were watching a *Wheel of Fortune* rerun on the television.

"Excuse me," Grandma said to the women. "I might move here, and I was wondering what you thought of the place."

"They use powdered eggs at breakfast," one of the women said. "They tell us they're real eggs, but I know a powdered egg when I see one."

"And they buy cheap toilet paper," another woman said. "Single ply. And it's all because of that Geoffrey Cubbin."

"And he was a womanizer," the first woman said. "He was having affairs with some of the ladies here."

"You mean some of the ladies who live here?" Grandma asked.

The woman nodded. "There have been rumors."

"I wouldn't mind having an affair," Grandma said.

"Good riddance to bad rubbish," the woman said. "He's gone, and he's not coming back."

The women all nodded in agreement.

"You don't know that for sure," Grandma said. "He could pop up."

"He better not pop up here," the woman said. "It wouldn't be healthy for him, if you know what I mean. We would have put a hit out on him but he stole all our money."

"Let's move on to the exercise area," Carol said, steering Grandma away.

"Do you have any idea what happened to Geoffrey Cubbin?" I asked Carol. "I understand he had his appendix removed and then disappeared from the hospital."

"I don't know anything about that," Carol said. "I have my hands full here, trying to keep the crew from mutiny."

We toured the rest of the building, talked to about forty people, got a brochure and an application from Carol, and returned to the Firebird.

"I could have my own bathroom if I lived here," Grandma said. "That's on the plus side. On the other side I wouldn't have anything to do at night.

How would I get to the funeral home for viewings?"

"Yeah, and those Cranberry people were all cranky," Lula said. "They should be giving them more than one glass of wine at dinner. They should be putting Kahlúa in their coffee in the morning. And if they find Cubbin toes up in a Dumpster they should start the investigation at Cranberry Manor because he's not a popular guy there."

Lula drove us back to Trenton and dropped Grandma off at the hospital.

"Don't shoot anyone," I told Grandma.

"Only if I have to," she said, straightening her wig. "I'll call when I need a ride home."

"I'm hungry," Lula said, driving off. "I could use a healthy lunch like nachos from the convenience store on Olden."

"That's not healthy."

"It's corn and it's got cheese product. That's two of the major food groups."

"If we wait until we get back to the office we can stop at Giovichinni's and get a salad."

"A salad? What do I look like, an alpaca? I'm a big woman. I can't keep going on a salad. I need salt and grease and shit."

I had to get into a slinky little black dress tonight. I wasn't up for salt and grease and shit. "Giovichinni will add all that stuff to your salad. Just ask for it."

"Yeah, but I'll have to pay extra."

I have no willpower. If Lula stops for nachos, I'll get them too. Or even worse, I'll get a couple hotdogs.

"My treat," I said.

"That's different then. Here we go to Giovichinni."

Giovichinni's Deli and Meat Market is just down the street from the bonds office. My family has shopped there for as long as I can remember, and it ranks on a par with the funeral home and the beauty salon for dishing dirt. Lula parked at the curb and we went straight to the deli counter. I got a salad with grilled chicken, and Lula got a salad with barbecued pork, extra bacon, blue cheese, and a side of macaroni and cheese.

"I'm glad you suggested a healthy salad," she said, moving to checkout. "This is just what I needed."

I made a large effort not to grimace. Her salad was a heart attack in a takeout carton. And it looked fabulously delicious. I was going to have a hard time not ripping it out of her hands.

"What's new?" I said to Gina Giovichinni when I got to the register.

"Annette Biel is preggers. We're starting a pool for birth weight and if it looks like her husband or Reggie Mangello."

"She's been seeing Reggie Mangello?"

"He did some drywall for them nine months ago when they fixed up their cellar."

"Anything else? Anything about Geoffrey Cubbin?"

"The guy who ran off with the old people's money? Nope. Haven't heard anything worth repeating."

"I'm looking for him. Let me know if you hear something."

We took our salads back to the office, along with a Greek salad for Connie. Nothing for Vinnie. He'd be out having a nooner with a duck or getting a good whacking from Madam Zaretsky.

"I checked the cabs," Connie said, digging into her salad. "No one had a pickup at or near the hospital the night Cubbin disappeared."

"He didn't drive himself," I said. "His car was in his garage. And he couldn't walk far in his condition. So he had to have help."

"True," Connie said. "Or someone could have snatched him."

"I can almost believe a post-op patient could manage to get himself to the elevator and not get noticed. I'm having a hard time seeing someone kidnap a patient and get him out the door."

"Maybe he went out the window," Lula said. "And then he got collected."

"He was on the fourth floor," I said. "That's a long way down."

Lula shoveled in barbecued pork. "Yeah, he would have had to be encouraged. And it would have made a good *thump*. If he landed on cement his head would've cracked open like Humpty Dumpty, but I'm pretty sure there's grass all around the hospital. So no point poking around, looking for brains."

It was a gruesome possibility, and it didn't make total sense, but it was as good as any theory I had. "If you wanted to kill Cubbin, wouldn't it be easier to do it after he left the hospital?" I asked Lula and Connie.

"Maybe it was some old lady who was already in the hospital for being so old," Lula said.

I speared a tomato chunk. "If she was that old she couldn't get him to the window and shove him out."

"How about that old lady who was playing cards," Lula said. "If she was in the hospital, she could have shoved him out. She had rage going for her. We should check to see if she was in the hospital."

"Have you looked at his relatives?" I asked Connie.

"His parents are deceased. One sister, married, living in Des Moines. A brother in the Denver area."

"Any recent credit card or bank activity?"

"None."

I finished my salad. It was okay, but Lula's looked a lot better.

"No way," Lula said, inching away from me. "Don't be looking at my salad like that. You made your choice. You got your plain ass grilled chicken. Not my fault you got no imagination."

I slouched back onto the couch. "I don't know where to go from here with Cubbin. I could do surveillance on his house, but I don't think he's going back there. Instinct tells me he's either dead or in Tierra del Fuego. And I can't access him in either of those places."

"I have a couple more skips that came in today," Connie said. "And you still have Melvin Barrel at large. Why don't you clean up the small stuff while you wait for something to break loose on Cubbin?"

I took the new files from her and skimmed through the paperwork. "Brody Logan. Took a hammer to a police car and turned it into scrap metal."

"I like it," Lula said. "Why'd he do it?"

"Doesn't say."

"We could find him and ask him," Lula said. "Where's he live?"

"Doesn't say."

"He's homeless," Connie said. "Usually hangs around Third Street and Freemont. Sleeps under the bridge abutment with a bunch of other homeless people."

My eyebrows lifted a quarter of an inch. "Vinnie bonded out a homeless person? How will the guy pay for his bond?"

"Apparently he has some sort of religious artifact

that's worth a lot of money, and he used it as collateral."

"Why is he homeless if he has this thing worth money?"

Connie shrugged and did a palms-up. "Don't know."

The other FTA was Dottie Luchek. She'd been arrested for solicitation at the KitKat Bar, and hadn't shown for court. "This has to be wrong," I said to Connie. "This woman looks like an apple dumpling. And she gives her age as fifty-two."

"A 'ho can come in any size," Lula said. "There's nothing wrong in a 'ho looking like a apple dumpling, and being of a certain age." She leaned over my shoulder and looked at the photo. "That don't look like a 'ho," she said. "I never seen a 'ho look like that. And I've seen a lot of different kinds of 'ho. I wasn't even the same 'ho every day. I had a whole 'ho wardrobe. I had schoolgirl 'ho, and nasty 'ho, and nun 'ho. But I never had this 'ho. This 'ho looks like she just baked her own bread this morning. If some actress played this 'ho, it'd have to be Doris Day."

I shoved the two new files into my messenger bag and hung the bag on my shoulder. "Gotta go. People to see. Things to do."

"I'll go with you," Lula said. "Which one of these losers you gonna see first?"

"Dottie Luchek. She's in Hamilton Township."

SIX

DOTTIE LIVED IN A neighborhood of small single-family houses with backyards large enough for a swing set, a Weber grill, and a picnic table. The yards were fenced for dogs and kids. Landscaping wasn't lush, but it was neat. We parked on the street and walked to her door.

A pleasantly plump woman who was clearly Dottie answered our knock. "Yes?" she asked.

I introduced myself and gave her my card. "You missed your court date," I told her. "We need to take you downtown to reschedule."

"Thank you. That's very nice of you," she said, "but I've decided not to go to court."

"Hah!" Lula said. "Good one."

"I appreciate your point of view," I said to Dottie, "and you don't have to go to court, but you *do* have to reschedule."

"Why?"

"Because," I said.

Because that's how I got paid. And because once

she walked into the municipal building she'd be re-arrested and she'd need a new bond to get released.

We were standing at her open front door and could see some of the house behind her. It was modestly furnished. It was neat and clean. And it looked homey, just like Dottie.

"It looks like you got a comfortable home here," Lula said to Dottie. "How come you were hookin'?"

"I thought about it a lot," Dottie said, "and it seemed like a good career choice. My husband, George, passed two years ago, and suddenly there was no money coming in. I tried to get a job, but I didn't have any luck at it. And then I remembered how George always told me I was good in bed. So prostitution seemed like the logical choice. It was that or lose the house."

"What about your family?" Lula asked. "You have kids?"

"Two. Marie Ellen and Joyce Louise. They're in college. University of Wisconsin."

"Are they home?"

Dottie shook her head. "They're in Wisconsin. They have summer jobs there waiting tables."

"So how'd the hookin' go for you?" Lula asked.

"Terrible. The first man I approached was a policeman. That's when I got arrested."

"That's what happens when you're an amateur," Lula said. "People think being a 'ho is easy, but it takes a lot of skill. You gotta keep your eyes open and be a judge of character."

"He looked like a nice man," Dottie said. "He was wearing a tie."

"Probably what you need is a business manager," Lula said. "Or as we say in the trade, a pimp."

"Jeez Louise," I said to Lula. "Don't tell her that. Hasn't she got enough problems?"

"Just trying to be helpful," Lula said. "After all, it's my area of expertise." Lula looked over at Dottie. "I used to be a 'ho. I was a good one too."

I checked my watch. "We need to move along. You can swap professional secrets in the car."

"I'd like to talk more," Dottie said, "but I don't want to go back to the jail. It smelled funny."

I was getting a bad feeling about this apprehension. I was going to have to handcuff Dottie Luchek and muscle her into the car. She'd be sobbing and begging and moaning, and someone would surely see her and call my mother to complain about me.

"Bring a can of air freshener with you," I said. "Maybe a nice scented candle."

"Yeah, and some hand sanitizer," Lula said.

"That's a wonderful idea," Dottie said. "Wait here. I'll be right back."

"Excellent thinking," Lula said to me. "She wasn't gonna go, and we were gonna have to drag her apple dumpling ass all the way to the car. Which would have been a shame since she seems like a nice lady."

We were on the front porch, and I heard a cupboard door open and close from deep in the house.

Another door slammed shut. I looked at my watch again. I wanted to get to the courthouse before the end of the day. There was the sound of a large door rolling up, and I realized it was the garage door. "Damn!"

"She must be coming out the garage door," Lula said. "Don't she know this door's still open?"

"She's running," I said.

I took off for the garage, and reached it just as she backed out. Her car came out fast, she laid rubber, and sped down the street.

"Hunh," Lula said. "I didn't see that one coming. Where do you suppose she's going?"

"I'm guessing she won't go far. She'll probably park a couple blocks away and call her neighbor to find out if we're still here."

"So we could be sneaky, and one of us could drive away, and one of us could hide out here, since she didn't bother to lock up her house."

My phone rang and an unfamiliar number appeared.

"I got your granny, and I'm turning her over to the police if you don't get her out of my sight in the next ten minutes," the caller said.

"Who is this?"

"Randy Briggs. Who else would be calling? And you're lucky I'm head of security here. Anyone else would have shot her."

"What did she do?"

"What *didn't* she do. Just come get her!"

"I'm on my way, but I'm in Hamilton Township. It might take more than ten minutes. And do *not* call my mother."

"That don't sound good," Lula said. "What was that about?"

"Just drive me to the hospital."

Twenty minutes later, as Lula idled in the Central parking lot, I ran in to retrieve Grandma. I found her handcuffed to a chair in Briggs's office. Her wig was tipped to one side, and I'm pretty sure I saw steam coming off the top of her head.

"What's going on?" I asked Briggs.

"She's a menace," he said. "She set off a fire alarm, and then I found her at a nurses' station, trying to get into the patient database."

"I would have done it too, if this idiot hadn't come along," Grandma said. "I was real close."

"Thank you for not calling the police," I said to Briggs.

"Don't thank me. I didn't do it out of the goodness of my heart. I'd be a laughingstock if one of the police beat hacks heard about an arrest. The headline would be 'Little Man Tackles Old Lady.' Or the gold standard, 'Short Stuff Sticks His Nose in Old Lady's Business.' "

This didn't evoke a good mental picture. "I agree. Not good publicity for the head of Central security. Unlock the cuffs and we'll be out of here."

"I'm not getting near her," Briggs said. "She's an animal. She ripped my shirt and went for my gun."

"That's a big fat lie," Grandma said. "I don't need your gun. I got one of my own."

Briggs handed the key over to me, I got Grandma out of the cuffs, straightened her hair, and herded her past Briggs and out of his office. We crossed the lot, I loaded Grandma into the Firebird, and Lula took off.

"How'd it go?" Lula asked Grandma.

"I got some good stuff," Grandma said. "And I had shrimp salad for lunch. They make a real good shrimp salad. Mitch McDoogle was there with two of his lodge buddies, and he didn't even recognize me. It might have been on account of his cataracts, but I still had a pretty good disguise."

"What did you find out?" Lula asked.

"I got the name of the night nurse that was check-ing on Cubbin. Her name's Norma Kruger. I heard a group of nurses talking about her at lunch. And I heard her name before. She gets around, if you know what I mean. I've never seen her because she only works the night shift, but I think she's a looker. Rumor is she disappears into the broom closet with some of the doctors."

"Well, a girl's gotta do what a girl's gotta do," Lula said.

"Yeah, and I wouldn't mind doing it," Grandma said. "I just got trouble finding a man that don't have a heart attack opening the condom package. They gotta make it easier to get them dang things open. It gets to be depressing. There's paramedics that know me by name."

"What else did you find out?" I asked Grandma.

"A couple other people disappeared like this. One was a year ago. And another was right after. I was going to get names for you, but Shorty interrupted me."

Interesting stuff, but I didn't actually care how many people disappeared from Central in the middle of the night. I cared about finding Cubbin. Preferably alive, because dead meant a lot of extra paperwork.

"Did anyone talk about Cubbin?" I asked Grandma. "Like where he might have gone?"

"No. They were mostly busy talking about Nurse Kruger. They said she bought her boobs. And one of the nurses at the table said she didn't see how Kruger could afford a boob job when all her money went up her nose."

"Honestly," Lula said, turning in to the Burg. "A cokehead nurse. What's this world coming to?"

"Did you go out of the house in your disguise?" I asked Grandma.

"No way. Your mother would have a cow if she saw me in this. Thanks for reminding me," Grandma said.

She took her wig off, stuffed it into her purse, and put her sweater on over the pink tank top.

Lula looked at Grandma in the rearview mirror. "Weren't you supposed to be at the beauty parlor?

How are you gonna explain your hair? You got hat hair."

Grandma rolled her eyes up as if she could see the top of her head. "I didn't think of that. Maybe you should drop me off at the beauty parlor, and I'll have Dolly do a quick set. I can walk home from there."

• • •

Aside from the occasional wedding I don't have many reasons to get dressed up. I own a sexy red dress with a swirly skirt that I put on when there's the possibility of dancing. I have a blue dress that I think is flattering and that I wear to events my parents will also be attending. And I have a very dressy, very slinky black sheath that I bought on sale, on impulse, and have been saving for the right moment. I hadn't anticipated that the right moment would be an assignment to guard Ranger's body, but what the heck. A moment is a moment.

I was ready and waiting at six o'clock, wondering about the appropriate etiquette for a paid date. Was I supposed to meet him in the parking lot, or was I supposed to let him collect me from my apartment? The issue was resolved when he knocked once and opened my door.

He stepped inside and looked at me. His eyes were dark, his expression serious. "Nice dress."

The unspoken message was that he wouldn't

mind seeing me take it off. And there was a part of me, looking at Ranger in his perfectly tailored black tux, that thought it might not be a bad idea. There was also another part of me, the part between my ears, that scolded me for considering such a thing. I was in a relationship with Morelli, trying to determine if he was my future, and good Catholic girls don't engage in spontaneous dalliances even if the guy in question is beyond hot. Plus I'd spent forty-five minutes on hair and makeup, and steamy Ranger sex would leave me with ten inches of frizz.

"Thank you," I said, slightly breathless, quickly moving past him, through the doorway, into the hall.

• • •

Ranger was driving his black Porsche 911 Turbo. The car was fast and sexy and sometimes the ride was a little rough, a lot like Ranger. He was never especially talkative, usually staying in his zone, always alert, keeping his thoughts hidden. This was fine because if I knew his personal thoughts about me I'd probably hyperventilate and faint. He didn't break the silence until we hit the Atlantic City Expressway.

"We're attending an awards dinner for a man who's been active in the Atlantic City community," Ranger said. "And we're keeping an eye on Robert

Kinsey. He's one of the speakers. He owns an electrical supply company in White Horse, and he lives in Hamilton Township."

"A client?"

"A friend."

"I didn't know you had friends."

"Funny," Ranger said.

"So not only do you have a friend, but he's the sort of guy who speaks at awards ceremonies."

"He's marrying Amanda Olesen. Her father is getting the award."

"Okay, that would explain it."

"I was in the Middle East with Kinsey. We were part of a small unit of specialists. Kinsey and I bailed when our tour of duty was up. The rest of the unit went career military. Three weeks ago Kinsey and I started getting cryptic threatening messages ending with a code known only to our unit."

"You don't know who's sending the messages?"

"No. I haven't been able to trace them down."

"Do you think they're serious?"

"The unit wasn't made up of a bunch of guys with a sense of humor. If they said they were going to blow up a building or wipe out a terrorist cell you knew they would do it."

"And this person is threatening to do what now?"

"So far it's just a vague threat. Nothing specific. If it wasn't for the code I wouldn't take it seriously. But the truth is, all of these men are capable of doing just about anything. At least they were when I knew them."

"And you?"

"I was part of the unit, and I fit the profile. We were all handpicked."

"Will any of the others be there tonight?"

"No others were invited."

Ranger pulled into the casino garage, parked by the walkway leading into the building, and looked at the small evening bag I had on my lap.

"No gun?" he asked, knowing my .45 wouldn't fit in the bag.

I felt the heat go to my cheeks. He was paying me to watch his back, and it never occurred to me to take my gun. "No gun," I said. "Sorry."

He opened the hidden drawer under his seat and removed a small semi-automatic. "See if this fits. It's a Ruger .38 with a trace laser. It carries six plus one rounds."

I dumped everything out of my bag, and the gun just barely fit in. "This is serious," I said.

"It could be. So far it's just annoying."

SEVEN

WE LEFT THE CAR and entered the casino, following signs to a private room on the second floor. The carpet was red and gold. The chandeliers were ornate crystal. The walls were covered in gaudy gold fleur-de-lis wallpaper. The lighting was bright to accommodate the seniors with macular degeneration. We passed an entrance into the gaming area, and the noise of the slot machines blasted out at us.

We found the room for the Olesen party, had our names checked off at the door, and moved inside. It was a large space with décor identical to that of the public area. Round tables seating eight people each were set up with gold tablecloths and white and gold flower arrangements. I did a fast count and came up with twelve tables. A few people had found their name tags and taken their seats, but the majority were socializing, drinks in hand. Waiters were circulating, passing hors d'oeuvres. I took a glass of champagne and a mystery appetizer, and we slowly made our way through the crowd.

"Are you recognizing anyone?" I asked Ranger.

"No one from the unit," he said.

His hand was at my waist. He bent his head and leaned close when he spoke. If I had a second glass of champagne it would be easy to forget I was working and instead think this was an occasion for flirting. Best not to have a second glass of champagne. Best to concentrate on the cocktail sausages and tiny spicy meatballs.

Ranger introduced me to Kinsey. He was shorter than Ranger, and softer. Not entirely out of shape, but he had a few extra pounds that rounded out his face and belly and made him more approachable than Ranger. He had brown hair cut short. He was in a rented tux, and he looked like he'd rather be at a barbecue.

"This is a nightmare," Kinsey said. "I hate this stuff. And my wedding is going to be even worse. If I can get through the wedding I'm home free."

"Are you having a big wedding?" I asked him.

"Ten bridesmaids," he said. "Is that big?"

"It's a village," Ranger told him.

Amanda Olesen crossed the room and stood next to Kinsey. She was blond and pretty and soft in the same way Kinsey was soft. And she was clearly in love. There was something about the way she watched Kinsey, really listening when he spoke, smiling when she was near him.

I wondered if I looked like that when I was with Morelli or Ranger. It would be a good thing with

Morelli, and a disaster with Ranger. And truth is I was a tiny bit jealous of her happiness. It would be wonderful to be that confident and excited about the future. My future was sort of a mess.

I looked up at Ranger and saw he was watching me. "What?" I said.

"You just did a massive eye roll and you grunted."

"Heartburn from the champagne."

At eight o'clock we found our table. It was one table away from Kinsey and to the side of the room.

"You're sitting with your back to the wall," I said. "You arranged this seating so you could keep your eye on Kinsey, didn't you? Do you think something bad will happen tonight?"

"I'm being cautious."

"That's more than I can say for the guy next to me. I just sat down and he has his hand on my leg, inching up my skirt."

Ranger looked around me to scope the guy out. "Do you want me to shoot him?"

"Maybe later."

The man was ninety if he was a day. Sparse white hair, splotchy skin showing several scars where cancer had been cut out, some drool escaping from the corner of his mouth.

"Excuse me," I said to the drooler. "Your hand is on my leg."

"What?"

"Your hand. It's on my leg, and I'd like it removed."

"Can't hear you," he said. "Got a hearing problem in that ear."

I leaned in and caught the attention of the woman sitting on the man's other side. "Are you with this guy?" I asked.

"I'm his wife," she said.

"He has his hand on my leg."

She reached for a roll. "Better you than me."

I rapped the drooler on his hand with my spoon, and the hand was withdrawn.

"Problem solved," I said to Ranger.

"Too bad," he said. "I haven't shot anyone all day. I was hoping for later."

"Tell me about the cryptic messages."

"A few words written on plain white paper and sent through the mail. Things like *Your death won't come easy,* and *I will grant you salvation through pain.* The last message received was *It will start soon.*"

"That's creepy. Have you reported this to the police?"

"Not yet. No real crime has been committed."

The man next to me had his hand back on my leg.

"Itsy bitsy spider climbed up the waterspout," he said, his fingers walking their way up to the waterspout.

"Your wish is going to come true," I said to Ranger. "Shoot him."

He stood and pulled my chair out. "Change seats with me."

I took Ranger's seat and looked around. Everything seemed normal enough. No obviously deranged Special Forces guerrilla guys lurking about. Waiters were serving the entrée and pouring wine. The meal consisted of a chunk of steak, mashed potatoes, green beans and carrots. Straight from the massive casino kitchen. In deference to the fact that the owner was in the room the chef had ordered up a sprig of parsley and an artistic swirl of gravy on each plate.

I had a few bites of steak and some green beans. I tasted the potatoes, but couldn't get excited about them.

"Waiting for dessert?" Ranger asked.

"I had a ton of hors d'oeuvres. And the mashed potatoes taste funny."

Ranger was watching Kinsey, who'd already cleaned his plate and was looking uncomfortable and flushed practically to purple.

"Does Kinsey have high blood pressure?" I asked. "He's sweating, and his face is the color of the pinot noir."

"Stay here," Ranger said, scraping his chair back. "Keep your eye on the room."

By the time Ranger reached him, Kinsey had slumped in his chair and his face was deathly white. Ranger got him to his feet and moved him through a side door and out of the room. No one paid attention. People were eating and talking. Amanda followed Ranger.

I kept watch for five minutes, and when Ranger didn't return I went to the side door. Kinsey was on the floor in the hall, doubled over in a fetal position. Amanda was on her knees beside him. A man in a suit was also on his knees beside Kinsey.

"What's wrong?" I asked Ranger.

"Stomach cramps and nausea."

I didn't feel all that great either, but I wasn't sick enough to curl up on the floor. I walked a short distance and found a chair. I was light-headed and sweating, and I was working hard at convincing myself I wasn't going to throw up. I realized I was losing the *no throwing up* argument, managed to find the ladies' room in time, and sent a bunch of Swedish meatballs and cocktail wieners into the casino sewage system. Ten minutes later I was back in the hall, and paramedics were strapping Kinsey onto a gurney.

"How's he doing?" I asked Ranger.

"They're taking him to the hospital to run some tests. The house doctor thinks it might be appendicitis." He slid an arm around me. "You're almost as white as Kinsey."

"I need air. I took one look at Kinsey on the carpet and got sick."

Ranger got me as far as the parking garage, and I threw up again.

"Jeez," I said. "I'm really sorry. I don't know what's wrong with me."

"Let's get you into the car, and we'll follow Kinsey to the hospital and get you checked out."

"I don't want to go to the hospital."

"Babe, you're green."

"Yeah, maybe I shouldn't have eaten all those cocktail wieners."

Ranger stopped and stood hands on hips when he got to the Porsche. A circle with what looked like a double cross sliced by a line had been spray-painted onto the driver's side door. Just below it was a skull and crossbones.

"What is that?" I asked.

"It's the insignia from my unit. And it's the sign for poison. It's a message."

I had my arms wrapped across my stomach and I was doubled over. "Oh boy," I said. "This isn't good."

Ranger coaxed me into the car. "Stomach pains?"

"Yeah. Is appendicitis catching?"

"No. You haven't got appendicitis. We changed seats, and you got the plate that was intended for me. If I'm reading the message correctly, you and Kinsey were poisoned."

Something halfway between a sob and a groan escaped from my mouth. "I don't want to be poisoned. Am I going to die?"

"Not on my watch," Ranger said. "Hang on. I'm taking you to the medical center."

He chirped his tires and flew out of the garage and onto the street. He drove two blocks, and I clapped my hand over my mouth. "Pull over! I'm going to be sick. *I'm going to be sick!*"

"You're going to have to be sick in the car. I'm not stopping."

I had lots of junk in my car. Fast food bags and cookie boxes. Ranger had nothing. Ranger's car was pristine. Ranger had nothing to contain the last remnants of meatball that were about to leave my stomach. So I did what any woman would do in an emergency. I threw up in my evening purse, all over Ranger's gun.

"Good catch," Ranger said. And he put his foot to the floor.

• • •

They were off-loading Kinsey when Ranger pulled into the ER drive-through. Amanda and her father were standing to the side. Ranger helped me out of the car, I put my hand on the rear quarter panel to steady myself and retched. Nothing left in my stomach to come up.

Ranger eased me into a wheelchair and corralled Amanda's father.

"I think Kinsey and Stephanie might have been poisoned," Ranger said. "Have the medical people work on that assumption. I'm going back to the casino to see if I can find the source."

Ranger kissed me on the forehead. "Don't let them remove your appendix."

My stomach was sore but not cramping, and I was weak but no longer nauseous. I went through the routine of talking to nurses, an intern, and finally a resident. I had my blood pressure checked, and a blood test taken. I accepted an icky drink to settle my stomach, but I refused more invasive tests. I was feeling better as time went on. Amanda came to check on me at regular intervals and to report on Kinsey.

An ER's waiting room isn't wonderful at the best of times, and this wasn't the best of anything. In the short time I was there I watched a gunshot victim roll through, a guy get wheeled in with a broken leg and a bloody foot wrapped in a T-shirt, and a very old woman complaining of chest pains being brought in by an equally old man. I was overjoyed when Ranger finally walked through the door.

"You're looking better," he said, standing in front of me.

"I'm feeling better."

"And Kinsey?"

"He seems to be okay, but they're keeping him overnight as a precaution. What did you find?"

"I spoke to the waiter who served you and Kinsey. The plated meals come up from the kitchen on large three-tier rolling carts. Special diet and allergy plates are marked with a name and a seat number. Kinsey and I had plates with an allergy marker."

"How did they get an allergy marker?"

"No one knew. I'm guessing someone slipped in and put something in the food, probably the mashed potatoes, and stuck the marker on the plate."

"And no one noticed?"

"I was in the kitchen. It's massive and chaotic. Anyone could walk into that kitchen in a chef coat or a waiter's uniform and have total access to the food, and unless they were seven feet tall and wearing a red clown nose no one would remember them. The food from your plate had already been discarded, but I requested to have someone inspect the kitchen for possible contamination."

"I'd really like to go home."

"Are you sure you're okay?"

"They gave me some stuff to drink and took a blood test. And they told me I was good to go, but to call if I had further problems."

He pulled me to my feet, wrapped an arm around me, and walked me to the Porsche. I sunk into the passenger seat and closed my eyes for a moment, happy to be going home, relieved that the poisoning episode hadn't been worse. Ranger got behind the wheel and drove us back to the Expressway. Traffic was light, and the interior of the car was dark and would have felt intimate if I didn't smell ever so slightly of upchucked meatballs.

"I realize I'm getting paid," I said, "and I don't

want to seem unappreciative, but this was a sucky date."

Ranger glanced over at me. "We've had better. I'm sorry this happened to you. I didn't expect poisoning. I just wanted another set of eyes in the room."

"Have you been in contact with the rest of your unit?"

"There were seven of us. One was killed in the line of duty. Two are out of country. The other two are on the West Coast. Everyone claims not to have told anyone the code. And so far, Kinsey and I are the only ones receiving the messages."

"Someone's fibbing."

"The envelopes were postmarked in Philadelphia and Camden. I ran the four remaining men through the search system and no one has relatives or business ties in the area."

"So what next?"

"I wait."

• • •

Ranger pulled into my apartment building lot and parked next to Morelli's green SUV. On the surface Ranger never showed much emotion over my relationship with Morelli. From what I could tell he neither respected it nor resented it. Mostly he ignored it.

"You have company," Ranger said.

"It seemed like a good idea yesterday when I had to break the date."

Ranger walked me into the building, escorted me to the elevator, and pushed the button for my floor. "Say hello to Morelli for me."

I let myself into my apartment, Bob rushed up to me, slammed on the brakes, took a big sniff, and backed off.

Morelli was watching from the couch. "That's not a good sign," he said. "Did you fall into the Dumpster again?"

"I got sick. Food poisoning." I held a plastic bag up for him to see. "I threw up in my evening purse. They bagged it for me at the hospital."

Morelli got to his feet. "I have to hand it to Ranger. He knows how to show a girl a good time. Is there anything I can do for you? Pepto-Bismol? Tums? French fries?"

"I need a shower."

Morelli got happy. "I'll help."

"No! I don't need a sexy shower."

"I can give you a non-sexy shower."

"No, you can't. It's not in your genetic makeup."

"How are you going to feel after the shower?"

"Tired," I told him.

"Before I forget, Schmidt thinks something is off with the Cubbin case. He's watched the security tapes from the hospital, and he can't figure how Cubbin got out."

"Grandma said there've been budget cuts, and

she thought the security cameras might not be working."

"The hall camera and the elevator cameras were working. If Cubbin left his room he would have been caught on video."

"How about the window?"

"No sign of impact below the window," Morelli said.

"Vinnie's going to be out a lot of money if I can't find Cubbin. And I could use the recovery fee."

"That's a nice dress," Morelli said. "Do you need help getting it off?"

"No!"

EIGHT

"SO HOW'D YOUR BIG date go?" Lula asked when I walked into the office.

"It wasn't a big date. It was business."

"I wouldn't mind doing some business with him. I swear he's the finest man ever made."

Connie looked up from her computer. "Did I miss something?"

"Stephanie had a date with Ranger last night," Lula said.

"It was business," I told Connie. "He needed someone to attend an event with him. It wasn't social."

"It don't have to be social to be sexual with Ranger," Lula said. "Unfortunately I don't know firsthand, but I have a active fantasy life."

"If you don't have any leads on Cubbin you might try to find Brody Logan," Connie said to me. "He's got a medium high bond, and he's got his collateral. Vinnie made the mistake of not confiscating it when he bonded him out."

I pulled the file out of my bag and glanced at it. "It says here 'religious icon.' What does that mean? Is it a cross? A picture of the Virgin Mary?"

"It's a tiki," Connie said. "It's three foot high and carved out of some sacred Hawaiian tree."

"I thought a tiki was one of them thatched huts they got in the Bahamas," Lula said. "They serve the best drinks at them tikis."

"Different tiki," Connie said.

"Do you have a picture?" I asked.

"No, but I think if you've seen one tiki you've seen them all. How different can a tiki be?"

"I never seen one," Lula said.

"I have," I told her. "They had one at the hotel when I was in Hawaii. They sort of look like a piece of a totem pole."

"This might be a good time to get Logan," Connie said. "He's probably still hanging out under the bridge."

"You got big bags under your eyes," Lula said to me. "You sure you didn't have a night of hot love with Ranger?"

"Positive. I got food poisoning and threw up three times."

"Bummer," Lula said. "That probably put a crimp in his style."

I hung my messenger bag on my shoulder and turned toward the door. "I'm off." I looked at Lula. "Are you coming with me?"

"Yeah, I'm hoping to see the tiki."

I took Hamilton to Broad and turned off Broad at Third Avenue. The Freemont Street Bridge was two blocks down Third. It was a good location for someone like Logan because it was close to a city soup kitchen, and the blocks around the soup kitchen had a lot of panhandling potential. I parked on the street, and Lula and I got out and walked across a rough patch of rogue weed and assorted trash. The bridge itself spiraled overhead, connecting Third Avenue to the freeway. A slum had developed under the bridge, with cardboard box huts and plywood shanties. Three men stood smoking in the shade.

"It's like a little town here," Lula said. "I bet it could be cozy in one of them cardboard boxes except for the rats. And probably they got no cable."

"They're also missing indoor plumbing."

"Maybe they got a box designated for that."

The men watched us approach. One of them looked drugged out and crazy. The other two just looked tired.

"Howdy," Lula said. "How's it going?"

"The usual," one of them said. "What's up?"

"We're looking for Brody Logan," Lula told him. "Is he here?"

No one said anything, but one of the men nodded toward a small bedraggled tent. I gave him a couple dollars and went to the tent. I squatted down and pulled the flap away. "Brody?"

"What?"

He was wearing a faded orange T-shirt and jeans, and sitting cross-legged in front of the tiki. Two red patches instantly colored his cheeks, and his eyes went round in what I took for panic. I introduced myself and showed him my ID.

"Oh man," he said. "Give me a break. I'm real close."

"Close to what?" I asked.

"To getting this guy home. He's like a tiki, you know? He's supposed to be living in this cool shrine, having the good life, takin' in the volcano vibes. Problem is some idiot snatched him and smuggled him out of Hawaii in a bag of dirty laundry. Seemed like a good idea. Like the tiki would be a conversation piece and get the dude chicks. And like the tiki would enhance the dude's tent. But turns out the tiki isn't turned on by Jersey. So now he's bummed and havin' like a hissy fit and bringing this idiot dude bad juju."

"Are you the idiot dude who smuggled him out?" I asked.

"Yeah. Wow, you're smart. How'd you know that?"

"Lucky guess."

"Tiki and me have been working the bridge traffic and the Starbucks crowd, and I've almost got enough saved up to get us back to Hawaii. So going to jail doesn't fit into the plan."

"I want to know why you trashed the cop car," Lula said.

"The stupid cop took Tiki."

"The wooden thing."

"Yeah. He has a name besides Tiki but I forgot it so I call him Tiki."

"The tiki is named Tiki?"

"He doesn't mind," Logan said. "He's cool with it. Anyway, Tiki was sitting in front of Starbucks waiting for me to come back with a cinnamon latte, and the cop picked him up. The cop said Tiki looked stolen, but I think he just wanted Tiki. Like the cop was the one doing the stealing. Like the cop had a tiki fetish or something. I came out and about freaked when I saw Tiki locked up in the cop car. And Tiki was freaked too. *Let me out, let me out,* he was saying."

"You heard it talking?" Lula asked.

"Yeah, of course. Well, you know, in my head. That's how Tiki always talks to me."

"He talkin' to you now?" Lula wanted to know.

"Not now, but before you came he was telling me he wanted eggs for breakfast."

"How's he take his eggs?" Lula asked.

"Usually scrambled. And some wheat toast."

"I bet you smoke a lot of weed," Lula said. "Maybe do some 'shrooms."

"No way. I'm pure. Maybe in the past, you know, but Tiki doesn't like that stuff."

"Good to know," Lula said. "Back to the cop car. Why'd you bash it in?"

"Well, at first I just smashed the window to get

Tiki out, but then I got into it, like it was a rush. I mean, have you ever trashed a cop car? It's the best."

"It got you arrested," I said.

"Yeah. I look back at it now, and I think it was Tiki messin' with my head, telling me to trash the car. I shouldn't have taken him away from Pele."

"Who's Pele?" Lula asked.

"She's the volcano goddess. She lives in Kilauea, and this guy here's one of her dudes. So you see how I'm on a holy mission, right?"

"Why don't you just FedEx the dude back to Pele," Lula said.

"It don't work that way. I have to put the tiki dude in the right spot. I gotta say words over him. Like how I'm sorry I put him in with my dirty laundry, and how now he and Pele can get it on."

"You'll have a chance to explain all that to the judge," I said. "And if you don't have any priors you might get away with community service."

"Uh-oh," Logan said. "I might have had a few substance indiscretions."

"Guess you're goin' to the pokey, then," Lula said.

His eyes darted from me to Lula and back to me, and he bolted, lunging out of the tent, knocking me over. "No!"

I scrambled to my feet and ran flat out, but I couldn't catch him. Logan dodged traffic on Third and disappeared down the street.

Lula came clattering after me on her four-inch Via Spiga spike heels. "He's a fast bugger," she said, bending at the waist, trying to catch her breath. "You should have just shot him."

"He's unarmed."

"Yeah, but he dissed you."

"I'm going back for the tiki," I said to Lula. "At least Vinnie will have his collateral."

The three men were still standing in the same spot, still smoking, when Lula and I returned to the shantytown.

"How'd that go?" one of them asked.

"He got away," Lula said. "He could really run."

"He got motivation," the man said.

I crawled into Logan's tent and took the tiki. "Me too."

"Uh-oh," the man said. "He's not gonna like you take the tiki. That tiki talks to him."

I carted the tiki across the field, put it into the backseat, and clicked a seat belt around it.

"Good thing your Uncle Sandor had seat belts put into this car," Lula said. "Otherwise Tiki would be rolling around back there."

I got behind the wheel, plugged the key into the ignition, and jumped when someone rapped on my window.

It was Ranger.

"You left the contents of your purse in my car last night," he said, handing me a plastic baggie.

"Thanks. And I have your gun." I pulled the Ruger out of my bag and gave it to Ranger.

He held the gun flat in his hand and looked at it. "It smells like orange blossoms."

"I washed it and sprayed it with air freshener."

"You washed it?"

"I wore rubber gloves and scrubbed it with my vegetable brush. It was . . . icky."

He yanked open the driver's side door, pulled me out of the car, and kissed me. The kiss involved tongue and a hand on my ass, and made my nipples tingle.

"I can always count on you to brighten my day," Ranger said.

Ranger drove off, and I got back into the Buick.

"That was hot," Lula said. "Imagine what he'd do if you washed his *Glock*."

"I'm a little flustered," I said. "What was I doing before Ranger knocked on the window?"

"You were gonna drive somewhere."

"Do you know where?"

"You didn't say, but we could ride around and look for bad guys."

I went back to Broad and took Broad to Stark Street.

"This here's a good choice," Lula said. "There's always lots of bad guys on Stark Street."

I was looking for one in particular. Melvin Barrel. I drove the length of Stark, all the way to the no-man's-land where the redbrick row houses are covered with gang graffiti, the insides are gutted from crack fires, the rats are as big as barn cats, and the human inhabitants hide in the shadows.

I made a U-turn and did another pass down Stark. I slowed when I got to Barrel's rooming house, idled in front of the house for a moment, and was about to drive away when I saw Barrel on the next block, walking toward us.

"Do you see him?" I asked Lula.

"Yeah, I see him. And he don't see us. He's texting on his cellphone, not paying attention."

I cut the engine, and Lula and I got out and went to the sidewalk. I tucked cuffs into the waistband of my jeans for easy access, put my illegal stun gun into my back pocket, and got a grip on my pepper spray.

"What's the plan?" Lula asked. "How about I distract him by offering him some 'ho services, and then you could sneak up behind him and give him a thousand volts. How's that sound?"

"Sounds good. Make sure you turn him around so he doesn't see me."

I slipped into the doorway of a building, Lula headed for Barrel, and Barrel stepped off the curb still texting. A shiny black Mercedes sped down the side street and hit Barrel straight on. Barrel got punted about ten feet, and the Mercedes ran over him. My stomach instantly got sick and my breath caught in my throat.

"Ow," Lula said. "That gotta hurt."

The Mercedes came to a stop, and two men got out. They were all blinged up in gold chains and flashy running suits, and the one had a lightning bolt cut into his hair.

Lula and I ran into the street and joined the men who were standing, staring down at Barrel. Barrel wasn't moving, and he had tire tracks across his chest.

"That's Melvin Barrel," the driver said.

The other guy squatted down for a closer look. "Yep. It's Barrel all right."

"Is he okay?" Lula asked.

"Looks to me like he's dead," the guy said.

"The idiot walked right in front of my car," the driver said. "Who does that?"

"He was texting," Lula said.

"Well, he's not texting no more," the driver said. He pulled out a gun and shot Barrel five times. "That's for hitting my car, asshole."

Lula and I sucked in some air and stumbled back about ten feet. And the two guys got into the Mercedes and drove away.

I punched 911 into my cellphone with a shaky finger and reported the accident. I called Morelli and reported the accident. And then Lula and I stood guard over the body so it didn't get scooped up by God-knows-who like the last time we were on Stark. On a personal level, I didn't actually care what happened to Barrel. As a professional, if the body disappeared my payday went with it. And as a woman, I was slightly nauseous.

A patrol car was the first on the scene. It was followed by the EMT truck, Morelli, and two more cop cars.

Morelli parked and sauntered over to me. "Your FTA has tire tracks on his chest."

I made a small grimace. "Two guys in a Mercedes drove over him."

"Technically it wasn't a hit-and-run, though," Lula told Morelli. "They stopped, but they just didn't stay. They only stayed long enough to shoot him."

"He got run over by the Mercedes, and then he got shot?" Morelli asked.

"That's right," Lula said. "But it was recreational shooting. Barrel was already dead from being run over."

One of the uniforms was cordoning off the area with yellow crime scene tape. The two EMTs were shuffling around, waiting for the medical examiner to show up and take over. A small crowd was gathering, gawking at Barrel.

Morelli turned his attention to me. "You do understand that your life isn't normal, right?"

"Barrel was texting and he stepped off a curb without looking," I said.

"But you were here," Morelli said. "How does it happen that you're always right in the precise spot where disaster strikes? Your car's been blown up how many times? And it's never your fault. Remember when you fell off the fire escape into dog diarrhea? And the time you dated a serial killer?"

"I liked that serial killer," Lula said. "He could make a damn good pork chop."

"Is there a point to this?" I asked Morelli.

"No," he said. "I'm venting. It scares the crap out of me that I'm in love with you."

"Aw, that's sweet," Lula said.

I thought so too. It was kind of a backhanded admission, but it made my heart get fluttery. The sight of Barrel lying on the ground oozing body fluids snapped me back to the moment. I took my phone out of my bag. "You don't mind if I take a picture of this guy with my cellphone, do you? I need to prove he's dead."

"Knock yourself out," Morelli said. "Last time an FTA of yours went dead you asked the EMTs to drive him to the courthouse."

"There's a lot of paperwork when the FTA is dead," I said. "It's easier when you can have him show up in court."

I took my pictures and gave Morelli a detailed description of the Mercedes driver. The medical examiner was on the scene, and the crime scene photographer was at work. Lula was looking like she was ready to break out in hives.

"I'm moving on," I said to Morelli. "Things to do. Will I see you tonight?"

"Dinner at seven. My house. I'll get Chinese."

NINE

LULA AND I CLIMBED into the Buick, I rolled the engine over and pulled into traffic.

"I almost forgot about Tiki back there," Lula said. "You don't suppose he really talks, do you?" She swiveled in her seat. "Hey, Tiki, how's it goin'?"

I stopped for a light and glanced at Lula. "Well? Is he saying anything to you?"

"No, but I think he might be smiling. Hold on here. Something's coming through. He's telling me it's lunchtime and he wants a bucket of chicken."

"Tiki said that?"

"Well, *someone* said it. It was in my head."

"It might have been you *thinking* it."

"Yeah, but I'm pretty sure it had a Hawaiian accent."

Cluck-in-a-Bucket was all the way across town. I took Broad to Hamilton, and we made a fast stop for chicken. Lula got a bucket of extra crispy, a side of fries, and a side of slaw. I got a biscuit. My stomach wasn't in top form after last night's poisoning.

We took the food to the office, and I lugged Tiki in, along with my biscuit.

"We had a good day," Lula said to Connie. "We had all kinds of success. Do you want a piece of chicken? I got the big bucket in case I had to share."

Connie passed on the chicken, and Vinnie popped out of his office.

"What kind of success? Did you get Cubbin?"

"Not yet," Lula said. "But we got Melvin Barrel."

"Melvin Barrel is good," Vinnie said. "Does he want to get rebonded?"

"Probably not," Lula said. "He's dead."

I showed Vinnie the picture on my cellphone.

"Are those tire tracks on his chest?" Vinnie asked. "And bullet holes? Christ, how many times did you shoot him?"

"I didn't shoot him," I said. "He got hit by a car, and the driver got out and shot him . . . five times."

"And we went after Brody Logan too," Lula said, digging into the bucket of chicken. "Except he got away."

I set the tiki on Connie's desk. "Logan ran off, so I confiscated his tiki."

"That's the tiki?" Vinnie asked, eyes bulging out of their sockets. "Are you nuts? You brought the tiki *here*?"

"I thought you wanted it."

"Yeah, but not here! That thing's evil. It's a bad influence."

"That could be true," Lula said. "I was planning

on just getting a couple pieces of chicken, and it told me to get the big bucket."

I did such a gigantic eye roll I almost fell over.

"Get that thing out of here, and go find Cubbin," Vinnie said. "I've got enough problems without a tiki putting ideas in my head. Lucille has me going to Sex Addicts Anonymous."

"How's that working for you?" Lula asked.

"It's a nightmare. I go there, and I'm in a room filled with perverts. It's like being in a bakery where everything is free and you can't eat anything."

"Speaking of bakery, I wouldn't mind having some dessert," Lula said. "I need something sweet to get my mind off the grease and salt attack I'm having."

I hefted Tiki and tucked him under my arm. "I want to talk to Mrs. Cubbin again. We can stop at Tasty Pastry on the way."

Ten minutes later Lula came out of Tasty Pastry with a box of Italian cookies, six fresh-made cannoli, and a bag of donuts.

"That's a lot of dessert," I said.

"I just wanted a cookie. I was gonna get one of them black-and-whites, but Tiki couldn't make up his mind."

"Tiki told you to buy all this?"

"Yeah. I'm pretty sure it was Tiki. It was like someone was whispering in my ear."

"That's ridiculous. You're using Tiki as an excuse."

"I don't think so. I definitely heard someone whispering." Lula selected a cannoli. "I don't usually get cannoli, but Tiki had a good suggestion here." She held the box out to me. "You want one? They're good for you on account of there's dairy in them."

"Sure," I said. "Give me a cannoli."

I ate my cannoli while I drove to Susan Cubbin's house. Okay, I get that it's not the perfect marriage, but it seems to me if anyone had a lead on Cubbin it would be his wife. Wives know things. They snoop around. They especially snoop around if they think they're getting screwed out of money.

I parked in front of the white ranch with the black shutters, told Tiki to behave himself, and Lula and I went to the door.

"You want me to go looking in the windows?" Lula asked.

"No!"

I rang the bell and waited. No answer. I rang again. Nothing.

"Maybe she's shopping," Lula said. "Taking her mind off her troubles. The other possibility is she fell down the stairs and broke her hip and can't get up like that lady in the commercial. In which case we have a obligation to break in and help her. Least that's what Tiki says."

"I'm surprised you can hear Tiki when he's in the car and you're in the bakery or standing here on the porch."

"Yeah, he's got good range for a chunk of wood."
Lula pushed on the door and it swung open. "Hunh,
look at this. The door's not locked. It wasn't even
all closed."

I stepped inside. "Hello," I called. "Anybody
home?"

No answer.

Lula followed me in and closed the door. "Look
at the bottom of the stairs. That's where they land
when they fall."

"This is a ranch house. There are no stairs."

Lula looked around. "You're right. I never
thought of that."

I walked through the house to the kitchen. Susan
Cubbin had decorated the house in American
Farmhouse style. Upholstered pieces were slip-
covered in ill-fitting floral fabric. End tables looked
like they'd been beaten with a chain. The chande-
lier over the trestle dining room table was fash-
ioned to look like a wagon wheel.

"Only thing missing from this house is chick-
ens," Lula said. "Maybe she's got some in the backyard."

I looked in the fridge. "No food," I said. "Ketchup,
mustard, mayo, but no milk or orange juice."

"Sounds like your house," Lula said.

"Yes, but Susan cooks. She has spices, and pots
and pans, and a waffle iron." I opened the door to
the pantry. Flour, sugar, rice, breadcrumbs, oatmeal,

graham crackers, macaroni. "She cleaned the perishables out of her refrigerator."

"Like she was going on a trip," Lula said. "Maybe her husband sent her a check, and she went on vacation."

The counters were clean. A cat's water bowl and food dish were in the dish drain. There was a landline phone on the counter. A basket with assorted scraps of paper and miscellaneous receipts sat next to the phone. One of the receipts caught my attention. It was a printout from an online store selling surveillance equipment. On Thursday, Susan had bought binoculars, a camera with motion sensors, and a remote-controlled audio amplifier.

"Susan was going to snoop on someone," I said.

I opened the door leading to the attached garage and flipped the light on. No car. I walked through the rest of the house. The guest bedrooms looked like they were seldom used. No clothes in the closets and dressers. No toiletries in the bathroom. No room designated as a home office. I investigated the master bedroom last. The bed was made. I went through the dresser drawers and bathroom medicine chest. Nothing out of the ordinary. Hard to tell if anything was missing.

I opened the closet door in the master, and a monster jumped out at me. He was easily 6'6". He had long snow-white hair, bushy white eyebrows, and one blue eye and one brown eye. And he had a stun gun.

"It's the Yeti!" Lula screamed. "Lord help me."

The next thing I heard was *zzzzzzt*. And I was incapacitated, on my back on the carpet.

It took a couple minutes for my brain to unscramble and start sending coherent messages to my nerve endings. My head cleared and I looked over at Lula. She was sprawled next to me, and she was twitching.

I got to my hands and knees, and then to my feet. "Hey," I said to Lula. "Are you okay?"

"Yuh," Lula said. "Did I wet myself? I hate when that happens."

I leaned against the dresser, taking deep breaths while my muscle memory returned. The house was quiet. No one walking around. No one slamming doors. No one making Yeti sounds. I carefully made my way to the closet and looked inside. It was a large walk-in. Geoffrey Cubbin's clothes were on one side, and Susan's on the other. Again, nothing looked out of the ordinary.

Lula was on her feet, adjusting her boobs, tugging her skirt back into place. "What the heck was that about?" she asked. "That scared the crap out of me. I thought she just had a cat. Nobody said anything about having a Yeti."

"That wasn't a Yeti. It was a big albino guy."

"I don't think so. I know a Yeti when I see one. I saw a Yeti at Disney World. It's like Chewbacca but it's all white."

"A Yeti is an Abominable Snowman. The Himalayan version of Bigfoot."

"Yeah."

"That's not what you saw. You saw a big, hairy albino guy."

"Maybe he was an Abominable Albino."

"That works for me. Do you have your gun with you?"

Lula pulled a Glock out of her purse. "We going Abominable Albino hunting?"

"Yes."

I made another pass through the house with Lula close on my heels, gun in hand. We went through every room, and opened every door. Nothing jumped out at us.

"He flew the coop," Lula said when we got back to the front door.

I took a moment to look around one last time. "Where's the cat? Susan had an indoor cat. Where is it? And where's the kitty litter? I think Susan split and took the cat with her."

"If I had a Yeti hiding in my closet I'd take the cat and go someplace else too," Lula said.

We left the house and sat in the Buick, eating cookies, thinking about where to go next.

"I can't shake the feeling that the clue to Cubbin is in the hospital," I said. "There's got to be something we missed. If we could find out how he got out of the hospital, we might be able to find out where he went."

"Yeah, and you could find that out on your own because I don't want to go back into the hospital and get more cooties. Besides, I might need to go shopping. I heard Junior Moody got some new merchandise last night, and he'll be open for business in the projects this afternoon."

"What kind of merchandise?"

"I don't know, but he usually has good stuff."

Junior Moody was a small-time opportunistic vendor who operated out of the trunk of his Cadillac Eldorado. Depending on what had been hijacked, robbed, or shoplifted, Junior might be selling cubic zirconia earrings, Cuisinart toasters, Hello Kitty watches, or Izod shirts.

"I'll drop you off at the office. Call me if he's got evening purses."

TEN

"BE CAREFUL OF TIKI," Lula said when she got out of the Buick. "Don't listen to him when he tells you to order a extra pizza."

"No worries."

I put the Buick in gear and slid a glance at Tiki in the backseat. "Well?" I said.

Nothing. No pizza advice. No requests to be returned to the volcano. No complaints that the seat belt was too tight.

I took Hamilton to Greenwich, turned onto Joy, and swung into the hospital garage. I told Tiki under no circumstances should he open the car doors to strangers, locked him in, and headed for the building. I walked through the lobby and went straight to Randy Briggs's office.

"Oh jeez," he said when I walked in. "Now what?"

"I want to talk."

"I'm working."

"Looks to me like you're surfing porn sites."

"A lot you know. I'm doing research."

I sat in the chair opposite him. "Tell me about Geoffrey Cubbin. How'd he get out of the hospital?"

"You're trespassing in my office."

"If you don't talk to me I'm sending Grandma back here."

Briggs closed his eyes and groaned. "Don't do that." He opened his eyes and looked at me. "I've got a good job here. I don't want to lose it. Give me a break."

"Aren't you curious about Cubbin?"

"No."

I looked past Briggs to his bulletin board. The two missing-patient pictures were still posted there.

"Who's the other missing patient?" I asked.

He turned and looked at the picture. "Floyd Dugan. He was a boxer. Trained out of the gym on Stark Street. He got caught with a pound of heroin in his car. He said it was planted. I'm surprised you don't recognize him."

"Why was he here?"

"Hernia operation. I inherited a file on him."

"Can I see it?"

"No," Briggs said.

"I'll scream rape and tell everyone you grabbed my boob."

"That's ridiculous. I can't even *reach* your boob." He jumped off his booster seat and went to the file cabinet behind his desk. "In the past three years this hospital has had four people go AWOL in the middle of the night. No one seems to think that's unusual. Turns out people don't like being here." He pulled four files and handed them over to me. "Read them fast. They're supposed to be confidential."

I flipped through Geoffrey Cubbin and Floyd Dugan. Both men had been accused of crimes and released on a bail bond. They got sick while they were bonded out, went to the hospital, and were never seen again. Didn't show up for court. Never returned home, made any credit card charges, or withdrew money from a bank account. Craig Fish was their surgeon.

The third guy was a homeless man who was hit by a car, kept overnight for observation, and disappeared before daybreak.

Willie Hernandez disappeared hours after having a kidney stone removed. He'd been arrested for domestic violence and was awaiting trial. And he was in the country illegally. Craig Fish was the surgeon.

"They all had a reason to disappear," I said. "And three out of the four were operated on by Dr. Fish."

"You've heard of lawyers chasing ambulances? He's the medical equivalent. Behind his back they call him 'Dr. Stalk' and 'Slash.' And it's rumored he isn't above removing a healthy appendix if business is slow."

"I met him. He seemed nice."

"Who said he wasn't nice? Everyone loves him. He's just a little aggressive about acquiring patients."

I gave the files back to Briggs. "Thanks for letting me see these. They're all open cases, right?"

"Right."

"And no one ever figured out how the patients left the hospital?"

"No. I don't think anyone cares a lot. They're gone. End of story."

"It's weird."

"It could be ingenious. Someone's in the hospital, and he's in trouble. He wants to disappear. And some sympathetic nurse or orderly is happy to make it happen for a price."

"What about the homeless guy?"

"I don't know about the homeless guy. He doesn't fit my profile."

"So we might have a theory on how three out of the four got help disappearing, but that doesn't explain why none of these people got caught on a security camera when they left."

"I looked at the tapes. I even looked to see if Cubbin could have been disguised as a nurse, but I didn't see anything."

"Did you look at any of the other tapes?"

"They aren't available. The hospital only keeps the tapes for six months."

I stood and turned to go. "Thanks again."

"Don't mention it. And I mean *don't mention it.*

I'll swear on a Bible I never showed you the files. In fact, I never even *talked* to you. You weren't here."

"Understood."

I left Briggs and took the elevator to the fourth floor. I walked past the nurses' station and slowly made my way down the hall, glancing into the rooms. They were standard semi-private hospital rooms. Privacy curtains, a chair for each bed, hospital tray tables. Painted a bilious green and tan. Many of the rooms had only one patient.

"This must be a slow time of the year for you," I said to an aide. "A lot of the rooms are only half full."

"This is the surgery floor, and most people get sent home same day or next day. It's too expensive to stay longer. Years ago when the hospital was built people stayed a week or two after surgery."

"Were you here when Geoffrey Cubbin disappeared? I read about it in the paper. I guess he decided to leave early."

"He was gone when I came in that morning. Everyone was scratching their head wondering where he could be. No one saw him leave. I guess he didn't want to stand trial."

"Did he have a roomie when he was here?"

She thought for a moment. "No."

I traveled the length of the hall, retraced my steps, and went back to the nurses' station. "Is this the only elevator?" I asked the aide.

"There's a service elevator, but it's not available to visitors," she said.

I went back to Randy Briggs.

"Jeez," he said. "I thought you left."

"I have another question. Is it possible Cubbin left via the service elevator?"

"No. I would have seen him from the hall video. It has a clear shot of the service elevator."

"Damn."

"Tell me about it. I'm on the job for two months and some idiot disappears. Lucky for me no one seems to care. Except for you. You're a real pain in the ass."

I gave him the finger.

"Nice," he said. "Very classy."

I left the hospital and drove back to the office.

"I want to talk to Cubbin's night nurse," I told Connie. "Her name is Norma Kruger. Can you get me some information on her?"

Connie typed the name into one of her search programs and the information started to pour in. She hit PRINT and in thirty seconds I had a two-page bio.

"Divorced, no children, thirty-four years old, owns a condo in a building not far from the hospital. Everything else is blah, blah, blah. No litigation or derogatory comments. I don't see a mortgage or car loan."

"Looks like she pays cash," Connie said.

"How does she do that on a nurse's salary?"

Connie shrugged. "Good divorce settlement?"

"And there's talk she does some recreational substance abuse."

"She might have something going on the side," Connie said. "Maybe she gives a really good sponge bath, and she gets tips."

"Maybe the sponge baths are so good Cubbin followed her home and never left."

"That would be convenient." Connie squinted in the direction of the large plate glass window at the front of the office. "I think someone's trying to break into your car."

I swiveled my head and followed Connie's line of vision. Sure enough, Brody Logan was at work with a crowbar.

"It's Logan," I said, on the move. "He wants Tiki."

I burst out the door, swung my messenger bag, and caught Logan on the side of the head. The crowbar flew out of his hand, and he staggered sideways. I lunged for him, but he jumped away and took off. I didn't bother chasing him. I knew I couldn't catch him.

"He's fast," Connie said. "Next time you need to zap him."

Connie went back into the office, and I looked the car door over for crowbar damage.

Ranger parked behind me and walked over. "What's going on?"

"Someone tried to break into the Buick."

"The Buick is enchanted," Ranger said. "It's impervious to damage and breaking and entering. Why would someone want to steal it?"

"It's a classic."

"Besides that."

"He was after the tiki in the backseat. It's sort of his."

"I have good news and bad news," Ranger said. "What do you want to hear first?"

"The good news."

"Actually I lied about the good news. It's all bad. Kinsey got another message. This time it was written on his living room wall. He found it when he came home from the hospital."

"You didn't get one?"

"No. I feel neglected."

"It would be hard to get to your living room," I said. "Being that it's in a building more secure than the Pentagon."

"You managed to get in."

"You allowed me in."

Ranger smiled. "I don't have a lot of fun. I can't afford to waste an opportunity."

"You threatened to throw me out the window!"

"I was playing."

"You weren't playing when you got in bed next to me."

"No," he said. "The play ended."

We considered that for a moment, and I thought it best to move on.

"Is there more bad news?" I asked him.

"Kinsey and his fiancée are worried the wedding has a bull's-eye on it."

"Good thought. I'd be worried too."

"Glad you understand the problem, because they want to replace one of the bridesmaids with you. They thought it was a good idea to have someone undercover, close to the bride."

"No. No, no, no. I don't want to be a bridesmaid. Been there, done that. I'll have to wear some awful dress, and it won't fit me. And I'll have to do that stupid step, stop, step, stop all the way down the church aisle. And there's the rehearsal dinner."

"You'll be on the payroll," Ranger said.

"You couldn't pay me enough."

"Babe, everyone has a price."

I locked eyes with him. "What about you? Do you get to be a bridesmaid too?"

"I'm the best man."

I was momentarily speechless. "Were you always the best man?"

"Yes."

"Holy cats."

"Can we get serious? Get past the deal with the dress? Kinsey has asked me to help with security for the wedding. As a professional I agree that it would be a smart move to include you in the bridal party. As someone who is very fond of you and has already gotten you poisoned, I'm not entirely excited about the idea. If you feel uncomfortable doing this for reasons that go beyond the dress I'll understand. Whether or not you take this assignment has to be your choice."

"If I get poisoned again I want a bonus."

"Deal. The wedding is next Saturday." He handed me a card. "The dress will need to be fitted. Here's the address of the bridal salon. Sooner would be better than later."

A text message came in on his phone, he turned on his heel, got into his Porsche, and drove off.

I looked at Tiki in the backseat. "Do *not* say *anything*."

I shoved the card into my back pocket and drove to Norma Kruger's condo complex. The two-story faux Colonial buildings were originally designed as apartment units. The buildings had been converted to condos when mortgage money was easy to get, and now in a more difficult economy I was guessing a lot of the units were being rented out. From what I could tell each unit had two parking spaces assigned by house number. Most of the spaces were empty. This was a complex of young professionals who were working at this time of day. Except for Norma Kruger, who worked the night shift. A red Jaguar convertible occupied Norma's parking space. I pulled in next to the Jag and cut the engine. I walked to the door and rang the bell.

Norma Kruger answered with a raised eyebrow. Not overjoyed to see me. Suspicious of my intent.

Possibly I looked like I was selling religion door-to-door.

"What?" she asked.

"I'd like to talk to you about Geoffrey Cubbin."

"Are you a cop?"

"Bond enforcement."

She gave a bark of laughter. "You mean like Dog the Bounty Hunter? Aren't you supposed to be decked out in leather?"

"We don't all dress like Dog," I said.

"How disappointing."

Norma Kruger was pretty in a hard-as-nails dominatrix kind of way. She had shoulder-length very blond hair, parted in the middle, tortured into waves, tucked behind her ears. She was wearing jeans and a T-shirt, and she obviously didn't need a bra to keep her boobs in perfect position and looking perky.

"I'm told you were the night nurse on duty when Cubbin disappeared."

"Is this going somewhere?"

"I'm trying to get a grip on how he got out of the hospital."

"You and everyone else. All I know is I saw him at two A.M. and he was gone at six A.M."

"Did you talk to him when you saw him at two?"

"No. He was sleeping. I didn't wake him."

"People don't just disappear into thin air," I said. "How many people were working on that floor between two and six?"

"Two nurses. Julie Marconni was with me. She was working the other side of the hall."

"And she didn't see anything either."

"Nope."

"I understand Cubbin was Craig Fish's patient."

"Almost everyone is Dr. Fish's patient. He keeps busy."

"Is he a good doctor?"

"He hasn't personally operated on me, but I'm told he's excellent."

I gave Norma my card. "If you think of anything that might be helpful I'd appreciate a call."

"Sure."

I returned to the Buick and rolled out of the condo complex.

"That was supremely unhelpful," I said to Tiki. "She told me nothing new. And I didn't get any special vibes from her on Craig Fish. This is getting discouraging."

Tiki had no words of wisdom, so I thought I might find inspiration in a bottle of wine. Or even better I could stop at Mexicana Grill on the way home and have a margarita. Free up the old brain cells, right?

Halfway through the margarita I was thinking a second margarita would be great. And I actually was feeling a little amorous, so I called Morelli.

"Hi there, hot stuff," I said. "I'm in a bar and I want to get you naked."

"Exactly how many drinks have you had?"

"One. And one more on the way. And I'm going to order nachos, which I'll share if you let me see your underwear."

"How could I pass up a deal like that? Where are you?"

"Mexicana Grill."

Ten minutes later Morelli pulled up next to me and snitched some of my nachos.

"Hey," I said, "you can't have any of those until I get a look."

Morelli grinned at me. "You're trashed."

"It's all Tiki's fault. He told me to do this."

"Who's Tiki?"

"He's a sacred carving from Hawaii. It's a long story."

"And Tiki told you to stop at a bar and get trashed?"

"Yes! He made it sound like a good idea."

Morelli paid my tab, wrapped an arm around me, and hauled me off my bar stool. "Where's Tiki now?"

"In my car. He wanted to come into the bar with me but I thought that was too weird."

Morelli walked me to my car and looked in at Tiki. "This is the guy who suggested the bar?"

"I know he looks innocent enough, but he's diabolical."

"He's a chunk of wood."

I unlocked the Buick, unbuckled Tiki, and handed him to Morelli. "He's also my ticket to Brody

Logan. Logan wants Tiki back. So instead of trying to chase down Logan, all I have to do is wait for him to come for Tiki."

"Clever. Did Tiki tell you that?"

"No. I thought of that all by myself."

Morelli unlocked his SUV. "We'll pick the Buick up tomorrow morning. Who thought about ripping my clothes off, you or Tiki?"

"It might have been me. And you still haven't let me look at your underwear."

Morelli held the door for me. "As soon as we get in the car."

"Do I get to touch things?"

"Oh yeah. Touching is encouraged."

ELEVEN

IT WAS SUNDAY MORNING, and Morelli and I were at his little kitchen table enjoying a leisurely breakfast of coffee and leftover Chinese takeout. Morelli isn't opposed to sleeping over in my apartment, but truth is, it works better for us to be in his house. My hamster, Rex, is self-sufficient with his water bottle and cache of food. Bob, not so much. Morelli has a yard for Bob plus a twenty-five-pound bag of dog kibble. Morelli also has a toaster and food in his refrigerator.

Morelli was always the bad boy wild child, and I was always the mostly good girl. Not to say I didn't have my moments in high school. And I for sure was never as good as my sister, Valerie. Still, an odd reversal took place when I wasn't looking, and I now find myself on the short end of maturity and financial stability.

I heard Morelli's front door open and close, and then footsteps coming our way. Bob jumped out of his dog bed, ran to the back door, and whined to get out.

"I've never seen him do that," I said to Morelli. "He always rushes to see who came in."

Morelli stood and let Bob out. "It's probably Grandma Bella. He's terrified of her."

Bob wasn't the only one terrified of Bella. *Everyone* was terrified of Bella, including me. She was whacko, making with the evil eye and putting spells on people. Okay, so it was a stretch to think she could make someone break out in boils just by looking at them cockeyed, but there were enough bizarre coincidences to make you want to err on the side of caution and not piss her off.

Bella marched into the kitchen. As always, she was wearing a black dress, black stockings, black low-heeled shoes. Very old school Sicily. Her white hair was pulled back into a bun, she wore no makeup, and her eyebrows were thick and black, forming a unibrow. She could have been an extra in a *Godfather* movie, speaking broken English and using offensive Italian hand gestures. It was as if the longer she lived in the country, the more Sicilian she became.

She plunked a casserole down onto the table. "It's Sunday. Why you not at church?" she said to Morelli. "And what this woman doing here?"

"Having breakfast," he said. "You remember Stephanie."

Bella narrowed her eyes at me. "Slut. You keeping my grandson from church."

"Last time I was in church it was Christmas mass," Morelli said.

Bella made the sign of the cross. "Holy Mother, help him. He good boy but he weak." She shook her head. "All the Morelli men weak."

"Thank you for the casserole," I said.

"I not give it to you," Bella said. "I make that for my grandson. You eat his casserole and bad thing happen to you. Warts." She spotted Tiki sitting on the countertop. "What's this?"

"It's a Hawaiian wood carving," Morelli said.

"You don't have statue of the Virgin in your house but you have this silly thing," Bella said. "You know nothing. I give it the eye. I fix it good."

We heard a horn honk from the street.

"Did my mother drive you here?" Morelli asked Bella.

"No. That's Mrs. Giovi. We're going to second mass."

Morelli put his arm around Bella and guided her back through the house to the front door. "Say hello to Mrs. Giovi for me."

I heard him throw the bolt after Bella left.

"Too late to lock the door now," I said when he came back to the kitchen. "You've got a casserole that'll give me warts, and she put the eye on Tiki."

"Too bad about the warts," Morelli said. "The casserole looks pretty good."

There was no way in heck I was touching it.

We walked Bob, and then got into Morelli's SUV to pick up my car at the Mexicana Grill.

"Have you heard any more about Geoffrey Cubbin?" I asked Morelli when he stopped for a light.

"Only that he hasn't surfaced. I don't think he's a priority with Schmidt. He's counting on you to find him."

"That's not a good plan. I'm at a total dead end. I know there's something wrong at the hospital but I haven't a clue what it is. Four people have gone missing in the last three years. Dr. Fish operated on three of them. All mysteriously disappeared in the early morning. All had a reason to want to disappear. Geoffrey Cubbin, Floyd Dugan, and a guy named Hernandez. It's been suggested someone at the hospital might be helping with the disappearance process for a bag of money."

"Not a big payday in medicine anymore," Morelli said. "I could see where that might lead to entrepreneurial activities."

"And there's a giant albino involved. Lula and I went to talk to Cubbin's wife, and this guy jumped out of a closet at us. Lula thought it was a Yeti."

"What did Cubbin's wife say about it?"

"She wasn't home."

"I don't want to hear this. You did B&E on Cubbin's house, didn't you?"

"Actually I just did 'E.' The door was unlocked."

"That makes all the difference," Morelli said.

"Are you being sarcastic?"

"Yes!"

"Anyway, it looks to me like Susan Cubbin took off with a bunch of newly purchased surveillance equipment. And this big guy with white hair and one blue eye and one brown eye was snooping in her house."

"What happened after he jumped out of the closet?"

"He tagged Lula and me with a stun gun and that was the last we saw of him."

"You got stunned?"

"Yeah. This wasn't one of my better weeks."

Morelli swung into the Mexicana Grill lot and parked next to the Buick. "Do you suppose we could spend some time exploring other employment options for you?"

"Such as?"

"An office job. Retail. Housewife."

"Is that a proposal?"

"Not entirely. Thought I'd throw it out there to see how it sounded."

I looked at Morelli. "Well?"

"It sounded scary."

"Kind of took my breath away," I said.

"I'll test drive it again next week and see if it gets more comfortable."

"Do you have plans for today? Do you want to go to the beach?"

"The beach would be good," Morelli said. "I'll pick you up in an hour."

• • •

I had my bikini on under my shorts and my T-shirt. I had a floppy hat, sunscreen, sunglasses, beach towel, plus all the usual other stuff in my tote bag. My doorbell bonged while I was searching for my flip-flops. I gave up the search and answered the door.

"You're early," I said to Morelli. And then I realized it wasn't Morelli. It was Brody Logan with a large knife.

He jumped into my apartment, and I stumbled back.

"I want Tiki," he said.

"I don't have Tiki," I told him. "I left him at a friend's house."

"I don't believe you. What's your friend's name?"

"I'm not telling you."

"Tell me or I'll cut you up into tiny bits."

"I don't think so."

"I could do it," he said. "I have this knife. It's not just any old knife either. It's a ceremonial knife."

"It looks like a butcher's knife."

"It used to be a butcher's knife, but now it's a ceremonial knife on account of it's being used for a righteous purpose. It's like a holy tool now."

I had my stun gun sitting on my kitchen counter.

If I could get Logan to relax his guard and I could get to the stun gun, it would be my holy tool against his holy tool.

Logan craned his neck, looking around. "Where's Tiki? I don't see him."

"I told you. He's not here. How did you get here, anyway? And how did you find out where I live?"

"I googled you. You're like famous. There were all these articles about how you burned down a funeral home, and how your apartment got fire-bombed."

"The funeral home was an accident. And technically I didn't start the fire."

"Hey, I can totally relate. Like, I burned down a forest once, and it wasn't my fault. We were just smokin' some weed and next thing VROOOM forest fire."

I took a step back, getting closer to my kitchen. "I thought you were homeless, living under the bridge. Did you take a cab here? Do you have a car?"

"No, man. I didn't take a cab. Cabs cost mucho dinero. I'm saving my money to get Tiki and me back to Hawaii. I stole a car."

"Clever," I said. "Good thinking."

He tapped the side of his head. "This ain't my first rodeo."

I could see the flash of strobe lights projecting from the lot below us. Logan saw it too.

"Whoa, there must be an emergency," Logan

said. "Like a fire, or some old dude had a heart attack."

He moved out of the small foyer into my living
room and went to the window, and I grabbed my
stun gun.

"It's a police car," Logan said. "And here comes
a second. And they're checking out a car. I bet
there's drugs in it. Or maybe it's stolen. Man, this is
so cool." There was a moment of silence. "Uh-oh,"
he said. "That's my car they're looking at. You're
gonna have to give me a ride back to the bridge."

He turned and faced me, and I lunged at him
with the stun gun. He shrieked and slashed at me
with the knife. The tip caught me on the arm, and
a bright red line instantly appeared from my elbow
to my wrist.

Logan's eyes went wide. "Oh jeez, I'm mega
sorry. You need like a Band-Aid or something."

What I needed was an entire box of Band-Aids. I
didn't think the cut was especially deep, but it was
long and dripping blood on the carpet. I took my
arm into the kitchen and wrapped a bunch of paper
towels around it.

"Are you going to be okay?" Logan asked. "Like
should I call 911?"

"Not necessary," I told him. "It's not that deep."

"Okay, then," he said. "I guess I'll be going."

"No!"

Too late. He was out the door and sprinting
down the hall.

I had the paper towels held in place with elastic bands, and I was looking for my Band-Aids when Morelli walked in.

"What the heck?" he said. "What did you do?"

"Brody Logan was here looking for his tiki, and he accidentally nicked me with his ceremonial knife."

"You've got your entire arm swaddled in paper towels and there's blood all over your floor."

"It was a big nick."

Morelli carefully unwrapped my arm, rinsed it off, and patted it dry. He applied first-aid ointment and rewrapped the arm in paper towels since the three Band-Aids I found weren't going to do the job.

"We'll stop at the drugstore on the way and get a better bandage," he said. "Do you still want to go to the shore?"

"Of course!"

• • •

I woke up with a slight sunburn and an arm wrapped in surgical gauze. It was Monday. A workday. And Morelli's side of the bed was empty. The room was dark, but there was light shining from the hall. I could smell coffee brewing. I rolled out of bed, got dressed, and shuffled down the stairs and into the kitchen.

Morelli was at the little table with his coffee,

toast, and cereal, and the morning paper. I kissed him on the top of his head and dropped a slice of bread into the toaster.

"You're up early," he said.

"Lots to do today."

"How's the arm?"

"It feels fine."

"Looks like Ranger was busy last night. An electrical supply warehouse was firebombed. Apparently it was a Rangeman account, and one of Ranger's guys was on the scene when it happened and was pretty badly burned."

I took the paper from Morelli and read the article. "This is Robert Kinsey's warehouse. He was my Friday night security assignment."

"Someone's not happy with him," Morelli said.

"Clearly." I spread strawberry jelly on my toast and poured out a mug of coffee. "I don't know much about it. Just that he's worried. He's getting married next Saturday, and Ranger and I will be doing security again."

Morelli took his cereal bowl to the sink and rinsed it. "I have to go. Monday morning meeting." He unlocked the drawer by the back door, removed his Glock, checked it out, and clipped it onto his belt. "Try to stay safe."

"Has Bob been out?"

"Bob's done everything he needs to do. Francine Lukach will be here at noon as usual to walk him."

I finished my breakfast, retrieved my tote bag,

and grabbed Tiki. "I'd leave you here," I said to Tiki, "but I'm afraid his Grandma Bella will return and perform a ritual sacrifice, turning you into a pile of ash."

Probably it was my imagination but I swear I felt a shiver run through Tiki. I went to the door, looked out, and realized I didn't have a car. My car was parked in my lot. The sun was barely up. Lula would still be asleep. It would be awkward to ask my father to come get me after a night of gorilla sex with Morelli. Too far to walk, especially lugging a three-foot tiki. I could call Ranger but that was even more awkward.

My phone rang and I grimaced at the number. Ranger.

"I need to talk to you," he said. "Where are you? Your car is in your lot, but your bag is at Morelli's."

"You have my bag bugged?"

"You didn't know?"

"No!"

"Now you know. Where are you?"

"I'm at Morelli's house. I'm stranded."

Disconnect.

I looked at Tiki. "He's coming," I said.

TWELVE

TIKI AND I SAT on the front stoop of Morelli's house and waited for Ranger. Lights were on in the house across the street. Morelli wasn't the only one up in his neighborhood. This was a neighborhood of hardworking people. Sleepy-eyed kids were eating breakfast, and stuffing their backpacks with favorite things to take to daycare or Grandma's house. Adults were organizing and watching the clock. Morelli's neighbors were nurses, clerks at the DMV, line operators at the button factory, plumbers, mechanics, and dental assistants. The houses were modest. Cars were economy models. And like the Burg this was an emerging immigrant neighborhood of multigenerational families. Lots of Italian and Eastern European cultures. A smattering of Russian. Some Portuguese. And, lately, Hispanic.

Ranger's low-slung Porsche 911 eased around the corner and glided to a curbside stop. I scooped Tiki up and wedged him into the small cargo area behind the seats.

"Garage sale?" Ranger asked, looking at Tiki.

I buckled myself in. "It's a Hawaiian wood carving put up for bond. I'm carrying it around because Vinnie thinks it encourages bad behavior and doesn't want it in the office."

Ranger's attention turned to me. "How about you? Is it encouraging bad behavior in *you*?"

"It might be."

Ranger's mouth tipped into a smile.

"That's an evil smile," I said to him.

"You're at your best when you're a little bad, babe."

I felt a rush of heat remembering times spent with Ranger. "A distant memory," I said, trying to sound aloof but pretty sure I wasn't pulling it off. "What did you want to talk to me about?"

"Kinsey's warehouse was firebombed last night."

"I read about it in the paper. The article said one of your men was burned."

"He was inside, checking on an alarm. Whoever fired off the rocket knew he was in there. The Rangeman SUV was parked at the door."

"Is your man going to be okay?"

"Yes. It could have been worse. Second-degree burns on his arms. The other burns were superficial."

"Do you have any idea yet who's doing this?"

"No. The code was secret but it's been years since the unit was disbanded. Someone might have had too much to drink and talked too much. Someone might have shared his life story with a woman and not thought anything of it. My instincts tell me one of the men is involved, but it's not a given fact."

"It's someone clever," I said. "This person knew you were going to be at the dinner. And they knew when your man would be inside the warehouse. Could it be someone inside Rangeman?"

"It's possible. More likely it's someone who knows how to listen or hack into a system. Everyone in my unit had access to that technology."

"Could someone hack into *your* system?"

"Not easily." Ranger swung into my apartment building lot and parked next to the Buick. "Rehearsal and dinner is seven o'clock on Friday. The wedding is at four on Saturday. You need to be careful. It's hard for anyone to get past my security, so there's a possibility this person will go after people close to me who are more vulnerable."

I wrestled Tiki out of the Porsche. "Understood. Thanks for the ride."

Ranger leaned across the seat and snagged my wrist. "I'm giving you another opportunity to walk away from this."

"I can't do that. I can't walk away."

• • •

I took Tiki to my apartment and set him on the kitchen counter next to Rex. I gave Rex fresh water and hamster food, added a chunk of carrot, and told him I loved him just in case he was feeling neglected.

I took a shower, dressed in clean clothes, and headed out with Tiki. Lula was already at the bonds office when I arrived.

"What happened to your arm?" she asked.

"Freak accident. Nothing serious."

"You look annoyed," Lula said. "Is Tiki getting you into trouble?"

"No. Tiki's fine. It's Cubbin. The disappearing thing is gnawing at me. It's not like he was walking in the woods and disappeared. The guy was in a hospital. There were video cameras. There was limited access. Two nurses were on duty."

"How about if one of the nurses sneaked him out," Lula said.

"I wouldn't be surprised. I talked to Norma Kruger, and she didn't give me a warm fuzzy feeling. Problem is, even if Kruger helped him, it doesn't explain how Cubbin got off the surgical floor, or why he wasn't picked up on camera. Briggs and the police looked at the tapes."

"Kruger could be a magician, and she could have given Cubbin the Cloak of Invisibility," Lula said. "Harry Potter had one of those. I saw it in the movies."

"That would be a long shot," I said to Lula.

"Even so, we could go snoop on her," Lula said.

Connie looked up from her computer. "And you should try Dottie Luchek again. It's not a high bond but it would be good to clear it." Her attention shifted to the front window. "It's Logan again, trying to get into your Buick."

Connie grabbed a shotgun from the cabinet behind her. Lula whipped out her Glock. And we all ran to the door. Logan turned, went wide-eyed, and took off.

Lula shoved her Glock into the waistband of her spandex skirt. "What we should do is set Tiki out on the sidewalk and give Stephanie a big butterfly net."

I couldn't get excited about the butterfly net, but setting a trap for Logan wasn't a bad idea. I'd think about it after I got Cubbin out of my head.

"I'm going to do a drive-by on Nurse Norma," I said to Lula.

"I'm with you," Lula said. "I bet I could tell from looking at her if she had the Cloak of Invisibility."

I unlocked the Buick and got behind the wheel. "If we get to talk to her, let's dial back on the Cloak of Invisibility. It's a little *out there*."

"Gotcha. You won't hear anything about it from me. My lips are sealed. I'm locking them shut and throwing away the key."

"Good."

"No way will I say anything about the Cloak of Invisibility. Even if she brings it up I'm not joining in the conversation."

"Good."

"You're gonna have to tell me if you want me to

say something, 'cause otherwise I'm not saying nothing."

I did a U-turn when there was a break in the traffic. "When are you going to start saying nothing?"

"When we get to her door. I'm saving myself for then."

• • •

I turned left at Olden and cut across town. I drove into Kruger's condo complex and crept past her address. The Jag was in the assigned spot. Curtains were drawn.

"We gonna knock on her door?" Lula asked.

"I don't think so. She looks shut down. She works the night shift so she's probably sleeping."

"We should come by at night when she's working and see if she's all locked up. You know, just check on everything for her so she don't get robbed."

"It would be our civic duty."

"Damn skippy," Lula said.

I made a loop around the parking area and noticed a rust-riddled van parked across from Kruger's apartment. A blond woman was behind the wheel. It was Susan Cubbin.

I parked next to the van and got out. "Stay here," I said to Lula. "I'll only be a minute."

I opened the door to the van and stuck my head in. The cat was sleeping next to Susan, and I could see the kitty litter on the floor behind the seat.

"Hey," I said. "What's up?"

"I'm looking for my jerk husband, that's what's up. What's up with you?"

"Pretty much the same thing. Why are you parked here?"

"He's with the nurse. It's the only explanation. I don't know how she got him out of the hospital, but she's got him squirreled away somewhere. Have you seen her? She's probably made her powder room into a sex dungeon."

"So you're following her around?"

"No. I'm watching her condo. I'm waiting for a sign that he's in there. As soon as I know for sure, I'm going in like gangbusters."

"Do you have her condo bugged?"

"No. I bought some stuff, but I don't know how to use it. It didn't come with instructions."

Susan Cubbin was almost as good at snooping as Dottie Luchek was at hooking. Which was to say she was no good at all.

"Lula and I went to see you yesterday," I said to Susan. "The front door was open and there was a big guy with white hair in your house."

"A realtor?"

"I don't think so. He looked more like a maniac."

"They're not mutually exclusive," Susan said. "I put that piece of junk up for sale. I'm sure it was a realtor."

The cat stood, turned around three times, and settled back down.

"How can you be sure Nurse Norma has your husband on ice here?" I asked her. "Maybe she has him someplace else."

"She doesn't go anywhere else. She works all the time. If she's not here then she's at the hospital or The Clinic. I followed her there the first day. She's at The Clinic from four in the afternoon until six o'clock."

"Is this clinic attached to the hospital?"

"No. She's moonlighting. It's a private clinic on Deeley Street, and it's called The Clinic. At least it says 'The Clinic' on the sign, but I didn't see any patients going in or out. It might be one of those research places. There are a lot of them on that Route 1 corridor going to Princeton."

I gave her my business card again, and I went back to Lula in the Buick.

"Well?" Lula said.

"It's Susan Cubbin. She's hunkered down looking for her husband and the five million dollars. She's got her cat with her and a sleeping bag in the back."

"Where's she going potty?"

"I didn't ask."

"That would have been my first question," Lula said. "I'm interested in stuff like that."

"Have you ever heard of Deeley Street?"

"No, but I can find it on my cellphone."

Lula tapped the address in and we watched while the phone searched.

"Here it is," Lula said. "It's off Route 1. Looks like it's just before Quaker Bridge Mall. Are we going there? We could stop at Quaker Bridge and get one of them big salty soft pretzels and a Blizzard."

"That would be great," I said. "And we could get a couple cheeseburgers."

"Don't forget the fries."

"Do they still make supersize? I need supersize."

"Drive faster," Lula said. "I'm about to have the big O just thinking about the fries."

I reached the mall in record time, parked, and Lula and I jumped out of the car and ran to the food court.

We hit the burger place first, and Lula pulled a wad of money out of her purse. "I want two of everything on your menu," she said to the girl behind the counter. "And hurry up because I have to put in my order at Dairy Queen and Dunkin' Donuts."

"Yeah, me too," I said. "I want the same."

The counter girl stared at us. "Am I getting punked?"

"Say what?" Lula said.

"Omigod," I said to Lula. "What are we doing?" I grabbed her arm and pulled her away from the counter. "We're out of control."

"I don't feel out of control," Lula said.

"Have you ever ordered everything on a menu before?"

"Do I have to answer that?"

"I'm going to the sandwich place and I'm getting a turkey club."

"That don't sound like a lot of fun."

"You can eat whatever the heck you want, but I have to get into a bridesmaid dress on Saturday, and I don't want to look like a whale."

Lula tagged after me to the sandwich shop. "Who's getting married?"

"Ranger's client. The same one we did security for last Friday."

"So this is a bridesmaid job? You're like a undercover bridesmaid. Like in *Miss Congeniality*. Remember that movie? Sandra Bullock was a FBI agent that they made into a beauty queen. I loved that movie."

I got a turkey club and a bottle of water, and Lula got ham and cheese, a bag of chips, and a soda.

"I think it was Tiki sitting in your backseat that made us crazy for all that food," Lula said. "You might want to think about giving him back to Logan, on account of he's going to make us fat."

Tiki fell into the same category for me as Grandma Bella and Catholicism. I couldn't bring myself to be a true believer and have complete faith, but I had fear. There was the irrational possibility of the existence of a power beyond my comprehension.

"I can't give him back. I need the recovery money."

"Yeah, but Tiki might be more trouble than he's worth. Money isn't everything."

"The only people who say that are people who have enough money to pay the rent."

We finished eating and went back to the Buick and Tiki.

"Look at him," Lula said. "He's smirking. I know smirking when I see it." She pulled attitude and leaned in to him. "Well *ha ha* on you, because we didn't eat all that food. We had a nutritious meal of a sandwich."

"That's telling him," I said. "Buckle up and we'll try to find The Clinic."

THIRTEEN

IT WAS THE MIDDLE of the day and Route 1 wasn't especially challenging. No gridlocked traffic. No nutso drivers weaving in and out of lanes trying to cut three minutes off their drive time. No one giving everybody the finger because they had a crapola day at the office. I cruised along, following Lula's directions.

"It's coming up," she said. "Take the next light and you'll be on Willow, and then turn onto Deeley."

We were in one of the many light industrial complexes that line the highway. Most of the buildings were medical arts. A plumbing supply company. A FedEx facility. And The Clinic was off by itself at the end of a cul-de-sac. It was a medium to large two-story stucco building painted a sick green. There were no cars in visitor parking. No lights shining from any of the windows. No signs indicating what sort of clinic it might be. I parked to the far side and we sat looking at the building.

"According to Susan Cubbin, Nurse Norma spends two hours a day here," I said to Lula.

"It's kind of out of the way of the hospital."

I called Connie and gave her the address. "See if you can find something called The Clinic."

Five minutes later Connie called back. "It's a private clinic for surgical recovery. Usually that means it's a spa type facility where wealthy men and women can hang after cosmetic procedures like face-lifts and liposuction. Two doctors are listed on staff. Abu Darhmal and Craig Fish."

"Anything else?"

"I did a superficial search. Do you want me to go deeper?"

"Yes, but there's no rush."

I pulled the key out of the ignition. "Let's go say hello."

"Okay, but if I get one whiff of hospital cooties I'm out of there."

I walked to the door and looked inside. Small vestibule. Dark. The front door was locked. I couldn't see beyond the vestibule.

"You sure Nurse Norma comes here?" Lula asked. "Don't look like nobody's home."

I rang the bell and waited. I rang a second time. Nothing. We walked around the building, but the blinds were drawn and we couldn't see in any of the windows. An underground garage entrance in the back was sealed off by a roll-down door. There was also a metal fire door in the back. It too was locked.

"Guess there aren't a lot of ladies getting their fat sucked out today," Lula said. "Business doesn't look all that good."

We went back to the car and sat there.

"What are we waiting for?" Lula asked.

"I don't know. I guess I'm waiting for something to happen."

"Looks to me like that could take a while."

"I'd like to see what's in this building."

"You thinking it could be Cubbin? Like they could have him in here hanging by his thumbs until he tells them where he's got the money stashed?" Lula said.

"It's a possibility."

"I bet I could get us in."

"Yes, but you'd break something. There's a keypad on the front door. At four o'clock Nurse Norma is going to show up and punch in her code."

"And all we have to do is watch and get the code."

I turned the key in the ignition. "I'm going to move the car to the next lot so Norma doesn't see it, and then I'm going to come back and find a place where I can see the keypad."

"You got binoculars?"

"Yep."

I parked around the corner and left Lula with Tiki. It wasn't quite two o'clock, so Lula had time for a nap and I had time to investigate some of the other buildings in the area and ask about The Clinic.

I went to FedEx first.

"I'm looking for The Clinic," I said. "I was told it was in this park but I can't find it."

"It's all by itself at the end of the street," the woman behind the counter said. "If you go out of our lot and turn left and keep going you'll find it. I've never been in it myself, but they drop off here once in a while."

"I'm applying for a job there and the ad was vague. What kind of a place is it? The ad just said they were looking for a med tech."

"I don't know what they do. They won't ship anything for months, and then they'll send out a bunch of cold packs and that'll be it. Probably they use other shipping companies."

Myron Cryo Industries was The Clinic's closest neighbor. Myron was in a large sleek black glass cube, separated from The Clinic by a clump of trees and shrubs. The lobby was high-gloss onyx and polished chrome. The guy working the reception desk was in a suit that had me thinking he moonlighted at a Holiday Inn.

"I'm supposed to be applying for a job at The Clinic," I said to him, "but it doesn't seem to be open for business. The front door is locked and no one answers. Did they move or something?"

"As far as I can tell that's normal for The Clinic. It always looks closed."

"Do you know what they do there? It didn't say in the ad."

"Don't know. I've never seen anyone go in or go

out. Our security guard says sometimes he hears the garage door going up."

I walked to the end of the cul-de-sac, where there was another wooded area, and I was able to lose myself in the foliage. I leaned against a tree and waited, suspecting this was wasted effort. Nurse Norma was most likely going to enter through the garage.

At four Norma's Jag cruised down the street, turned in to the private drive at the side of the building, and disappeared around back. I heard the garage door roll up, and I dropped my binoculars back into my messenger bag. So much for this brilliant idea.

I stayed in place and watched the building for signs of activity. After ten minutes I heard the garage door roll up again, and a black Cadillac Escalade with dark tinted windows appeared from the back of the building and motored down the street. I couldn't get a good look at the driver but I copied the plate and called Connie to trace it.

Lula was asleep when I reached the Buick. I rapped on the window to jolt her awake, and she snapped to attention.

"Who? What?" she said.

I slid behind the wheel and cranked the engine over. "I wasn't able to get the front-door code, but shortly after Norma arrived I saw an SUV drive away from the building. Norma was replacing someone."

"Did you see who was in the car?"

"No, but I got the plate. Connie's tracing it for me."

"So how are we going to get in this place?"

"There's a mail drop box in the back of the building next to the garage door. It's designed to receive package deliveries. It isn't locked from the outside because no one could possibly get into it. If it isn't locked from the inside we might be able to shove Briggs in and have him unlock a door for us."

"You think he'd do that?"

"A patient disappeared. That's a major security breach, and Briggs can't even explain how it happened. I'm sure he'd like to solve the mystery."

"I thought he said no. Like I thought nobody at the hospital cared."

"I don't believe it. They have to care. It's embarrassing. It's bad business. And Briggs is head of security. I mean, how does it look on your résumé that you lost a patient?"

"I see your point. Do you think he'll fit?"

"It was a pretty big drop box."

"When are you going to do this?"

"Tonight."

"I'm in," Lula said. "I don't want to miss this."

• • •

I stopped at the hospital on the way back to the office. Lula waited in the car and I ran in to see Briggs.

"Are you nuts?" Briggs said when I explained my plan. "I'm not doing that. And by the way it's demeaning. How would you like to be stuffed into a drop box?"

"I wouldn't fit," I said.

Briggs narrowed his eyes at me. "I bet I could get you in."

"Let's not get nasty over this. You lost a patient, and I'm offering to help you."

Briggs took a moment. "And you think Cubbin is in The Clinic?"

"It's possible."

"Okay. I'll do it, but I swear if you ever tell anyone you stuffed me into a drop box I'll shoot you."

"Fine. I'll meet you in the FedEx parking lot at nine o'clock."

I returned to the car and plugged the key into the ignition.

"Well?" Lula asked. "What did he say?"

"He's going to do it."

"Wow, just like that?"

"He said he'd shoot me if I told anyone we stuffed him into a drop box. What's with all this shooting stuff? Have you noticed there's a lot of shooting going on? Something should be done about it."

"Like what?"

"We should stop shooting people! There has to be a better way to solve a problem."

"I guess," Lula said. "But personally, I like shooting someone once in a while. Nothing serious. Like maybe just shooting someone in the little toe. I've done that a couple times."

I cut my eyes to the rearview mirror and glanced at Tiki. He was still strapped in and he looked benign, but I didn't trust him. I thought he might be encouraging thoughts of shooting.

Connie was packing up to leave when we got back to the office. "The black Escalade belongs to Abu Darhmal, the second doctor listed at The Clinic. Darhmal is forty years old and has a Ph.D. in biochemistry from the University of Maryland. No medical degree that I could find. He's originally from Somalia. Looks to me like he has a green card but isn't a U.S. citizen. I could find no address other than The Clinic. He taught at college level before settling in at The Clinic four years ago. No wife or other dependents. He was accused of human trafficking four years ago but was acquitted. Probably why he left academia." Connie handed me the report.

"Maybe Nurse Norma is *doing* Dr. Darhmal," Lula said.

"She'd have to *do* him fast," I said. "He left immediately after she got there."

"The Clinic is even sketchier," Connie said. "It's listed as a medical recovery facility, but that's it. No hours of operation. A phone number that goes directly to voicemail. It's owned by a holding company. Franz Sunshine Enterprises. Franz Sunshine is the president. He's also president of FS Financials. Sunshine bought the Clinic building at auction four years ago. Its assessed assets come to just under five hundred thousand dollars. That's not a lot for a viable business."

Connie gave me that file as well. "I'm out of here," she said. "There's a glass of wine waiting for me somewhere."

"I'm out of here too," Lula said.

I checked my watch. It was almost six o'clock. Too late to try the bridesmaid dress on for size. I'd have to do it tomorrow. I left the bonds office and drove to my parents' house.

"Just in time for dinner," Grandma said when I strolled into the kitchen.

"That was my plan," I said, setting Tiki onto the kitchen table.

My mother was spooning mashed potatoes into a bowl. "What is that?" she asked. "It looks like a totem pole."

"It's a Hawaiian tiki," I told her. "Vinnie took it as security on a bond and I'm babysitting it because he didn't want it in the office."

"It's cute," Grandma said. "It reminds me of a big tater tot."

I looked over my mother's shoulder. "Pot roast?"

My mother nodded. "With mashed potatoes, green beans, and gravy."

"And chocolate pudding for dessert," Grandma said.

I set a plate for myself at the table and helped carry the food in.

"Have you heard any more about Geoffrey Cubbin?" I asked Grandma, taking my seat.

"Nothing about Cubbin," she said, "but there's talk going around that some residents of Cranberry Manor were planning to kidnap him and squeeze some information out about the money."

"Do you have names?"

"Nope. Just the rumor. I heard about it at the bakery this morning when I went for coffee cake."

I forked a slab of meat onto my plate. "Those people are pretty old. Hard to believe they'd be able to kidnap Cubbin."

"They want their money back," Grandma said. "And they haven't got a lot to lose. If they get arrested it's not like they'll spend a lot of years in prison. Most of them have one foot in the grave already."

I helped myself to potatoes. "I'll go back to Cranberry Manor tomorrow and dig around," I told Grandma. "See if you can get me a name."

"You bet," Grandma said. "I'm on the job."

"Gravy," my father said. "I need more gravy."

My mother jumped up and scurried into the kitchen with the gravy boat. At first glance it would seem that she was waiting on my father, but truth is she was happy for an opportunity to go to the kitchen to refresh her "ice tea."

My family doesn't spend a lot of unnecessary time on body functions. We eat and we leave to do other things. My father has television shows to watch. My mother and my grandmother have dishes to wash and the kitchen to set straight. I helped in the kitchen and by seven-thirty I was on my way.

I had Tiki on the seat next to me guarding the bag of leftovers. I called Morelli and asked if he was interested in pot roast and chocolate pudding. He asked if I was delivering the food naked. I said no. And he said he wanted it anyway.

He was at the door when I parked. He was in his usual outfit of jeans and T-shirt. He had a five o'clock shadow going that was two days old. And he looked better than dessert.

I handed him the bag of food, he dragged me to him, and he kissed me with an indecent amount of tongue and ass grabbing.

"I haven't got a lot of time," I said. "I'm meeting Lula at nine."

"I can be fast," Morelli said.

"Not fast enough. I'm just dropping off."

He looked in the bag. "Yum."

"You used to say that about me," I told him.

"Cupcake, you're still *yum*, but we've got chocolate pudding here. That's serious competition."

I returned his kiss. "Gotta go."

"Where are you going?"

"You don't want to know."

Morelli immediately turned from playful boy-friend to serious cop. "Tell me."

I studied him for a moment. It would be good to

confide in him and tap in to his expertise. He was smart. And he had more experience than I did. Unfortunately I was about to do something not entirely legal, and I'd compromise his cop ethics if I told him. Not that Morelli didn't sometimes bend his ethics to suit the occasion. It was more that I never knew when he would bend and when he'd handcuff me to the bedpost to keep me from committing a crime.

"I need to get into a building," I said. "And it's locked except for a large drop box for mail."

"How large is the drop box?"

"About as big as Randy Briggs."

Morelli's face creased into a grin. "You're kidding."

"No."

"Why is this building so important?"

"I think Geoffrey Cubbin might be in there."

"You have reasons for thinking this?"

"Yep."

"Then why don't you just break in and announce yourself? You have that privilege as a bail bonds agent."

"If he's not in there I want to be able to snoop around."

"I didn't hear any of this," Morelli said. "And I want you to call me when you get home."

"Deal."

FOURTEEN

I WAS THE FIRST to get to the FedEx lot. Lula arrived a few minutes after me. Randy Briggs drove up a few minutes after Lula. We all had penlights and pepper spray. We were all dressed in black, just like in the movies. And we all felt sort of stupid. Okay, maybe not Lula, but definitely Briggs and me.

"We'll go in Lula's car," I said. "We'll park in Myron Cryo's lot and cut through the band of trees. I drove around the cul-de-sac when I first got here and there are no cars parked in front of The Clinic and no lights shining from any of the windows."

Lula killed her lights at the entrance to the Cryo lot and glided to a stop close to the greenbelt. We all piled out and crept through the trees and shrubs to the blacktopped driveway that led to The Clinic's underground garage. There was a single light shining over the garage entrance. And there was a light in a room at the far end of the second floor.

The drop box was next to the roll-down door.

The metal fire door was to the other side of the drop box. I opened the drop box door, clicked my penlight on, and took a look inside. It was going to be a tight fit for Briggs.

"I'm not crazy about this," Briggs said. "What if I get stuck? What if I get caught?"

"If you get caught just tell them some college kids kidnapped you and put you in the box for fun," Lula said. "Probably happens all the time to you little people."

"I got a gun," Briggs said to Lula. "I could shoot you."

"You don't scare me," Lula said. "My gun's bigger than your gun."

"Oh yeah?" Briggs said. "Haul it out and we'll see who's got the bigger gun."

"Jeez Louise!" I said. "Here we go with the gun stuff again. Stop the gun stuff! *There's no gun stuff!*"

"She don't understand the joys of shooting," Lula said to Briggs.

"She hasn't got enough rage," Briggs said. "She needs more rage."

"You're going to see rage if you don't stop talking and get in the box," I said to Briggs.

"Alley-oop," Lula said, lifting Briggs up and sliding him in feetfirst.

"I don't fit," Briggs said.

"Sure you do," Lula told him. "Just squish down a little."

Lula put her hand on top of Briggs's head, compacted him into the box, and closed the door.

"See," Lula said. "I knew he'd fit."

There was a lot of swearing and banging around inside the box and then silence.

Lula and I waited, staring at the box.

"You think I should open it and look inside?" Lula asked. "If he's dead I'm not pulling him out. Bad enough I just ran the risk of getting Briggs cooties. I'm not getting dead cooties. They're worse than hospital cooties."

I opened the box and looked inside. Empty.

"I think I hear something," Lula said. "Sounds like he's working at the lock on the door."

My cellphone rang. It was Briggs.

"Hang tight," Briggs said. "I can't reach the deadbolt. I'm going to get something to stand on."

A minute later Briggs opened the door, and Lula and I scooted into the building. The garage was dimly lit. Two cars were parked in the garage. The black Escalade and a white panel van. We took the stairs to the first floor, and I cautiously poked my head out the door and squinted into a dark hall.

"Stay here," I said to Lula and Briggs. "I'm going to investigate."

I tiptoed down the hall, looking into empty, unfurnished rooms with en suite handicap bathrooms. I was thinking that the building had been designed for use as a nursing home, but probably never had any residents.

The hall was bisected by a nurses' station from which a short corridor led to the small lobby and main entrance, and to the far side of the nurses' station were more unused, unfurnished rooms.

I retraced my steps and took the stairs to the second floor. The hall was dark, but I could see light spilling from a room on the far side of the center foyer. I'd been nervous as I walked the first floor. The nerves kicked up to heart palpitations and nausea when I stepped into the second-floor hall. The rooms on either side of the hall were obviously offices. Two of the offices were furnished and looked like they were being used. I didn't want to take the time to snoop in the offices. The rest of the offices were empty.

I crossed the center foyer, held my breath, and opened a door to a fully equipped lab. I assumed this belonged to Darhmal, the biochemist. There were two hospital type rooms across from the lab. Beds were made. No one in them. No sign that anyone occupied either of the rooms. No personal possessions. No toothbrush in the bathroom. No water glass.

I could hear a television droning in the room at the end of the hallway. I swallowed back panic at the knowledge that someone probably was in the room. Cubbin maybe. More likely whoever owned the two vehicles in the garage. There were two doors opening onto the television room. Not a normal hospital room, I thought. It was most likely a dayroom for staff or a rec room for patients who didn't exist.

I had one more door to open. It had a numbered keypad on it. No window in the door. I gently pushed against it. Unlocked. I stepped in and flicked my penlight on. I wasn't sure what I was seeing at first. It took me a moment to realize it was an operating room. My experience with operating rooms is little to none, but to my untrained eye this looked very complete and high tech. There were cabinets with drugs and syringes, refrigeration units, gas tanks, autoclaves, surgical equipment trays, high-powered lights, a hydraulic table, computers, and a bunch of mysterious machines.

I heard a phone ring in the television room. Heard a man's voice answer the phone. My heart stopped dead in my chest for a beat, and I started to sweat. I had the penlight in one hand and my phone in the other. Lula and I had done the drill before. If I opened the line to her it meant I was screwed.

Hard to hear what the man was saying over the noise of the television, but it sounded like a social call. There were no shocked or angry exclamations. I stepped out of the operating room, tiptoed to the first door, and carefully peeked in. It was the Yeti with his back to me. No one else in the room.

I whirled around and speed walked the length of the hall. I was almost at the stairs when I heard the Yeti yell.

"Hey! What the hell? *Stop right where you are.*"

I bolted the last couple steps, ducked into the stairwell, flew down the stairs, and ran past Lula and Briggs.

"Time to go," I said to them.

I kept running, through the garage, out the door, across the driveway to the patch of trees. I could hear Lula and Briggs behind me. We were all breathing heavy when we piled into the Firebird. Lula put the car in gear and peeled out of the lot.

"What happened?" Lula wanted to know, racing to the FedEx lot. "Did you see Cubbin?"

"No," I said. "I saw the Yeti. He was watching television, and he caught me creeping down the hall. I think I might have wet my pants."

"You saw a Yeti?" Briggs said. "Isn't that one of them Bigfoot things?"

"Actually what I saw was a six-foot-six albino with one blue eye and one brown eye," I told him.

"We're onto something," Lula said. "This is big. We're like *crime solvers*. We should have our own television show. What do we do next?"

"I don't know," I said. "I need to go home and have a glass of wine and stop hyperventilating."

"Just remember who got you into the building," Briggs said. "I want to be there when you get Cubbin. And I don't want to be left out of the television show either. Little people are sexy now. Have you seen *Game of Thrones*? We're hot."

I left Lula and Briggs and drove out of the industrial park. I didn't have hands-free phoning in the Buick so I waited until I was home to call Morelli.

"I'm home," I said.

"How did it go?"

"I didn't get arrested or shot at."

"That's good."

"I don't know what to think of The Clinic. It looks like it's set up for business. It's got offices, and a lab, and an emergency room, and rooms for patients, but there are no patients."

"And no Cubbin?"

"I didn't see him. I saw the albino."

"The guy who stunned you?"

"Yeah."

There was a big awkward silence in which I imagined Morelli was trying to get a grip on himself.

"And?" Morelli asked.

"And he saw me but I ran away."

"Did he follow you?"

"I don't think so. I checked for a tail."

I had Tiki sitting on my dining room table, and he was telling me to go back to the Mexicana Grill for a bucket of margaritas.

"Bad Tiki," I said.

"Are you talking to the wood chunk?" Morelli asked.

"Only a little."

• • •

I woke up pleased with myself that I'd ignored Tiki's margarita suggestion. I was able to snap the top snap on my jeans, and I felt right with the world. No residual nausea from the night's adventure. I'd almost gotten caught, but almost doesn't count, right?

I worked my way through a bowl of cereal and a mug of coffee while I constructed a mental to-do list for the day. First up was Dottie Luchek. Then I might take a look at Franz Sunshine. And I wanted to go back to Cranberry Manor. I was forgetting something, but I couldn't nail it down. It wasn't Melvin Barrel. His case was closed. It wasn't Nurse Norma. Susan Cubbin was staked out on that one, though I thought she made the wrong choice. I didn't think her husband was doing the sex slave thing with Norma Kruger.

I rinsed my dishes, brushed my teeth, grabbed Tiki and my messenger bag, and opened my front door. There was a note tacked to it.

Fear not. I will cleanse you of the evil. You will burn and your soul will flee the body he's contaminated.

I had a moment of scramble brain, followed by the sort of cold terror that only the criminally insane can inspire. And then I remembered the other item on the list. I needed to go to the bridal salon and get the bridesmaid dress fitted.

I ripped the note off the door and stuffed it into my bag. I returned to the kitchen, took my .45 out of the brown bear cookie jar, and spun the barrel. No bullets. I'd have to mooch some from Connie. I slipped the gun into the side pocket of my messenger bag, locked up my apartment, and took the stairs to the lobby.

I was a little freaked walking to the car. I didn't feel good about the whole burning-and-soul-leaving-body thing, so I was looking around for incendiary devices and being careful.

I put Tiki on the seat next to me and took off for the office. "You have to help me out here," I said to Tiki. "I can't be distracted by donuts and margaritas. If I don't stay sharp we could both end up as a big pile of ashes."

Traffic was light and fifteen minutes later I docked the Buick in front of the bonds office and called Ranger.

"I had a note tacked to my door this morning," I told him, trying to keep my voice even. I didn't want to sound like a freaked-out girl, but my hand was shaking as I read him the message.

"I got something similar," Ranger said. "Would you consider staying with me until we solve this? It would be easier for me to keep you safe if you were under my roof."

Very tempting. Ranger's private apartment in the Rangeman building was beyond comfortable. It was professionally decorated in soothing earth shades. The furniture was all clean modern lines. The kitchen was sleek and stocked with food thanks to his housekeeper. The shower had limitless hot water and Bulgari Green shower gel. The king-size bed had thousand-thread-count sheets. And then there was Ranger. He was total eye candy and surprisingly easy to live with as long as you understood that his energy would always dominate his space. Not to mention Ranger in bed. If I allowed myself to think too long about Ranger in bed I'd be on the road to Rangeman, foot to the floor.

"Thanks for the offer but I'm going to pass," I said. "It would be complicated."

"Babe," Ranger said. And he disconnected.

I looked over at Tiki. "You could have persuaded me," I said. "Where are you when I need you?"

FIFTEEN

CONNIE WAS ON THE phone when I walked into the office. Lula was on the couch, reading *Star* magazine.

"It's the cellulite issue," Lula said. "I love the cellulite issue."

Connie got off the phone, typed something into her computer, and sat back. "The charges have been dropped on Dottie Luchek. The cop said he misunderstood her intentions."

"Hah!" Lula said. "Translation is she ran into him again and gave him a free BJ."

So my list had just gotten shorter.

"I'd like to take a look at Franz Sunshine," I said, "but I can't come up with an angle."

"You could just walk up to him and come right out with it," Lula said. "He's a busy mogul. He might not know there's a Yeti living in his investment property. He could be happy you brought it to his attention."

I looked at Connie. "Do you think?"

Connie shrugged.

I hiked my bag higher onto my shoulder. "I'll play it by ear."

"Me too," Lula said. "I'm going with you. I want to see what a Franz Sunshine looks like."

FS Financials was located in a high-rise on State Street in the middle of town. I parked on the street, and Lula and I took the elevator to the fifth floor.

"This is a swanky building," Lula said. "This Franz guy must be doing okay."

FS Financials occupied half of the floor. The door was frosted glass with the lettering in gold. I had my hand on the doorknob, and I still had no idea what I'd say to Franz Sunshine.

"Well?" Lula asked.

"I'm thinking."

"Honest to goodness," Lula said. "What's to think about? You just go in and make something up. You let me do it. I'm good at making things up. I used to make stuff up all the time when I was a 'ho. Like how you think it's cute that their dick has a crook in it."

"That might not be a good opener for Franz Sunshine," I said.

"Well, I got a lot more than that," Lula said, pushing the door open. "You just stand back."

Lula was dressed in flaming fuchsia today with hair to match. Skin-tight short black spandex skirt, fuchsia cap-sleeve spandex top showing acres of cleavage, five-inch stiletto heels, and her fuchsia hair was frizzed out to about a two-foot diameter.

She marched into FS Financials and politely asked to see Mr. Sunshine. The woman at the desk asked if Lula had an appointment, and Lula said actually Mr. Sunshine had missed *his* appointment so she was here doing a house call.

"Yes, but you still need an appointment," the woman said. "May I give him your name?"

"You certainly may," Lula said. "It's Lula, as in Tallulah. And you tell him that he's gonna want to see me firsthand."

Sixty seconds later Lula swung her ass into Sunshine's office with me trailing behind.

"Howdy," she said to Sunshine. "I appreciate your seeing me like this. I'm Lula and this here's my associate Stephanie. I want to talk to you about The Clinic. What the heck does it do anyway?"

Sunshine was older than Grandma Mazur. He was a shrunken man with a wisp of hair plastered to the top of his head, and rosacea spread across his face like the map of Europe.

"It doesn't do anything," he said with a thick German accent. "I bought it cheap. It's an investment."

"Well, I'm looking for a place to start my business and someone told me you had the perfect place."

"What kind of business are you starting?"

"I'm a 'ho," Lula said. "And I'm looking for a 'ho house."

"You thought The Clinic would make a good brothel?"

"Yeah. I was told it had lots of rooms, which is just what I'm looking for. I could have a wide variety of themes going on if you see what I'm saying. And it sits by itself at the end of the street so the neighbors wouldn't be complaining about noise and such. Not that a 'ho is real noisy, but sometimes depending on what a customer wants you might get carried away fakin' a orgasm. I drove by your property on the advice of my finance officer and it looked empty except for a car I saw go in."

"I have a security guard."

"This didn't look like no security guard," Lula said. "This was a lady with 'ho hair. So I thought maybe the building had a head start on my idea."

"Not that I'm aware," Sunshine said.

"You'll have to excuse me if this is a offensive question," Lula said. "But you got a real kraut accent, and it don't go with the name Sunshine."

"It's the American equivalent to Sonnenschein. How much would you be willing to pay for my building?"

"How much do you want?" Lula asked.

"Ten million."

"Say what? I'm a 'ho, not Donald Trump. I don't got that kind of money. Would you be willing to hold a mortgage?"

"We should go now," I said to Lula. "We have another appointment."

"What appointment you talking about?" Lula asked.

"The appointment you made with your doctor for that rash you've got all over your . . . you-know-what."

"Oh yeah, that appointment."

Lula stuck her hand out to Sunshine but he waved it away. No doubt worried about the rash.

"Well, I gotta go," Lula said to him. "I'll be back in touch if I can get hold of ten million."

We swished out of Sunshine's office, down the hall, and into the elevator.

"How'd I do?" Lula asked. "I was good, right?"

"Yeah. You were great. I almost fell over when you said you wanted to turn The Clinic into a whorehouse."

"That was genius on my part," Lula said. "When you think about it the building's perfect with all those rooms. And it's even got a lab so you could do your own disease testing."

We stepped out of the building and found a shiny black GLK-Class Mercedes SUV parked where my Buick had formerly resided. A guy dressed in Rangeman black stepped away from the car and handed me a key.

"Ranger wanted you to have this," he said.

I looked up and down the street. "Where's the Buick?"

"Hal took it back to Rangeman."

Another black SUV rolled down the street and stopped by my new car. The Rangeman guy got into the SUV. And the SUV drove off.

"It's like you got a hot fairy godfather," Lula said.

I remoted the Mercedes doors open. "Be careful what you say in here. He's probably got it wired for audio and video to go straight to the control room." I looked up to the sky, half expecting to see a Rangeman chopper hovering over my head.

I got behind the wheel, pressed the keyless GO button, and the phone rang.

"I have your Buick," Ranger said. "Do you want it stored here, or do you want it taken back to your parents' house?"

"Leave it at Rangeman. Tiki is in the backseat. Make sure nothing happens to him."

"There's a gun in the drawer under your seat. My recommendation is to carry it with you."

"I have my own gun."

"Is it loaded?"

I did a mental groan. "No. I forgot to get bullets from Connie."

"Babe," Ranger said. And he disconnected.

"I bet he finds you exasperating," Lula said.

"Mostly I think I'm an amusement."

I pulled into traffic and headed for Cranberry Manor. I now had hands-free capability so I called Grandma.

"Were you able to get a name for me at Cranberry Manor?" I asked her.

"Not exactly, but Binney Molnar's granddaughter used to work there, and she said Bill Smoot is the only one with a car. Seems like he'd be a good place to start on account of they had to get to the hospital somehow."

"Thanks."

"Over and out," Grandma said.

• • •

Lula and I entered Cranberry Manor through a side door, bypassing the reception lady, and located the lounge. A woman was sitting off to one side, reading. Two men were playing Scrabble. And people were watching television. I walked over to some cardplayers and told them I was looking for Bill Smoot.

"Figures," one of the men said. "The chicks always want Smooty. It's because he's got a car."

"Why don't you have a car?" Lula asked.

"I used to have one but it was a pain in the keester. This place is lousy with pigeons. They crap all over everything. I got better things to do than wash pigeon crap off my car."

"Like what?" Lula asked him.

"Like this. I got a lot riding on this game. Loser has to get tested for Alzheimer's."

"I guess that's assisted-living humor," Lula said.

"About Bill Smoot," I said. "Where can I find him?"

"He's probably sitting outside the dining room. He gets there early so he can get a good seat."

Lula and I left the lounge and followed the corridor to the dining room. The dining room doors were closed, and the sign on the door stated that lunch would be served at noon. Noon was a little over an hour away but people were already lining up.

"Your granny is right," Lula said. "It's good living here. You get to watch television, and someone makes your food, and it's real pretty. And everyone looks happy unless they're talking about Cubbin. I bet they give out good pharmaceuticals."

"What about the pigeons?"

"That would be a problem."

There were four men sitting on a couch by the dining room door.

"Would one of you be Bill Smoot?" I asked.

"Yep, that's me," one of them said.

He was about 5'7" with white hair and thick glasses. I put him at late seventies, possibly early eighties. He was wearing tan slacks and a three-button white knit shirt.

"I'd like to talk to you about Geoffrey Cubbin."

All four men leaned forward, eyes narrowed.

"Asshole," one of them said.

"I understand you went to see him?"

They exchanged glances, and I knew I'd found the hospital contingent.

"What's this about?" Smoot asked.

"I'm looking for Cubbin and I thought you might be helpful."

"Why are you looking for him? Are you a cop?"

"Fugitive apprehension agent."

"Hah!" one of them said. "Bounty hunter."

There were smiles all around. "All right then," Smoot said. "What do you want to know?"

"Did you go to the hospital to see him?"

"Yeah," Smoot said. "We were gonna beat the snot out of him until he told us where he had the money stashed."

"You'd beat up a guy who'd just had his appendix removed?"

Everyone sort of shifted in his seat.

"We didn't have a clear-cut plan," Smoot said. "We might have just slapped him around a little."

"So what happened?"

"Ernie over there spent some time on that floor a couple months ago so he knew the drill," Smoot said.

Ernie shrugged. "Gallbladder. Easy come, easy go."

"The night nurses come on at eleven. They punch in, skim over the charts, and then they watch movies on their iPads. Central isn't exactly an award-winning hospital," Smoot said. "So we figured we could sneak in after visiting hours when the nurses were snarfing down vodka-laced chocolate candies and tuning in to *Twilight* episodes. We took the stairs and everything was going to plan except when we got to Cubbin's room it was empty. No Cubbin."

"So what did you do?"

"We left. We got stopped by the night guard on the way out. I guess he caught us on one of the monitors. We acted all dumb and demented and confused and he helped us get to our car. And then we went to the diner on Livingston and then we went home."

"I know that diner," Lula said. "They got amazing rice pudding."

"I always get grilled cheese," Smoot said. "It's nice and greasy. They don't give you a lot of grease here at the Manor."

"Well, that's a strike against them," Lula said. "That and the pigeons. The bad news is adding up."

"I don't suppose any of you have any idea where Cubbin might be?" I asked.

"Vanished off the face of the earth," Smoot said.

Lula and I left through the side door and got into the Mercedes.

"I'm out of ideas again," I said.

"Not me. I got a good idea. I say we have lunch. I'm in a pizza mood."

A half hour later we were sitting at a table in Pino's, working our way through a basket of bread, waiting for our pizzas. Pino's is a bar and grill on the edge of the Burg. It's a cop hangout and it's the go-to place for pizza. The polished wood bar is dark and smells slightly of whiskey. The tables on the fringe and in the middle of the room have red and white checked tablecloths. The light is dim even during daytime hours. The aroma of garlic and pizza dough baking hangs in the air. Sitting in Pino's is like being in a time warp. After a few minutes you can't remember if it's day or night. After a couple beers you don't care.

"I think that Sunshine dude is fishy," Lula said, buttering a wedge of bread. "And why was the Yeti in Cubbin's house? I bet he was gathering up some stuff for Cubbin. My theory is they got Cubbin stashed away at The Clinic and they're waiting for the right time to get him out of the country. Cubbin's gonna give them a bag of money, and they're gonna send him to Denmark."

"Why Denmark?"

"Nobody would think to look for him in Denmark. Have you ever heard of anybody hiding out in Denmark? It's another one of my genius observations. I bet all those other people who disappeared are in Denmark too. It's perfect."

"The homeless guy?"

"Maybe not the homeless guy. I can't explain the homeless guy. He could be in Carteret."

"Okay, let's go with your idea. I see where Sunshine would be involved. It's his building. And I can see the Yeti. He's muscle. I can even see Nurse

Norma. She makes the contact. What I don't get are the two doctors. Where do they fit?"

"They could have gotten rooked into something that never happened. Like this was supposed to be a medical facility and it was one of them things seemed like a good idea. And they probably don't even know their good name could get besmirched."

"Besmirched?"

"Yeah, that means you got a smirch on it."

We'd ordered one pepperoni with extra cheese and one with everything they could find in the kitchen. The pizzas came to the table, and I started with a slice of the pepperoni.

"I got another good idea," Lula said, going for the pizza with the works. "I always get inspired when I eat, and my new idea is we bag on Geoffrey Cubbin. I'm thinking we'd be better using our time to go look for some other scumbag."

"Brody Logan is the only other live FTA right now."

"What's with that? We usually got a stack of skips."

I took a second piece of pizza. "I'm sure some more will come in."

"Yeah, if there's one thing you can count on in Trenton, it's crime."

We had half a pizza left over, and I thought it would be a nice gesture to take it to Susan Cubbin. And while we were at it we could see if anything interesting was going on with Nurse Norma.

SIXTEEN

THE VAN WAS STILL parked across from Norma's condo, and Susan was behind the wheel. She was smoking, staring straight ahead, eyes glazed.

"Hey," I said. "How's it going?"

"It's not going," she said. "My ass is asleep from sitting here."

"We had pizza for lunch and we couldn't finish it. You want some?"

"Sure."

I passed the pizza box to her through the open window. "Any change in Norma's routine? Has she had any visitors?"

"No. And no."

"Are you here 24/7?" Lula asked. "Where do you go to the bathroom?"

"I go home when she goes to work. I figure Jerk-face is sleeping then and isn't going to be out walking around."

"Jerkface as in Geoffrey?" I asked her.

"Yeah. Jerkface Geoffrey." She opened the lid on the pizza box and looked inside. "What's on this?"

"Everything," I said.

Susan finished her cigarette, tore a chunk of pizza off for the cat, and ate the rest of the slice.

"I know he's in there," she said. "The shades are never raised. I can practically smell him from here."

"That's a long way to smell someone," Lula said. "He must be a real stinker."

"I'm tired of sitting here," Susan said. "I'm going in tonight. Soon as she leaves, I'm breaking in."

"Do you know how to do that?" Lula asked. "No offense but you're sort of a amateur."

"I watched a video on YouTube. It's easy. It's called lock bumping. I'm all set with a key from the hardware store that's been filed down. And then all I have to do is hit it with a hammer."

"God bless YouTube," Lula said. "You don't even need to go to college no more because you could learn how to do everything on YouTube."

"She's going to come out any minute," Susan said. "You should go away or hide or something so you don't spook her."

Lula and I went back to the Mercedes and waited. After ten minutes Nurse Norma stepped out of her front door, locked it, got into her sporty car, and drove off. When she was out of sight Lula and I returned to Susan.

"Let's do it," Lula said to Susan. "Let's root out Jerkface."

Susan fished the bump key out of her purse. "Are you coming with me?"

"Hell yeah," Lula said. "Wild horses couldn't drag me away."

Susan cracked a window for the cat, and we all marched across the parking area to Norma's condo.

"I've never done this before," Susan said, "but it didn't look hard on the video."

"I've done it lots of times," Lula said. "I used to always break a window to get in, and sometimes when I'm not prepared ahead I still do that, but mostly I bump the lock now."

Susan stuck the key into the lock, tapped it with the hammer, and turned. Nothing.

"You gotta have a knack," Lula said. "Try again. You'll get the feel of it."

The lock tumbled on the third try.

"I did it!" Susan said.

"This could be the start of a whole new career for you," Lula said. "Being able to bump a lock opens up lots of financial choices."

"None of which are legal," I said.

"It's legal for *us*," Lula said.

I flicked the lights on. "Sometimes."

Susan still had the hammer in her hand. "Stand back. I'm going on a Geoffrey hunt, and when I find him I'm going to hit him with this hammer until he tells me where he hid the money."

We moved out of the small foyer into the living room. The furniture looked comfortable. Lots of shades of beige. Dark wood tables. Beanpot lamps. An orange chenille throw on the couch.

"This looks like a page out of a Pottery Barn catalog," Lula said. "I recognize all this. I get that catalog in the mail."

Susan stalked her prey through the rest of the house. She had steely eyes and a white-knuckle grip on her hammer. She opened closet doors and looked under beds, and swore when there was no Geoffrey cowering behind Norma's pink fuzzy bathrobe.

"If she finds her husband you might want to jump in and take control before she splits his head open like it was a walnut," Lula whispered to me.

I didn't think she was going to find her husband. I could pretty much tell from the living room that there wasn't a man in residence. No size 12 running shoes under the coffee table. No crushed beer cans or Doritos bags hanging out on end tables. The pillows on the couch were all plumped and lined up perfectly. And in the kitchen the dishes were inside the dishwasher and not left on the counter.

While Susan was looking for her husband I was looking for information about Nurse Norma. Drug paraphernalia, bank statements, travel plans, a phone number or an address written on a pad by the phone, compromising photos, something that would tie her to The Clinic. I didn't find any of those things but I now knew she wore lacy thongs, she used Bumble and Bumble shampoo, she fell asleep reading *Cosmo, Glamour,* and professional articles on Botox, thermal fat reduction, and heart transplants.

The thongs, shampoo discovery, and reading selections didn't tell me why Norma was going to The Clinic every day if there were no patients. And if Cubbin wasn't in Norma's condo or at The Clinic, where the heck was he? Oddly enough the one thing that tied it all together was the Yeti. He was in Cubbin's house, and he was in The Clinic.

"I can't believe it," Susan said, back in the middle of the living room after totally searching the condo. "He's not here. I was so sure he was here."

"We would have liked if he was here," Lula said. "Stephanie needs to buy a car."

"Do you have any other ideas?" I asked Susan. "Let's start fresh. Where would Geoffrey go to hide? Would he go to a relative? Would he go to the shore? Would he steal a car and drive to Phoenix?"

"He wouldn't go to a relative," she said. "They'd turn him in. They were horrified when he was accused of embezzling the money. And they were probably the reason he took the money in the first place. Geoffrey was sort of the schmuck of the family. He wasn't making a lot of money. He didn't have a glamour job. And then there was always the one-nut thing hanging over his head."

"You be surprised how many men only have one nut," Lula said.

"Yeah, well, he was the only one in his family

with one nut, and the rest of his equipment wasn't impressive. Unfortunately I don't know firsthand but I'm told his brother is hung like a horse."

"How about the shore?" I asked.

"I can't see him at the shore. It was never his favorite place. I don't know about stealing a car and driving to Phoenix. I guess he could do that, but it seems to me he'd be in some pain and wouldn't want to be moving around that much. He was never great with pain. Most likely he'd try to get out of the country. He always wanted to go to Australia."

"Does he have a passport?" I asked.

"I took his passport out of the safety deposit box and hid it."

"And it's still in your hiding place?"

"Yes."

"Maybe that's what the Yeti was looking for," Lula said. "Of course with the kind of money ol' Geoffrey stole he could buy a new passport."

"What will you do now?" I asked Susan.

"I guess I'll go home and wait to be evicted."

"Well, good news," Lula said. "That could take a while. I hear they're real backed up on foreclosures."

• • •

I dropped Lula at the office and cruised around the block, trying to decide what to do next. For the

better part of the day I'd forgotten about the gruesome note, but now that it was time to go home
I had a hollow feeling in my stomach. It was the
stretch of pavement between my car and the door
to my apartment building that bothered me most. I
felt vulnerable when I walked that stretch of pavement. I could delay the experience by eating dinner
with my parents, visiting Morelli, or dropping in
on Ranger, but eventually I had to get from my car
to my door. Better to do it sooner than later, I decided. It would be more dangerous when it was
dark.

I drove home, parked, and retrieved Ranger's
small Ruger from under the driver's seat. I walked
into my building with the gun in my hand and
hoped I wouldn't run into any of my fellow ten-
ants. I had a reputation for being the building's Ca-
lamity Jane, and I didn't want to enhance that
image. I made it safely to my door, slipped inside,
and threw all the bolts.

My apartment is mostly furnished with relatives'
discards. It won't get a spread in *Architectural Di-
gest,* but it's comfortable in a secondhand kind of
way. I can't cook, and I never have dinner parties,
so my dining room table serves as a computer desk.
I have a couch and coffee table positioned in front
of the television, and that's about it for interior
decorating.

I said hello to Rex and gave him a baby carrot. I
took a half-empty box of Frosted Flakes out of the

cupboard, settled in front of the television, and snacked my way through dinner. I was channel surfing, looking for a nine o'clock show, and I noticed a red glow coming from the parking lot. I went to the window and saw that Ranger's car was on fire. A second later my cellphone rang.

"Now what?" Ranger asked.

"Someone toasted your car. I imagine we know who did it. I don't mean to be ungrateful, but personally I think I was safer in the Buick."

Ranger disconnected, and I stayed at the window to watch the fire trucks arrive. Two Rangeman SUVs and a cop car followed the fire trucks. No need for me to go out. Rangeman would take care of it. I pulled my curtains closed, double checked the locks on my door, and went back to the Frosted Flakes and television, wishing I had a bottle of wine to help make it all go away.

SEVENTEEN

I COAXED MYSELF OUT of bed, shuffled into the bathroom, and stood under the shower, trying to get energized. It hadn't been a totally restful night. I'd had nightmares about fire and difficulty getting back to sleep. I ended the shower when I ran out of hot water.

I got dressed, went to the window, and looked down at the lot. Ranger's Mercedes SUV was gone. Uncle Sandor's Buick was back. I slogged into the kitchen. No more cereal. Ate it all last night. No point making coffee since there wasn't any cereal or milk. I filled Rex's bowl with hamster kibble, gave him fresh water, and hung my messenger bag on my shoulder. I opened my door and found another note. *Be prepared to die.* Crap. I returned to the kitchen and got Ranger's gun.

Twenty minutes later I reached the bonds office. My first stop was the coffeemaker. The box of donuts on Connie's desk was the second stop.

"You look like you need to visit the makeup

counter at Macy's and get some industrial strength concealer," Lula said to me. "I'm hoping there's a good story that goes with the bags under your eyes."

"Someone torched Ranger's Mercedes last night when it was parked in my lot."

"It should be illegal to do that to a Mercedes," Lula said.

"It *is* illegal," I said.

"Well, yeah, but you know what I mean. Did Mr. Tall Dark and Sexy come by to watch his car burn and console you?"

"No. I haven't seen him. He sent a couple guys to take care of it."

I finished off a Boston Kreme and went to the box for another donut.

"Any new skips come in?" I asked Connie.

"Arthur Beasley missed his court date. He's charged with indecent exposure. It's a small bond but he should be easy to find. He works at the nudie beach in Atlantic City."

This got Lula's attention. "There's a nudie beach in Atlantic City? I never heard of it."

"I have an address," Connie said. "I think it's new. It's attached to a casino."

"Is the casino nude too?" Lula asked.

"I don't know," Connie said. "And I don't *want* to know. Have you seen the people who go to Atlantic City? Would you really like to see them naked?"

"Anybody else?" I asked.

"Lauren Lazar. She got high on one of those new designer drugs and tried to sell her little sister to the night manager of the convenience store on Hyland. Apparently she had the munchies and wanted a bunch of Little Debbie snack cakes."

"I get that," Lula said. "Sometimes I think about doing some pretty bad shit for those Little Debbies."

I was working my way through a jelly donut when my cellphone buzzed.

"You gotta help me," Briggs said. "You gotta get over here. I can't believe this friggin' happened. I mean, what are the chances? I finally get a halfway decent job and it turns to doodie right in front of my eyes."

"What are you talking about?"

"I friggin' lost another one!"

"Another patient is missing?"

"You got it. Disappeared in the middle of the night just like Cubbin. Nobody knows nothing about it."

"Did you look at the video?"

"Yeah. Nada. Nothing. Zip. Zero. And I've personally gone over every inch of that floor. I've looked in every closet, under every bed, in all the bathrooms."

"He didn't go home?"

"No. The police looked. His wife says she hasn't

seen him. Not that she cares. They were in the middle of a divorce."

"And you want me to come to the hospital *why*?"

"To keep me from blowin' my brains out."

"It's not the end of the world, Randy."

"Easy for you to say. Just get over here. I could use some help. I had cops crawling all over the hospital. And now I've got a pack of reporters camped out in the lobby."

Seemed like a lot of fuss for someone who was only missing for a few hours. "Who did you lose?"

"Elwood Pitch."

Oh boy. Elwood Pitch was a state legislator who's been arrested for human trafficking. He was caught driving a U-Haul crammed with girls ages nine to fourteen. The girls had been smuggled in from Mexico via Port Newark and were told they'd be working as prostitutes. Pitch claimed he thought the truck was full of bananas. What he expected to do with the bananas was never made clear. Like Cubbin, Pitch was awaiting trial.

"Did Pitch get his appendix removed?" I asked Briggs.

"He didn't get anything removed. He was admitted with stomach pains and kept overnight for observation."

This was too weird. Two guys out on bail disappear in exactly the same way. Hard to pass it off as a bizarre coincidence.

"I'm on my way," I told him.

"Where we going?" Lula wanted to know.

"Central Hospital. Elwood Pitch checked in with stomach pains last night. They kept him for observation and he mysteriously disappeared."

"Get the heck out," Lula said. "What is this, Lose a Slimebag Month at that hospital?"

"Briggs wants me to hold his hand," I said to Lula. "He's having a meltdown."

"That don't sound like a lot of fun to me," Lula said. "If it's all the same to you, I'm gonna stay here with the box of donuts. I might even do some filing."

"Did Vinnie bond out Pitch?" I asked Connie.

"Yes. And it was a really high bond."

• • •

I parked in the hospital lot a half hour later, and I remembered that Tiki was in the backseat. Chances were slim that Logan would find me here, but I thought better safe than sorry, so I locked Tiki in the trunk. I reached the hospital entrance and felt terrible. I'd been locked in a trunk once and it wasn't good. And now I'd put Tiki in the trunk.

He's a piece of wood, I told myself. He doesn't have feelings. *Except he felt real.* Damn. I returned to the car and got Tiki and brought him into the hospital with me.

"It's about time," Briggs said when he saw me. "What have you got under your arm?"

"Tiki. I didn't want to leave him in the car."

"Why?"

"It's hard to explain."

"I bet."

We were in Briggs's office when Morelli strolled in. He was wearing a blue collared shirt, jeans, and running shoes. Other plainclothes cops wore dress slacks and dress shoes and sometimes a suit. When Morelli dressed like that he looked like a casino pit boss, so he had special permission to go casual. He pulled a chair out and slouched into it.

"What have you got?" Morelli said to Briggs.

"Nothing," Briggs said.

"Are you working missing persons?" I said to Morelli.

"Pitch was my collar. I worked with ICE to bring him down and I don't like that he's disappeared. I pulled four nine-year-old girls out of that truck. They were terrified and dehydrated and one of them was unconscious. They were smuggled into the country in a cargo container and then locked in that truck for ten hours. This is personal for me."

"Me too," Briggs said. "I look like an idiot. Security at this hospital sucks."

"Count me in," I said. "Vinnie bonded Pitch."

"Walk me through it," Morelli said. "What do I need to know?"

"There were two nurses on duty," Briggs said. "Norma Kruger and Julie Marconni."

"The same nurses that were on duty when Cubbin disappeared," I said.

Briggs nodded. "Yeah. And the times were the same too. Kruger checked on Pitch at two in the morning and he was sleeping. And then when she went in just before going off shift at seven he was gone."

"I was on the floor," Morelli said. "There are security cameras covering all exits."

"I watched the video," Briggs said. "I didn't see Pitch leaving."

Morelli looked like he'd had heartburn. If he had had Briggs downtown, locked in a little room, he'd have run over him like a four-ton dump truck. Sitting in Briggs's office on the first floor of Central Hospital required more diplomacy, and diplomacy wasn't Morelli's strongest attribute. I suspected Morelli wanted to grab Briggs and shake him like a rag doll until Briggs remembered seeing Pitch leave the building.

"I'd like to see the videos," I said to Briggs. "Maybe if we all look at them together something will pop out at one of us."

"Yeah, sure," Briggs said. "Good idea. I can pull them up on my computer."

Morelli shot me a look of gratitude that promised a back rub next time we were alone together, and we scooted our chairs around so we could see the screen.

Briggs brought four camera views up at once.

Two cameras on the fourth floor and two cameras that covered the exits. He ran the videos at high speed. When they were done we all sat there in silence for a full minute.

"Well?" Briggs asked. "Did you see anything?"

Morelli and I shook our heads. No one had left the floor. It was a snooze fest. Dim light. Nothing happening. Nurses occasionally walking around in uniforms that looked like they were designed by Disney. Very casual and cheerful. What ever happened to the starched white look with the hats? The only time you saw those uniforms anymore was in porno films.

Morelli turned to me. "Is there anything else I should be looking at here?"

"You should talk to the two night nurses. I never interviewed Julie Marconni, and it wouldn't hurt for you to grill Norma Kruger. I'm pretty sure Kruger is involved somehow."

"Who works security here on the night shift?" Morelli asked Briggs.

"Mickey Zigler. He's worked the night shift here forever. He comes on at six and goes off at six. We both do twelve-hour shifts."

"We'll be back at six to talk to him," Morelli said.

I glanced over at Morelli. "We?"

"We're in this together, Cupcake."

I thought Morelli was sexy as heck. And I was almost positive I loved him. Whether I could live with him was still up in the air. Whether I could work with him was highly unlikely. We'd tried to work together before and it hadn't turned out wonderful.

Morelli got Julie Marconni's and Norma Kruger's addresses from Briggs and stood to leave.

"Do you want to ride shotgun?" he asked me.

"No. You'll do better interviewing them without me. I'll catch up with you later this afternoon."

I carted Tiki back to the Buick and returned to the office.

"How'd it go?" Lula asked. "Did you have to get Briggs injected with happy juice?"

"No. Briggs was fine. We all watched the security videos together."

"Who's all?"

"Morelli was there. Pitch was his collar, and he's not comfortable that Pitch might have walked away."

"Oh boy," Lula said. "You're not gonna have to work with Morelli, are you? Last time you tried that he had to stop carrying his gun so he wouldn't be tempted to shoot you. And remember the time he chained you to a pipe in his cellar?"

On the positive side, the possibility that I'd be set on fire was a lot slimmer when I was with Morelli.

"I don't have much choice," I said. "We're after the same guy. And Morelli might be helpful. It's not like I'm making a lot of progress on my own."

"Long as I don't get caught in the crossfire," Lula

said. "Where is he now? He in the Buick with Tiki?"

"He's doing his own thing for a while."

"How did the fitting go?" Connie asked me. "What does the dress look like?"

I squinched my eyes closed and smacked my forehead with the heel of my hand. "I forgot all about it!"

"That's one of them subliminal things," Lula said. "You keep forgetting because you don't want to do it."

This was true. "I'll go now," I said. "And then I'm going to Atlantic City to get the guy at the nudie beach."

"I don't want to miss either of those things," Lula said. "I'll go with you."

The bridal shop was on Hamilton, not far from the Tasty Pastry bakery. I'd been there before on a couple other excruciating occasions when I was a bridesmaid. It was presided over and owned by Mary DeLorenzo. She had coal black hair pulled back in a bun. She was in her fifties. And she ate way too much pasta. She employed two cousins who served as seamstresses. They were imported from Italy and spoke no English beyond *S'cusa me* when they stuck you with a pin or pushed your breast out of the way to adjust the bodice.

The walls of the shop were lined with gowns in zippered plastic bags smushed together on racks.

One side was bridal and the other bridesmaid. Mother of the bride was in a separate room.

"This might not be so bad," Lula said, following me through the front door. "You got to look on the bright side. It could be a pretty dress. If I was getting married I'd have my bridesmaids in animal print. Zebra or leopard."

Mary DeLorenzo rushed over to me, all smiles, hoping for a new bride. I explained who I was and the smile faded a little.

"Of course," she said. "We've been expecting you. Let me get the dress. I'll bring it to the dressing room at the back of the shop."

Lula looked around at the cocooned dresses. "You want me to come back there with you? You might need a second opinion on this."

"Whatever."

"And remember to have a good attitude. You don't want to prejudge stuff. You go in expecting it to be bad and that's all you'll see."

"You're right. I need an attitude adjustment. I need to look forward to this. It could be fun. I'll be with Ranger. It'll be a party."

"Yeah. And I bet the dress is real classy. This is a pretty classy place in an Italian kind of way."

Mary bustled back with a zippered bag and ushered me into the dressing room. "This is so beautiful," she said. "We had to special order the fabric. And the bride was very specific about the color. She wanted something romantic."

"Romantic is good," I said. "Right?"

"Of course. It's a wedding." She pulled the dress out of the bag and fluffed it up. "This is going to be stunning on you."

It was a floor-length Pepto-Bismol pink taffeta dress with big puffy cap sleeves, a huge bow at the waist in the back, and a bell skirt.

I felt my eyes get wide and my mouth drop open.

Have a good attitude, I told myself. It'll look better once it gets off the hanger.

Lula was on the other side of the dressing room door. "How is it?" she asked. "Do you love it? Is it pretty?"

"I don't have it on yet," I said, swallowing down panic.

"Well, hurry up. I can't wait to see it. This is exciting."

Mary dropped the dress over my head and zipped it up. I had my eyes closed. I was afraid to look.

"Oh dear," she gasped. "It's just beautiful. It fits you perfect. It's as if it was made for you."

"Really?" I asked with my eyes still closed tight.

"It's your color."

"I don't wear a lot of pink," I said.

"It does wonders for your skin tone. Don't you want to open your eyes and look at it?"

"No."

"I want to look at it," Lula said. "Open the door so I can see. I bet it's ravishing."

Mary opened the dressing room door for Lula. "Ta-da!"

"Holy cow," Lula said. "That's the ugliest dress I ever saw."

"It's from the Little House on the Prairie collection," Mary said. "It's very au couture this year. And it comes with a matching bow for her hair."

I opened one eye and looked in the mirror. I bit into my lower lip and whimpered. The dress was two sizes too big, the bow made me look like I was starting kindergarten, and the color washed me out to vampire skin tone. It weighed about twenty pounds and it made swishing sounds if I moved.

"It's lovely," I said to Mary. "Is it fire retardant?"

"I don't know," Mary said. "No one ever asked that question."

"That dress is just wrong," Lula said. "You look like a pregnant flamingo."

I blew out a sigh. "What about the positive attitude?"

"That was before I saw the dress. Now that I'm seeing the dress I'm thinking you want to come down with some bad contagious disease. Something gives you a rash and makes your brain melt."

I smoothed the skirt out. "It isn't that bad."

"Yes, it is," Lula said. "It's an atrocity."

"I'll send Philomena out to make a few adjustments," Mary said.

"Go babysit Tiki," I said to Lula. "I'll be done soon."

Thirty minutes later we were on the road to Atlantic City.

"Don't say another word about the dress," I told Lula. "I don't want to think about it."

"I understand completely. That dress was a disaster."

"Not another word!"

"My lips are sealed. Zipped them up and threw away the key."

"This should be an easy apprehension," I said to Lula. "He's not a career criminal. Probably not armed."

"Especially if he's naked."

EIGHTEEN

THE NUDIE BEACH WAS at the end of the strip and attached to a casino that looked like it used to be a Walmart. I parked in the two-story garage, left Tiki in the car, and Lula and I walked through the casino to get to the boardwalk and the beach. A chunk of the beach had been screened off so as not to offend the modest people who weren't crazy about seeing eighty-year-old naked guys. There was a concession stand and a changing room that opened onto the beach. Admission was twenty dollars. I tried to badge my way through but the woman at the door wasn't seeing it.

"No one gets through without a ticket," she said. "I don't care if you're a cop, the tooth fairy, or Jesus Christ."

"That's blasphemy," Lula said to her. "You better watch what you say or you're going straight to hell. God don't like people implying he needs a ticket."

We went to the concession stand and bought

hotdogs, French fries, fried dough for dessert, and two tickets. We gave our tickets to the woman at the door and were allowed into the women's locker room. We were stopped when we tried to get onto the beach.

"This is an all nude beach," we were told by a large woman in a casino uniform. "You can't go out with clothes on."

"I'll only be a minute," I said. "I'm looking for Arthur Beasley."

"He's the bartender at the Surf Bar," she said, "but you still have to take your clothes off."

I showed her my credentials. "He's in violation of his bond. I need to return him to the court."

"That's all well and good," she said, "but you're gonna have to do it naked."

Lula and I retreated back into the locker room.

"I'm not going out there naked," I said.

"Yeah, I see the problem. It's sort of awkward trying to arrest someone with your hoo-ha showing. Kind of takes away the dignity of the apprehension procedure."

I looked at my watch. "We'll have to wait until he goes off his shift. We can catch him when he leaves."

"That might not be until five o'clock," Lula said. "I can't wait here that long. I got a big date tonight. I need to get ready. I don't even know what I'm gonna wear." Lula kicked her shoes off. "I'm going out there. I haven't got time to mess around with this."

She peeled her tank top off and shimmied out of her spandex skirt. She stuck her thumb into the waistband of her thong, and I clapped my hands over my eyes.

"What the heck are you doing?" she asked.

"Giving you some privacy."

"Girl, I'm taking my bare ass out onto that beach. I don't think you gotta worry about my privacy."

I uncovered my eyes but I looked down at the floor. I wasn't ready to see Lula naked.

"Uh-oh," Lula said. "I got a problem. Where am I gonna hide my handcuffs and stun gun?"

"You can't take your stun gun out there. Stun guns are illegal. You'll get arrested if you use it out in the open. You can hide the cuffs in a towel. They have a stack of towels by the door."

"Okay, here I go," Lula said. "I'll be right back with the little runt."

I sat on a bench and waited for Lula. Ten minutes went by. Fifteen minutes. Finally the door opened and Lula walked in all by herself.

"I couldn't get him," Lula said. "He didn't want to cooperate."

"What took you so long?"

"Well, first he was making drinks for everybody so I had to wait in line. And then it was hot out there, and I got thirsty, so I had a mojito. And what it comes down to is you gotta help catch him. He kept dancing away from me. I figure if one of us distracts him, the other one can sneak up from behind and cuff him."

"No way."

"It's not so bad. Once you get used to being naked you get to like it. It's real liberating. And there's parts of you feeling the ocean breeze that never felt the ocean breeze before. I might come back here on my own someday except I'm not sure it's worth twenty dollars. I might come back if they have a discount day."

"Someone will take my picture with their cellphone, and I'll be on YouTube."

"They don't let you take a cellphone out there. Anyways if you want this loser you're gonna have to get your clothes off."

I squinched my eyes shut and grunted. "Great. Fine. No big deal." I kicked my shoes off, ripped my T-shirt over my head, and shoved my jeans down to my ankles. I took the rest of my clothes off and rammed them into a locker along with our purses. I turned the key in the lock and slipped the rubber bracelet with the key onto my wrist. Lula and I each had cuffs.

"Maybe you should take your pepper spray," Lula said. "Just in case."

"The towels aren't that big. I can't carry everything. It's not like I have pockets."

"You could hide it in your you-know-what," Lula said. "It's just a little canister."

"Are you serious?"

"Just thinkin'," Lula said.

"Well, stop thinking. I have enough problems without you thinking."

"Boy, you get cranky when you take your clothes off. I'm not sure I want to go out there with you and have you ruin my good experience."

"We're working," I said. "We're not here to have a good experience."

I took a deep breath and stepped out of the locker room onto the beach. It was a beautiful blue-sky day and the surf was up. The beach was dotted with people sitting in beach chairs and stretched out on blankets.

"We must be at least thirty years younger than everyone out here," I said to Lula.

"Yeah," she said, "it's like someone sprinkled the beach with a bunch of raisins and a couple prunes. I never saw so much shriveled skin. This group makes Grandma Mazur look like a teenager."

The sand was hot under my bare feet and the sun felt warm on my skin. "You're right," I said to Lula. "It does sort of feel good to be out in the fresh air."

"Yeah, I love the shore. I wouldn't mind having a house here someday. I could look at the ocean all day long and listen to the waves."

I shielded my eyes from the sun and looked down the beach. "Where's the bar?"

"It's over at the far end, under that thatched roof.

You have to fight your way through the crowd to get to it. Old people like to booze it up."

"Is Beasley naked?" I asked her.

"Sure he's naked. Everyone's naked here."

We walked closer and I eyed the bar and the people milling around it. "We need a plan. Do you want to be the distractor or the cuffer?"

"I gotta be the distractor," Lula said. "He already knows what I'm up to and he'll be on guard if I try to sneak behind him. I figure I'll walk right up to him and he'll keep his eye on me. It's hard to miss all my big brownness."

Lula set off, plowing through the sand, and I circled around, hugging the perimeter. I was inside the bar area and directly behind Beasley when Lula elbowed her way up to the bar and got his full attention. I opened a bracelet and *click* it was on him. I went for the second wrist, he yelped, and threw a drink in my face. I blinked and swiped at my eyes. I felt him shove me aside and by the time I recovered he was outside the bar and running.

I sprinted after him, both of us having a hard time in the deep sand. He was distracted by the metal bracelet attached to his wrist, I took a flying leap, and snagged him by the ankle. We both went down face-first. I was holding tight to his foot, and I heard Lula yell *"INCOMING!"* I let go and scooted away just in time to see Lula hurtle over me, casting a massive shadow, and land on Beasley. "WOOF!" Beasley exclaimed on an explosion of air. And then he was completely still with Lula on top of him.

Lula climbed off, I cuffed him, and we rolled him over. His eyes were open, but I wasn't sure he was breathing.

"Sometimes it takes them a while to get air after I pounce," Lula said. She looked down at Beasley. "Are you okay?"

"Unh," Beasely said.

"He's okay, folks," Lula said to the crowd that had gathered. "You could go back to your sunnin' and drinkin'. Bar's open. Self-serve."

Beasley wasn't looking like he was going to get up anytime soon, so Lula and I each took a foot and dragged him to the locker room.

"This is the ladies' locker room," the attendant said. "You can't bring him in here."

"Wait here," I said to Lula.

I went to our locker and got dressed in record time. I took twenty dollars out of my purse, gave it to the attendant, and she happened to be looking the other way when we dragged Beasley into the locker room.

Lula got dressed, and we stood there looking at Beasley. We couldn't take him out onto the board-walk or through the casino naked, and we didn't want to go into the men's locker room to get his clothes.

"Only thing we got here is towels," Lula said.

"We could make him a diaper but I don't know how to hold it together."

"Garbage bag," I said. "Have the attendant open the broom closet and give you a big green trash bag."

Lula came back with the garbage bag, we tore a hole in the top, got Beasley up on his feet, and pulled the bag over his head. It came to about two inches below his privates.

"Lucky for us he's not hung like some of the old folks out there," Lula said. "Some of them would need a bag that comes to their knees."

We walked Beasley to the car and strapped him in next to Tiki.

"I got sand in my lady parts," Lula said. "Whoever thought a naked beach was a good idea never sat in one."

NINETEEN

I BROUGHT BEASLEY INTO the police station and ran into Morelli.

"I was just going to call you," Morelli said.

"I've been busy."

"So I see. Your FTA's dressed in a garbage bag, you have sand in your hair, and you smell like a piña colada."

"The guy I just handed over was a bartender at a nudie beach, and he threw a drink at me."

"You took him down on a nudie beach?"

"Yeah. Lula and me."

Morelli grinned. "Did you and Lula join in the fun?"

"We didn't have much choice. They wouldn't let us on the beach with our clothes on."

"Both of you full monty?"

"Yep."

"I'm a little turned on," Morelli said.

"I hate to disappoint you but it wasn't all that sexy. I have sand *everywhere*."

Someone stuck his head out of a room down the hall and yelled for Morelli.

"Coming!" Morelli yelled back. "I'll pick you up at your apartment at six o'clock," he said to me. "We can catch a fast burger and then talk to Mickey Zigler."

I dropped Lula at the office and continued on home. I brought Tiki into the apartment with me, set him on the couch, and turned the television on. I got into the shower and realized I'd turned the television on for a chunk of wood.

At a little before six I went downstairs to wait for Morelli. I stood in the lobby, where I felt relatively safe, and I called Ranger.

"Just checking in," I said. "I got another note tacked to my door this morning. Anything new with you?"

"More messages. This freak has a lot of anger."

"Me too," I said. "I tried my bridesmaid dress on today. It's pink. And it has a big bow over my ass."

I could sense Ranger's smile over the phone. "Looking forward to seeing it."

And he hung up.

After a couple minutes Morelli rolled into the lot, and I ran out to his SUV.

"Do you want to eat first or talk to Zigler first?" Morelli asked me.

"Let's get Zigler out of the way."

Morelli pulled out of the lot and drove toward Hamilton Avenue. "That would be my choice too."

"How did it go with the nurses?" I asked him.

"Julie Marconni is a zombie. She's a single mother who works the night shift and then goes home to take care of her three kids."

"Who's with the kids at night?"

"She has a roommate who teaches eighth grade. On the surface it sounds like a good arrangement, but Julie Marconni is a burnout. She was cleaning the house when I got there and she was dead on her feet. I suspect she sleeps a lot on the job. She's responsible for half the patients on the fourth floor, and none of her patients have gone missing."

"All the missing patients were Kruger's?"

"Yeah. Three years' worth of missing patients." Morelli stopped for a light. "I asked Kruger if she worked other jobs, and she said once in a while she took on a private client. I asked her if she worked at The Clinic and she said she spent a couple hours there five days a week but she really didn't do anything. She said if The Clinic ever got up and running she would be guaranteed a supervisory position."

"Do you believe that?"

"Yes, but I also think there's something bad going on, and Kruger's up to her armpits in it. She has a defensive posture when she's questioned, and things aren't adding up in her favor."

"Did she offer to give you a back rub?"

"No. She wasn't friendly. It was a short conversation."

"I would have given you a back rub," I said to Morelli. "I like the way your jeans fit. And I like your shirt when it's open at the neck a little like this."

I leaned in and kissed him just below his ear and above the shirt collar.

Morelli dragged me across the console and kissed me. Lots of tongue. His hand under my shirt. The driver behind us leaned on his horn, and Morelli broke from the kiss and moved forward.

"We could turn around and go back to your apartment," he said.

I retreated to my seat and stuffed myself back into my bra. "Is Zigler expecting you?"

"Yeah," he said on a sigh. "And Briggs is waiting for us."

"Then let's get the job done."

"My jeans aren't fitting all that great right now," Morelli said.

I noticed.

• • •

Briggs was in his office waiting for us with Mickey Zigler. Zigler was in his fifties. Gray hair in a buzz cut, barrel-chested, bloodshot eyes.

"Sit," Morelli said.

We all sat.

"What's your routine on the night shift?" Morelli asked Zigler.

"I make the rounds every hour. Between the rounds I watch the monitors. We got them all over the building and in the parking areas."

"That's a lot of monitors to watch," Morelli said.

"Not so much at night," Zigler told him. "Nothing happens. Once in a while we get something coming into the emergency room but usually they go to St. Francis. Especially if it's a shooting. St. Francis specializes in gunshot wounds. Mostly what I see is pigeons walking around in the lot. And sometimes kids making out in the parking garage."

"Who watches the monitors when you're making the rounds?" Morelli asked him.

Briggs answered. "No one. It's like that during the day too. There's no money in the security budget for two guys on a shift."

"So if someone knows when security is on the second floor and the nurses are sleeping on the surgical floor, it wouldn't be impossible to sneak a patient out," I said.

"Yeah," Zigler said, "except we reviewed all the video for the night when Pitch went missing, and it was all the usual stuff. Two to seven is the dead time. There aren't even pigeons walking around between two and seven."

"How long does it take you to make the rounds?" Morelli asked.

"A half hour. Unless something unusual happens,

it's a half hour on my feet going through the hospital and then a half hour watching the monitors."

"When you get to the fourth floor what are the nurses doing?" I asked him.

"They're usually at the desk, working on the charts or talking."

"Are they ever asleep?"

"I never saw anyone sleeping. Sometimes Julie looks a little zoned out. She has a tough life. But I never saw her sleeping."

"How about Kruger?"

"I never saw Kruger sleeping." He looked at Briggs. "Sometimes she disappears for a while."

"Where does she go?" I asked Zigler.

Zigler grinned. "Sometimes she gets the orderlies to diddle her in the dayroom. I figure it's none of my business, but since you asked."

"Do you have any idea how these patients disappeared while you were working security?" Morelli asked Zigler.

"No, sir," Zigler said. "I think it must have been aliens. You know how they can beam you up?"

"That's on television," Morelli said.

"Maybe," Zigler said.

I followed Morelli out of the hospital and we buckled ourselves into the SUV.

"Aliens," Morelli said. "I think he was serious."

"It *is* hard to explain." And hell, I was carrying a chunk of wood around with me that I almost believed was putting ideas into my head. I was ready to believe just about anything.

We called ahead to Pino's and ordered meatball subs. Morelli stopped at his house and got Bob and a six-pack of Bud. We picked the subs up and took everything up to my apartment. We were in front of the television, eating the subs, drinking beer, and watching a pregame show for the Mets. I heard something go *phoonf* from the parking lot and my living room window shattered.

Morelli vaulted over the couch, picked something off the floor, threw it out the shattered window, and a moment later there was a loud explosion from the parking lot.

I went to the window and stood next to Morelli. Three cars were furiously burning. One was Morelli's. The Buick was fine.

"I'm thinking about marrying a woman who gets rockets launched into her living room," Morelli said. "What's wrong with this picture?"

"You're thinking about marrying me?"

"I've been thinking about marrying you for ten years," Morelli said. "Do you want to explain this latest terrorist attack to me?"

"It's all a misunderstanding. Some nutcase guy thinks I'm in a relationship with Ranger."

"Are you?"

"In a relationship with Ranger? No! I'm working for him."

"And this is why the nutcase guy just fired off a rocket into your living room?"

"Yes."

"Do you know him by name?"

"Not exactly. Ranger's working on it."

Emergency vehicles were pouring into my parking lot. Fire trucks, EMTs, police cars.

"I suppose I should go downstairs and explain this to them," Morelli said.

"What will you say?"

"I'll say I haven't a clue. And I'm absolutely not going to tell anyone I picked it up and chucked it out your window." He turned when he got to the door. "I want you to call Ranger and tell him I'm not happy."

Bob and I watched the circus in the parking lot for a while and I called Ranger.

"Morelli wants me to tell you he's not happy," I said to Ranger.

"I already talked to Morelli."

"Was he happy?"

"No."

"Your guy shot a missile into my living room."

"Yeah, he hit Amanda Olesen's townhouse too. He shot it into her front window."

"Was anyone hurt?"

"No, but the townhouse was destroyed. Amanda and Kinsey were in the back of the house when the explosion occurred."

"Where are they now?"

"I have them in a safe house."

"Are they going through with the wedding?" I asked.

"They're trying to decide."

"They should cancel. It's too dangerous."

"Babe, you just want to get out of wearing the pink dress."

"True."

• • •

Bob and I were watching the game when Morelli finally came back to the apartment. I heard the door open and slam shut, locks were flipped, and Morelli went into the kitchen. A minute later he came to the couch with a beer in his hand.

"Well?" I asked.

"It was a direct hit on my car. There's nothing left of it."

I bit into my lower lip to keep from smiling. I didn't want to make matters worse by laughing at Morelli, but there was some humor to the fact that Morelli tossed the thing onto his own car. Of course, there was also the possibility that in my state of mild hysteria the line between horrible and hilarious was blurred, and it wasn't all that funny that Morelli blew his car up.

"Sorry," I said.

Morelli chugged down a bottle of beer. "It's you. You're a disaster magnet. I'm surprised this building hasn't been wiped out by a tornado. How could it possibly have escaped a tornado?"

"Maybe tomorrow."

"I'm serious," Morelli said. "You're like one of those people who keep getting hit by lightning."

"Hey, it's no picnic for me either. Do you think I like having rockets shot into my living room? Do you think I like getting poisoned, threatened with cremation, and forced into a pink taffeta dress?"

"Don't forget the stun gun," Morelli said. "You got stunned. And this all happened in *one week*."

I sucked in some air and burst into tears. "You're right," I said, sobbing. "And it's even worse. I got two more cars totally toasted and my arm slashed. I'm a walking time bomb."

"Oh jeez," Morelli said, putting his beer bottle down and wrapping his arms around me. "I didn't mean to make you cry. I hate when you cry. I got carried away with the disaster magnet thing."

"I'm a big, humongous mess! I need an exorcist."

He wiped away a tear that had streaked down my face. "You're not *that* much of a mess, Cupcake. And to tell you the truth I don't think an exorcist would help a lot. It's not like you're a biblical mess. You just have a knack for rolling in dog doo."

I wiped my nose on the back of my hand. "That's awful."

"It's not so bad. Bob rolls in dog doo, and we love Bob, right?"

"Yes."

"Well, there you have it." Morelli kissed me on the top of my head. "You know what you need? A beer. I could use another one too. Don't go away."

I watched Morelli trot off to the kitchen, and I was half worried he wasn't coming back. If I was in his shoes, I might be tempted to grab Bob and head for the hills. Of course Morelli didn't have a car so I guess that would slow him down.

At any rate, he was right. I needed a beer. And he was right about the dog doodie too. Even when I was a kid I had a knack for pushing the boundaries of common sense and normal behavior. I walked into the boys' bathroom in grade school because I was convinced I was invisible. I jumped off the roof of my parents' garage because I thought I could fly. And that was the tip of the iceberg.

And I'm still pushing boundaries, flopping around in water that's over my head. And here's the scary part that I wouldn't say out loud to anyone . . . I'm a little addicted to it. I like my crazy job and my disaster-prone life. Not that I want a bomb in my living room, but I've come to like the adventure. I was hooked into the challenge of the manhunt. And the occasional rush of adrenaline was sort of invigorating.

TWENTY

MORELLI AND BOB LEFT just as the sun was coming up. I gave Morelli the keys to the Buick, and told him I'd try to stay out of trouble. I went back to bed and woke up to blinding daylight and Ranger standing at my bedside with coffee. He was wearing Rangeman black cargo pants and T-shirt, and he was, as always, armed. He wore custom-tailored suits when he was talking to clients, but at all other times he dressed like the rest of his men.

"What the heck?" I said.

"I have a full day, and I need to talk to you."

"Is that coffee for me?"

"Yes."

I sat up and took the coffee. "What's going on?"

"I left keys to an SUV on your kitchen counter. I have someone coming over to fix your window. I got a call from the bridal salon that they were worried about your shoes. They wondered if you had pink shoes and they reminded you that you were wearing sneakers and not heels when you tried the dress."

I burst out laughing at the thought of Ranger taking the message.

"It's not funny," Ranger said. "One more message like that and I'll get my nuts repossessed."

"Anything else?"

"Yes. I've ruled out all but one man in my unit, and he's supposed to be dead. His name is Orin Carr, and he was the unit demo expert. He was reported killed in Afghanistan, but there are pieces of information in some of the notes that only Orin would know. Orin was the unit whackjob. He would walk through minefields with his eyes closed because he thought he had divine protection."

"How did he feel about fire?"

"He loved fire. He said it was the great purifier."

I sipped my coffee. "Are you close to catching him?"

"No. I'm chasing down a dead man. He isn't leaving any markers."

"Can I help?"

"Yes. Get the shoe thing straightened out so I don't have to talk to that woman again."

And he left.

I rolled out of bed, carried my coffee into the bathroom, and took a shower. A half hour later I was dressed in a black T-shirt and a short denim skirt that I hadn't worn since high school, and my phone rang.

It was Lula. "Where the heck are you?" she asked.

"We got Grandma here, and she's got big news. She's been snooping."

"What's the news?"

"You gotta hear it from Grandma. I thought for sure you'd be here by now."

Grandma got on the phone. "I went undercover to Cranberry Manor with Florence Mikolowski last night," Grandma said. "She was going to visit her friend Marion, and I told her I wanted to go along to see the place. So we were sitting there having a cup of tea and who do you think comes in? Susan Cubbin. Flo's friend knew her right off. And Mrs. Cubbin goes straight to the office her husband used to have and starts pulling open all the drawers and looking under the desk and in all the books in his bookshelf. And the whole time that young girl who took us around, what's-her-name, is trying to stop Mrs. Cubbin, and Mrs. Cubbin's having none of it. I tell you, she was on a mission. And we're standing there watching it all. And then Mrs. Cubbin is rummaging around in a file drawer, and she goes *Aha!* And she runs out of the office and out of the building."

"She found something!" I said.

"Yeah, she had a big folded-up paper in her hand. Like a poster or something."

Lula got back on the phone. "We gotta go see Susan Cubbin. I bet she knows where the money is. And it might be with her jerk husband."

"I'm on my way. Give me fifteen minutes."

I left Tiki with Rex, and I ran to the car with my messenger bag in one hand and a gun in the other.

"Look at you in a skirt today," Lula said when I walked in.

I took a cruller out of the box on Connie's desk. "I need to do laundry. This was the only thing left in my closet."

Lula looked out the window. "You have another new car."

"It's Ranger's. Morelli had to borrow the Buick."

"What's wrong with Morelli's SUV?"

"It sort of got blown up."

Everyone looked at me with their eyebrows raised.

"It's a long story," I said. "Not worth telling."

Grandma, Lula, and I trooped out of the office and got into the shiny, immaculate black Jeep Liberty.

"I'd like to know where he gets all these new cars," Lula said. "It's like they drop out of the sky. And the other question is, how does he get insurance when you keep blowing them up?"

"I don't blow them *all* up," I said.

I drove to the Cubbin house in Hamilton Township and parked in the driveway, behind the van. We went to the door and Susan opened it before I had a chance to ring the bell.

"I saw you drive up," she said. "Now what?"

"Just checking in," I said.

"I recognize the old lady," Susan said. "She was at Cranberry Manor last night. You want to know what I was doing, right?"

"I'm not so old," Grandma said. "I got a bunch of good years left in me."

"What *were* you doing there?" I asked Susan.

"I was looking for the money. What else would I be doing?"

"Did you find it?"

"When I find it, all you'll see is an empty house."

"What about the big albino? Has he been around?"

"The realtor?"

"I don't think he's a realtor."

"Whatever. Haven't seen him."

Grandma craned her neck to look around Susan into the living room. "This is a real nice house. I like your decorating."

"I did it myself. I was going for the Americana look."

"You got it," Grandma said. "What's with the suitcase in your living room? Are you planning a vacation?"

"No. I'm cleaning out my closet."

We left Susan and returned to the Jeep.

"I think she was fibbing about cleaning out her closet," Grandma said.

"Suppose you embezzled five million dollars?" I asked Grandma and Lula. "Where would you put it?"

"I guess it would be in a bank account somewhere," Lula said. "It's not like he robbed a liquor store. He probably took some here and there. That's a lot of money to take out of that dinky Cranberry Manor."

"I'd put it in a lot of different banks," Grandma said. "You gotta move it around and laundry it. And then I'd put some in Grenada and Jakarta and places like that."

"How do you know all this?" Lula wanted to know.

"I pick it up at Bingo. I sit with Angie Raguzzi. Her brother is in the investment business."

"Her brother is mob," I said.

"Yeah," Grandma said. "Angie says this economy is real good for the mob on account of they're the only ones loaning money to people. Of course if Cubbin was planning on going somewhere and wanted to take his money with him he could be collecting it all in hundred-dollar bills. It would take a couple suitcases to hold it all if you bundled it up nice and neat."

"You know that from Angie?" Lula asked.

"No. I got that from Tony Destafano. He's a bagman. He makes collections, and he's got it down to a science. He could tell you how many hundreds you could put in a brown grocery bag."

"He go to Bingo too?" Lula wanted to know.

"No. I see him at viewings. All them old mob guys are croaking. Pretty soon there's not gonna be any more mob. All the young guys are going into the hedge fund business."

"What are we gonna do now?" Lula asked. "Is it time for lunch?"

"Not nearly," I said. "I think we sit around the

corner and wait to see if Susan Cubbin drags her suitcase out to the van and goes somewhere."

"That would be a good plan," Grandma said, "but I gotta tinkle."

I drove to Dawn Diner so Grandma could tinkle. Lula got double rice pudding to go, Grandma got a piece of apple pie, I got a giant wedge of coconut layer cake, and we went back to Susan Cubbin's street. No van. Her driveway was empty.

"Maybe she had to run an errand," Lula said.

Yeah, maybe she ran an errand to Rio. I hear they do a lot of stomach stapling and fat suctioning there.

I parked half a block away, and we ate our food. An hour went by and no Susan Cubbin. I drove up to her house, walked to the front door, and looked in the window. No suitcase.

I took Grandma home. I dropped Lula off at the office. I called Mary DeLorenzo at the bridal salon and told her I had shoes. I was feeling sick after eating all the coconut cake, so I went home and took a nap. It was midafternoon when I woke up to my phone ringing.

"You're not going to believe this one," Connie said. "I just got a call from my cousin Frankie. He owns the pawnshop on Broad, and Susan Cubbin was in. She had a gold bar, and she wanted to know how much she could get for it."

"Get out!"

"Swear to God. Frankie said he took the bar and emptied his cash register into a suitcase she had with her. He called me because he knew we were looking for her husband."

I called Morelli and asked if he was making any progress with Elwood Pitch.

"I'm running down a ton of contacts and finding nothing," Morelli said. "I looked into The Clinic, and on the surface it seems to be legitimate. Franz Sunshine is writing it off as a loss on his taxes."

"There's more going on there than a tax loss."

"I agree. From what you've told me he has a security guard, a part-time nurse, and a perfectly maintained lab and surgical suite. He's using that building for something."

"Did you go in to take a look?"

"No. I have no justification for questioning them. I did a drive-by, and it looked locked up and empty."

I told him about Susan Cubbin, and I got silence on the other end.

"Are you still there?" I asked.

"I'm dumbstruck. A gold bar?"

"Yeah. In trade for a suitcase full of money."

I could hear Morelli laughing. "Just when life can't get any more insane someone comes along with a gold bar. I hope she kept her pawn ticket because I'm sure she got hosed. Gold is trading high."

I wandered into my living room and looked out my newly fixed window. Logan was sitting cross-legged on a small patch of grass at the beginning of my parking lot.

"I have to go," I said to Morelli. "I have to see a guy about a thing."

I hung up on Morelli, and stuffed a pair of cuffs into the waistband of my denim skirt on the remote possibility that I could catch Logan. I took the stairs down to the lobby, I stepped out the door, Logan saw me and ran away.

This whole deal with Logan was dragging. At this rate I was never going to get rid of Tiki. I really should go more proactive, I thought, but I had other stuff on my mind. Like Ranger's freak. I did a quick scan of the lot to make sure no one was aiming a rocket launcher at me, and I returned to my apartment.

I went into my bedroom, gathered up my laundry, and headed for my parents' house. My mom has a washer and dryer that don't require the insertion of money. Plus I'd get dinner.

• • •

"Look who's here," Grandma said when she saw me at the door. "You came on a good night. We got a ham."

I threw my laundry into the washer and helped set the table. My dad was asleep in front of the television, and my mom and my grandmother were in the kitchen. It's not a big kitchen but it gets the job done. Refrigerator with a freezer on the bottom. A four-burner stove with an oven. Small microwave on the counter. A sink and a dishwasher. The dishwasher is a recent addition but my mom and my grandmother rarely use it. They still do dishes by hand while they review the evening meal and gossip about the neighbors.

The kitchen is like Tiki. It's an inanimate object that seems alive. It smelled like apple pie and baked ham today. My mom had the windows open and a fan going, pulling in the scent from the geraniums in her window box. In the winter the windows will be closed and steamy from soup bubbling on the stove. It's been like this since the day I was born and I can't imagine it any other way.

My mom has squeezed a table and four chairs into the kitchen. My sister and I did our homework here. We ate breakfast here. And this is where important announcements were made. Engagements, pregnancies, college choices. This is also where I stomped and fumed over curfews, rolled my eyes at my parents' antiquated ideas, and plotted how to sneak out when they were asleep. My sister never did any of those things. She was the perfect child.

I moved out from under my parents' roof a bunch of years ago and I haven't been completely successful at re-creating this comforting and stabilizing environment for myself. I'm hopeless in the kitchen, and I never seem to have the time to build my nest. Holidays like Christmas and Easter sneak up on me and fly by before I can decorate my apartment and wrap presents. Maybe if it wasn't so easy to come back to my parents' home I'd work harder at building my own. On the plus side I have a hamster and a cookie jar. Okay, so I keep my gun in the cookie jar. But it's a start, right?

I sat at the little table across from Grandma and watched her shell peas. I could smell the ham heating in the oven with the brown sugar and mustard glaze, the ham studded with cloves and draped in pineapple rings, and I was ready to gnaw my arm off with hunger. Problem was, I couldn't stop thinking about Susan Cubbin and the gold bar. She shouted *Aha!* in her husband's office and next thing she had a gold bar. No way could I walk away from it.

"I have an errand to run," I said to my mother. "If I'm not here for dinner don't worry about it. I'll stop by later and get leftovers."

The van was in the driveway when I got to Susan's house. I went to the door, and Susan sighed when she saw me.

"You know," Susan said.

"I know you pawned a gold bar."

Susan pressed her lips together, and she blinked away tears. "He's dead," she said. "Jerkface is dead."

"Why do you think he's dead?"

"It's all here. All the money he stole from those people. It's all still here. He didn't run out on me. He went to the hospital, and he expected to come back. He had it hidden. It was in a place I would never have thought to look."

"Did you tell this to the police?"

"No. It's proof he was guilty, and I feel bad about it. I mean, isn't it enough that he's probably dead?"

"What about Cranberry Manor?"

"He hated that place. He said the old people were always complaining. And he said they cheated on everything. Cards, Bingo, taxes, Social Security. Half of them are collecting on dead relatives."

"It's still their money."

"I know, but I can't be the one to tell on him. It seems mean. He was my husband, and he wasn't so bad. He just had a lot of issues."

"Can I help?"

"Yes. You can help me figure out a way to get the money back to Cranberry Manor without making Geoffrey look like a monster."

"Give me some history."

"Come on in and I'll show you what I found."

I followed Susan to the dining room table and looked down at what appeared to be a blueprint for landscaping her yard.

"Yesterday I was sitting out back having a glass of wine and the sun kept reflecting off something in the yard. So finally I got up to see what it was and at first I thought it was a gold button that popped off something and got smashed into the grass. I tried to get it up, but it wouldn't come, and I kept digging away more grass and more grass, and what do you think I found?"

"A gold bar."

"Yes. And then it hit me. I remembered Geoffrey

was always talking about his big scheme to land-scape the yard, and how flowers were as good as gold. Five years ago he started working on this blue-print. He'd haul it out and work on it some, and then he'd file it away and go on to another project."

"I haven't seen your backyard. Is it filled with flowers?"

"No! That's the thing. He kept saying flowers were as good as gold but he only planted a few flowers. There were some bushes in the yard when we first moved in and they're still there too, but that's it."

"He was buying gold and planting it," I said.

"Yes. And he was marking off the locations of the bars on the blueprint. It hit me like a big brain-storm! Like *BLAM!* I went all over the house look-ing for the blueprint, and when I couldn't find it I went to his office. It was real smart of him, because when the police searched the office they didn't bother to take the landscape plan."

"Did you find all the bars?"

"I got all the ones that were marked on the plan. I don't know anything about the price of gold, so I don't know if all the Cranberry Manor money is there. It wasn't easy to get those stupid bars up ei-ther. It took me all night, working with a flashlight and one of those little shovels."

"Where are they?"

"In the kitchen."

I went to the kitchen and gaped at the bars. They were stacked up everywhere.

"How many are there?" I asked her.

"A hundred and thirty-three. Actually there were a hundred and thirty-four but I took the one so I could get a manicure. Digging up gold bars is hell. My nails were destroyed."

"I have to think about this," I said. "Keep your doors locked and your shades down so no one sees what you've got in your kitchen."

"There are so many of them," she said, looking at the bars. "I didn't know what to do with them."

"I'll figure it out," I told her. "Just lay low until I get back to you."

I left Susan, got behind the wheel, and broke out in a sweat. A hundred and thirty-three gold bars. At least five million dollars' worth of gold, stacked up in her kitchen. This went way beyond putting a couple hundred dollars under your mattress. This was mind-boggling.

I went back to my parents' house and ate the ham. At least I think I ate the ham. At some point I looked down at my plate and realized it was clean and I must have eaten something, but I couldn't remember. My mind was on the bars. It was hard to get past the fact that Susan Cubbin had five million dollars in gold in her kitchen. A dilemma I wasn't likely to face because the men I loved didn't have stolen gold bars buried in their backyards. At least none that I knew about.

TWENTY-ONE

I WAS SHOCKED OUT of sleep by someone banging on my apartment door. I rolled out of bed and padded to my small foyer. The sun was pouring into my living room. The day had started without me. I looked through the peephole and didn't see anyone. There was more pounding and I realized it was low on the door. I looked through the peephole again, this time down toward the floor. It was Briggs. I opened my door and he rushed in.

"A person could grow old standing out there," Briggs said. He squinted at me. "Are you still in pajamas? It's the middle of the day."

"It's eight o'clock in the morning."

"Well, it feels like the middle of the day. I've been up since three. I can't sleep. This disappearing patient thing is driving me nuts. And I think the hospital is interviewing security people. They're gonna fire me over this."

"I'm sure it's not that bad."

"Are you kidding? It's worse than *that bad*. They didn't want to hire me in the first place."

"Because you're short?"

"No. Because I'm incompetent. I have no qualifications. All I've got going for me is the short card."

"Better than nothing."

"Yeah, go figure."

I walked into the kitchen and got the coffeemaker working. "What do you want from me?"

"I want you to find these guys."

"I've been trying," I said to Briggs. "Do you want coffee?"

"Yeah. You got any eggs?"

"No."

"Toast?"

"No."

"Cereal?"

"No."

"What *have* you got?" he asked.

"Coffee."

"How do you live like this?"

I took two coffee mugs from the cabinet and set them on the counter. "I keep forgetting to stop at the store."

I gave Briggs his coffee, set him in front of the television, and brought Tiki in to keep him company while I took a shower. I wanted to help Briggs but I had nowhere to go. I was out of ideas.

I took as long as possible in the shower, drying

my hair, applying makeup. I wasn't eager to start my day.

"Hey," Briggs yelled from the living room. "Did you die in there? Let's go!"

I ambled out. "Where do you want to go?"

"The Clinic. I think you should bust in there and search the place. Dollars to donuts Pitch is in there."

"How am I supposed to bust in? No one answers the door."

"Break a window. Kick down the door. What the heck do I care? Just get in."

"Why don't *you* go in? You're the only one with a way to get in."

"I'm afraid I'll get caught trespassing or something. And then I'll for sure lose my job. You and Fatso break into places all the time. It don't matter with your job. And you got a cop for a boyfriend."

"I'll drive us out there, and we'll take a look, but I'm not breaking in."

"How about if something's going on?"

"Like what?"

"Like a helicopter landing. Or Pitch looking out a window? Or attack dogs patrolling the property."

"If we see any of those things I'll call Morelli."

"I guess that's okay," Briggs said. "I just don't want Pitch getting away."

• • •

I parked within sight of The Clinic, and Briggs and I watched the building for three hours.

"I'm hungry," I said. "And nothing's happening. I'm giving up on this."

"He's gotta be in there," Briggs said. "Where else would he be?"

"Switzerland?"

"There's a car coming," Briggs said. "Duck down!"

The car sped past us and turned in to the driveway to The Clinic's garage. We sat and waited and an hour later the car left The Clinic and drove down the road. I followed at a distance.

"This is big," Briggs said. "This is a new car. It's a silver Lexus. It wasn't in the garage that night. And it doesn't belong to Nurse Cokehead."

The Lexus left Route 1, cut across North Trenton, and pulled into the parking lot of the medical center where Craig Fish had his practice.

It was Craig Fish.

"This isn't earthshaking, since he's *supposed* to work at The Clinic," I said to Briggs.

"Yeah, but why would he go there if there were no patients? He must be checking on someone."

I drove across town, hit the drive-through window of Cluck-in-a-Bucket, ordered too much food, and stopped off at the office with a tub of assorted chicken parts and a bag of artery-clogging biscuits.

"Hey," Lula said. "It's Shortstuff."

"Hey," Briggs said. "It's Fatso."

I put the food on Connie's desk and got a bottle of water out of the fridge.

"Anything new?" I asked.

"Vinnie's in a state over Elwood Pitch."

"He's not the only one," Briggs said. "My job's on the line."

I took a piece of chicken. "Morelli's working on it."

My phone rang. It was Ranger.

"Babe," Ranger said. "The bridal salon woman called me again. Why is she calling me and not you?"

"Because she doesn't have my number?"

"I'll get even," Ranger said.

I actually was loving it. "What did she want?"

"She wanted me to remind you to pick up your dress."

Lula, Connie, and Briggs were watching me when I dropped my phone back into my bag.

"Who was that?" Lula wanted to know.

"Ranger."

"That explains the smile," Lula said. And she selected another piece of chicken.

I ate a piece of chicken and a biscuit, and I was thinking it might be a good idea to stop at the bakery on the way to the bridal salon. A donut would be the perfect ending to a really deliciously crappy lunch.

I loaded Briggs into the Rangeman SUV, we made a quick stop at the bakery, and I left him eating donuts in the car while I ran into the bridal salon.

Mary DeLorenzo brought the dress from the

back room. "Let's just try it on to make sure every-thing is perfect," she said.

"No time," I told her. "Things to do. I'm sure it's fine."

"You really should try it on," Mary said. "It's such an important occasion."

"I'll try it on at home. Promise." I grabbed the massive zippered bag and rushed to the door. I couldn't resist the opportunity and turned back toward Mary DeLorenzo. "Be sure to call Ranger and tell him I picked the dress up," I told her.

I tossed the heavy plastic bag into the backseat and slid behind the wheel.

"Did you ever check the morgue and the funeral homes to see if either of these guys turned up?" Briggs said. "Maybe we should take a walk along the river and make sure they're not washed up and lying there."

"I'm sure Morelli's checked the morgue. And Grandma would know if they were in a funeral home."

"What about the river?"

I glanced at him. "Do you want me to drop you off so you can check it out for yourself?"

"You'd drive away and leave me there, and I'd get mugged."

This was all true. "I'm going to take you back to your car, and my advice is to go home and take a nap. If I get any breaking news I'll call you. Prom-ise."

• • •

A lot of skip tracing is done on the phone and computer. For the most part Connie does the phone and Internet work and I do the legwork. I have some search programs on my computer, but Connie's programs are better. For lack of something better to do I ran Geoffrey Cubbin and Elwood Pitch through the system on my computer to see if anything new showed up. I got a big zero, and I was surfing Pinterest when Morelli dropped in.

"I got off work and thought I'd stop by to see if I'd missed any rocket or firebomb events," he said.

"You missed a bucket of fried chicken. It was the high point in my day."

Morelli sat across the table from me. "I went deeper on Franz Sunshine and found some interesting things. He has similar clinics in four other states. He owns two midsize jets. And he's the primary on seven different holding companies."

"Success isn't a crime."

"He's operating five businesses at a loss, but he can afford to keep two jets in the air."

"What about FS Financials?"

"It's in the black but it doesn't show the kind of profit that would offset his other expenses and losses."

"Creative bookkeeping?"

Morelli shrugged. "Hard to say, but it's one more reason to suspect The Clinic."

"Do you want me to go in with guns blazing?

Briggs thinks Pitch is in there. It's probably enough justification for me to enter."

"No! Let me see if I can dredge up a search warrant." He looked at his watch and stood. "I have to get home to let Bob out. Do you want to do something for dinner tonight?"

"I have the rehearsal dinner tonight."

"That's still on?"

"Unfortunately."

Morelli looked like he was contemplating cuffing me and locking me up somewhere. "And the wedding is tomorrow?"

"Yep. What are you doing tomorrow?" I asked him.

"Shopping for a new car," Morelli said.

"That's almost as bad as being in a wedding."

Morelli opened the front door to leave and Brody Logan was there. Logan shrieked and ran away down the stairs.

"What the hell was that?" Morelli said.

"Brody Logan. He wants Tiki."

"Does this happen a lot?"

"Define *a lot*."

Morelli dragged me up against him and kissed me.

"Was that *a lot* of a kiss?" I asked.

"Not as *a lot* as I'd like it to be."

I watched Morelli walk down the hall, and I closed and locked my door. Moving on to the next activity, I thought. Dinner with Ranger.

Ranger let himself into my apartment a little before seven o'clock. He was wearing black slacks, a black blazer, and a black dress shirt. He was perfectly tailored and pressed, and the cut of his blazer hid the black Glock at the small of his back.

I was pretty much matching in a black skirt, white silky blouse, and black jacket.

"I was told you picked your dress up from the bridal salon," Ranger said.

"I thought you'd want to know."

He smiled at me. "It made my day."

Ranger doesn't smile all that often so it's always either really wonderful or stone cold scary. This smile was a mixture of both.

I had a little black leather purse hanging from my shoulder. Ranger hooked his finger under the strap, tested the weight, and returned it to my shoulder. It was heavy enough to hold the Ruger.

I told Rex and Tiki I'd be back in a little while. I got to the door and hesitated.

"They'll be fine," Ranger said. "He's not going to hit your apartment again. He's already done that. Orin is going to kick it up a notch. He was the kind of guy who tortured bugs, pulling their legs and wings off one at a time. It was like foreplay for Orin, leading up to the kill. We were all thrill junkies but Orin was pathological. He got his thrills from the fear and suffering of his victims. He liked the kill but it was almost anticlimactic for him."

"Are you sure it's Orin?"

"Yes. He left a message on my phone this morning. I recognized his voice. He said it was time for him to come out of the shadows. He laughed his crazy Orin laugh, and he said I would see him soon."

"Did he say why he wasn't dead?"

"No. It wasn't part of the message."

"Do you want to tell me the rest of the message?"

"You'd rather not know."

I was sure this was true. I didn't even want to know what I already knew. I could have done without the whole ripping-wings-off analogy.

"Did he say why he was doing this now?"

"Only that the road here wasn't easy but he'd finally made it."

"Was he this crazy when you were serving together?"

"There were signs. Orin was a good man to have on your side and a very bad enemy. We all slept with one eye open, not just for whatever was out there but for Orin."

"The life you have now must seem tame compared to that."

"It has its moments. I had to talk to the bridal salon lady twice today."

He had his hand at my back, guiding me down the hall to the elevator and out of the building to his Porsche 911 Turbo. I suspected the car was brand-new. Hard to tell since it was identical to the last one, but its paint was unmarred, and it was lacking the aroma of horked-up cocktail wieners and meatballs.

TWENTY-TWO

THE CHURCH WASN'T FAR. It was in the Burg, and it was the Catholic church where I'd made my First Communion. It was the church where my family worshiped and I was supposed to worship. I went to Christmas mass and I was there for weddings and funerals but true faith was elusive for me. Catholic guilt was a constant. I made the sign of the cross and watched Ranger. He was comfortable here. He knew the rituals. He was raised Catholic just as I was.

"Do you attend mass?" I asked him.

"Not as often as I would like."

The answer surprised me. It had never occurred to me that Ranger might attend church. He was on the job 24/7, and he wasn't a man who easily accepted someone else's doctrine. Ranger made his own rules. Most of them were good rules, but they didn't completely line up with the Ten Commandments.

He wrapped his hand around mine, and we

walked down the aisle to the crowd of bridesmaids and ushers at the altar. Kinsey and Amanda were there. The parents were sitting in a pew. A priest and a wedding planner were organizing.

"We need the maid of honor to lead the bridesmaids to the back of the church," the wedding planner said.

"That's you," Ranger said to me.

"I'm the maid of honor?"

"Yes. That's why you have the special pink dress."

I gave him a sharp elbow to the rib cage and was pleased to hear him expel some air.

I lined up at the back of the church with the bride and the rest of the bridesmaids. The music started and we walked down the aisle. Step, stop, step, stop. Ranger was next to Kinsey, watching me walk toward him. His expression was serious and unwavering. Hard to imagine what he was thinking. And I hoped he had no idea what *I* was thinking, because I was having a hard time corralling my emotions. For a heart-stopping moment I imagined myself walking down the aisle to marry Ranger. It was one of those bizarre *what if* moments and was so disorienting that I almost stepped on the bridesmaid in front of me. It got a smile out of Ranger and a gasp from the bride, behind me. In the next instant I saw him scan the church, nothing moving but his eyes, and then he was back to me.

I left the altar on his arm after the practice ceremony. We were behind the bride and groom. Kinsey and Ranger were vigilant. Amanda looked shell-shocked. Everyone else seemed oblivious to the possibility of impending doom.

"Would Orin try to do something in a church?" I asked Ranger.

"He's crazy," Ranger said. "He'd do anything."

Ranger pulled a photo out of his jacket pocket. "This was taken a while ago but it will give you some idea what Orin looks like. Orin is standing next to me. He's the one with the sunglasses."

It was a picture of seven men in army fatigues. They all had rifles and they were smiling. Ranger hadn't changed much. Maybe he was a bit heavier now but not a lot. Different haircut. The same serious dark eyes. Orin was shorter. Stocky. Blond hair. Couldn't see his eyes behind the glasses. Dimple in his chin.

I memorized Orin, but I was most interested in Ranger. I'd never seen a photo of him at a younger age. And I'd never seen a photo of the men he'd served with for at least part of his time in the military. Ranger's apartment was beautifully decorated and his furniture was comfortable, but as a home it was sterile. There were no photos anywhere, no keepsake baseballs, no favorite coffee mug in the cupboard. Sometimes it felt like Ranger was just passing through this life, serving some purpose, not intending to stay long.

"What exactly is my role here?" I asked him.

"My best guess is that Orin will target Amanda

either tonight or tomorrow. Orin's ultimate goal is Kinsey and eventually me, but Orin will want to pull the wings off before the kill."

Oh God, it was the wings again.

"Kinsey will stay close to Amanda but there are times when you'll have to take over. He can't follow her into the ladies' room. He won't be with her tomorrow before the wedding. I have extra security in place but they'll be at a distance. You're the one who will be at Amanda's side."

I thought Ranger's confidence in me was flattering but unfounded. I was willing to give this my best shot, but I wasn't exactly Ranger. I wasn't even half a Ranger.

"Are you sure you don't want one of your men to go drag for this?" I asked him. "He'd be much more competent."

"I asked Tank but he declined. He said pink wasn't a good color for him."

• • •

The after-rehearsal dinner was held at Cedar Mill House. It was a nice restaurant in downtown Trenton that had no relationship to anything cedar and didn't look like a mill house. It was in a redbrick building with public dining downstairs and a private dining room upstairs. The adjoining building burned down three years ago and Cedar Mill House cleared the rubble away and used the space for a parking lot.

Ranger pulled into the lot and cut his lights. "I'm going to wire you for sound," he said, "and add another GPS unit."

"Another?"

"There's one in your purse."

"This is a new purse. This is the first time I've used it. How did you bug it?"

"I took a few precautions last night while you were sleeping."

"You were in my apartment last night?"

"Briefly."

"That's creepy. I don't want you looking at me when I'm sleeping."

"Babe, that's not the first time I've seen you sleep."

"But all those other times I knew you were watching me sleep."

"Not always," Ranger said.

"You waited until I was asleep so you could sneak in and plant all your secret listening gizmos, because if I was awake I wouldn't let you do it."

"It was expedient. I had to take over a patrol for one of the men last night. I only had a few minutes to plant the GPS. When I asked you to be my date I didn't realize it was going to turn into this. I put you in harm's way and now I need to try to keep you safe."

Ranger removed a small plastic bag from the

glove box. It contained a watch, a metal disk, and a roll of surgical tape.

"The watch looks like a sports watch but it has a GPS system and can transmit audio. You turn the audio on and off by pushing this button. You'll see a plus or a minus sign on the watch face telling you if the audio is sending. If you get into trouble you push the button, an alarm sounds in the control room, and we can listen in."

I took my own watch off, dropped it into my purse, and put Ranger's watch on my wrist. "Can I talk to you through the watch?"

"No. It just transmits. It doesn't receive."

The metal disk was approximately the same size as the watch face. Ranger ripped off a small piece of tape and stuck the disk to it.

"This is backup GPS. I'm going to put it inside your bra for now. If it gets uncomfortable you can move it to the small of your back. I'd like you to wear both devices until the threat is removed."

He opened two blouse buttons and traced a line along the top of my bra with his fingertip. He bent his head, brushed a kiss across my breast, and slipped his hand inside my bra. I think I might have moaned a little, and I steadied myself by sliding my hand up the inside of his thigh. It turns out that just because I think I could have a future with Morelli doesn't mean I'm entirely immune to Ranger's hotness.

He taped the disk to the underside of my breast,

and his thumb skimmed across my nipple. I'd once done the deed with Ranger in his Porsche but it involved an open driver's side door and my knee on the console. I knew this wasn't a possibility in the Cedar Mill House parking lot. Especially not with a madman stalking us, someone's high beams shining in Ranger's rear window, and my resolve to not be a slut.

"Rain check this," Ranger said. "We have company."

I made some clothing adjustments, and we followed Kinsey and Amanda into the restaurant. Besides the cars carrying the bridal party I counted two Rangeman SUVs in the lot and one more on the street.

We walked through the restaurant and up a flight of stairs. The private dining room, decorated in red and gold, was dimly lit, and seating was at three long tables. I was placed next to Amanda, and Ranger was across from us.

"I appreciate that you would take on this job," Amanda said to me. "I knew Robert was in Special Forces, but I was unprepared for something like this to happen."

"This has nothing to do with his Special Forces background," I said. "This is about mental illness. This is about a man with a problem, and for some reason that's beyond our control he's fixated on Kinsey and Ranger. We just have to be careful until Ranger catches him."

"Do you have a gun?" Amanda asked.

"Yes."

"Me too," she said. "I have a Beretta. What kind do you have?"

"A Ruger."

"Have you ever shot anyone?"

"Yes, but it was sort of an accident."

"You mean the gun went off when you didn't mean it to go off?"

"No. I mean he was shooting at me, and I shot him back."

"That doesn't sound very accidental."

"It wasn't planned," I said.

This subject was out of my comfort zone. My comfort zone ran more to bakery products, mascara, who was pregnant from my high school graduating class, and who was doing well on *The Biggest Loser*. I searched for a change of topic and came up short.

"You must be excited about the wedding," I finally said.

Amanda leaned closer and lowered her voice. "Can I confide in you? I'm nervous. I thought this would be the most fabulous thing. All my life I've dreamed about my wedding day. The gown. The walk down the aisle. The party after."

"And now?" I asked.

"I'm not sure. I love Robert, but marriage is so permanent."

It should be permanent. That's certainly the aspiration, but I knew firsthand it didn't always work that way. I'd been married for about ten minutes. I was hoping for longer next time around . . . if there was a next time around.

"I guess most brides have pre-wedding jitters," Amanda said. "I'm not even sure I did the right thing by having such an elaborate wedding. I almost wish we'd just gone off and gotten married."

"It'll all be great," I said. "You'll be a beautiful bride."

Amanda sipped at the wine that was set in front of her. "Have you ever thought about marrying Ranger?"

"Ranger and I aren't really a couple," I said.

"Right," Amanda said, rolling her eyes and smiling.

When Amanda rolled her eyes it was cute. In fact it was adorable, because Amanda was adorable. When I roll my eyes people are afraid I've had a seizure.

"I've seen the way he looks at you," Amanda said.

"Like I'm a disaster?"

"Like he can't take his eyes off you."

"We're friends," I said. "And sometimes we work together. I don't think Ranger is ready for a relationship."

Amanda glanced over at him. "He's very handsome," she whispered.

I nodded in agreement. Ranger is drop-dead handsome.

The first course was set in front of me. Green salad with croutons and chunks of tomato. Standard fare. Not especially tempting.

Ranger was next to the bride's mother, listening politely to her chatter. Occasionally he'd flick a glance my way but more often than not he was looking behind me, watching a waiter, scanning the room. I was doing the same, looking for someone with a dimple in his chin.

The main course was steak, vegetable medley, and mashed potatoes. I stared at the mashed potatoes and bit into my lower lip. I was hungry but not hungry enough to risk getting poisoned again.

"I have someone in the kitchen," Ranger said from across the table. "This should be okay."

TWENTY-THREE

IT WAS ELEVEN WHEN we left the restaurant. Two Rangeman SUVs followed Kinsey and Amanda, and another one followed Ranger.

"Did you think he would make a move at the restaurant?" I asked Ranger.

"I thought he would try something at the church. It could be that he's discouraged by the security force."

"I like Amanda. It was nice to get to know her. Will she be safe for the rest of the night?"

"She's with Kinsey. I have them back in the safe house. She should be okay." Ranger stopped for a light and looked over at me. "Would you consider spending the night at Rangeman?"

Oh boy. Desirable for a variety of reasons, the least of which was security, but I was remembering the conversation with Amanda about marriage. And I was remembering Morelli.

"Not a good idea," I said.

"You'd be safe there."

"Tempting, but I think I should go home tonight. I'm sure I'll be fine. It's not like I'm Orin's number one target."

"No, but you could be his number two target. Hal is following us. I'll leave him in your parking lot. And *do not* remove the GPS devices."

"Yes, sir."

Ten minutes later Ranger opened my door and stepped into my apartment. He did a walk-through, looking in closets and under the bed.

"Lock up when I leave and don't open your door to anyone," he said. "Are you sure you don't want me to stay?"

I hesitated for a beat. "I'm sure."

He traced a line down the side of my face with his fingertip. "Would you like me to change your mind?"

That got a smile from me. "No, but thanks for offering."

He stood outside my door and waited until he heard all my locks tumble into place, then he knocked once and left.

I glanced over at Tiki. "What do you think? Did I do the right thing?"

Tiki looked disgusted with the whole process, so I had the last beer in the fridge and went to bed. I'm not usually a restless sleeper but I had a horrible night. I was worried about Orin going after Amanda and Ranger and Kinsey. I thought it was remote that he would attack me. He'd made a show of sending a firebomb into my apartment but I wasn't convinced he cared about killing me or even torturing me. I figured I was tangential to his vendetta.

At daybreak I gave up trying to sleep. I forced myself out of bed and into the shower. An hour later I was on the road in search of breakfast. I was thinking something greasy and salty and totally unhealthy. Something fattening with cheese and a worthless piece of white bread. I pulled into Cluck-in-a-Bucket and ordered their breakfast sandwich and coffee. It was too early to go to the office. Connie wouldn't be there until eight o'clock and it wasn't even nearly eight.

Hal was in line behind me. I waited for him to get his order and then I pulled out into traffic. I returned to my apartment building, parked, and went back to talk to Hal.

"I need a nap," I told him. "You don't have to stay here."

"Ranger told me to keep my eye on you and that's what I'm doing," Hal said. "I get relieved at eight o'clock."

I trudged up the stairs and down the hall. I let myself into my apartment, relocked the door, and took my coffee and breakfast sandwich into the kitchen. Rex was sound asleep in his soup can. Tiki was on guard.

I ate the sandwich and sipped my coffee. "This is the day," I said to Tiki. "I have to get into the pink dress and march down the aisle today. I'd almost rather face Orin."

I turned to go into the bedroom and Orin was in front of me.

"Your lucky day," he said.

He resembled the man in the photo but there were significant changes. He'd lost weight and his face and hands were badly scarred. The dimple was still there, partially obscured by the scarring. One ear was almost completely obliterated. His eyes were very pale blue, almost colorless, and his pupils were shrunk to tiny pinpoints that hinted at total insanity. I sucked in air and the coffee sloshed out of my cup and onto the floor.

"Hideous, right?" he asked. "Do I scare you?"

I was unable to speak. My heart was pounding in my chest and I was suffocating, unable to breathe. He *was* hideous, not because of the scars but because of the eyes. The eyes were terrifying.

He was wearing army fatigues. His semi-automatic was holstered, as was a large knife. His chest was crisscrossed with ammo belts. Two grenades and packets of what I feared were explosives were strapped to the ammo belts with black electrician's tape. He was holding a black baton that at first glance looked like a flashlight, but there were two prongs where the light should have been. Heavy-duty stun gun, I thought. Not good news.

He swung the baton and knocked the coffee out of my hand, sending it flying toward a wall. I yelped, and he came at me with the baton. He hit me hard in the thigh, pressed the prongs against my side, and I crumpled to the floor.

When I came around I had my hands bound behind me with electrician's tape, and I'd been propped up against the under-sink cabinet in the kitchen. Orin was sitting on a dining room chair about three feet away, looking at me. He had a lighter in his hand. It was the kind you use to light a fireplace or a grill, and he was flicking it on and off.

"Do you like fire?" he asked.

"Sometimes," I said, working to keep my voice from trembling, not wanting to show fear. I thought about the watch on my wrist. I'd been too flustered to remember to press the button when Orin initially surprised me, and now it was under layers of tape and not accessible.

"It drives the devil out," Orin said. "That's why they used to burn witches. It returns everything to a pure state. It's the only way the soul can be released from the body in its most beautiful form."

"Does cremation count?" I asked him.

"Not if it's done after death. We must all suffer to achieve grace. It's important you understand this because you're going to suffer terribly. You're going to beg me to stop the suffering, but it will all be worth it to you. You'll die cleansed."

"Why me?"

"You've been chosen. Ranger chose you. So now I have to cleanse both of you."

"So this is about Ranger."

"He did a very bad thing. And he encouraged Kinsey to follow him. They abandoned the unit. When they left we were broken up and scattered to the winds."

"They left when their tour of duty was done."

"We were a brotherhood. It was a holy pact. While we were together we had divine protection. Once the bond was broken we were unprotected. These scars I wear are the result of that broken bond. I was attacked by the devil. It would never have happened if Ranger and Kinsey had kept us together. They did the unthinkable and now we're all at risk. The devil stalks us and I'm the only one who can set it right."

"Ranger thought you were dead."

"*Everyone* thinks I'm dead," Orin said. "I'm like a zombie."

His voice was flat and soft. No emotion. No emotion in his face. I wondered if he'd always been like that or if the craziness had reached critical mass and taken away all else.

"When the lesson happened I was in a truck in Afghanistan."

"Lesson?"

"The divine intervention that showed me the penalty for Ranger's sin. The day the devil was allowed to visit me."

I could feel goose bumps break out on my arm and a chill slide the length of my spine. As a bounty hunter I've come into contact with a good number of unhinged souls, but there was an otherworldliness to Orin that I hadn't seen before. A total detachment from reality that could only be described as cruel serenity.

"We were under fire and the truck took a hit," Orin said. "The impact was so violent the truck was tossed into the air and came to land in a field. There were five of us in the truck and everyone but me was blown to bits. Nothing left but bloody body parts. As it was I lost my foot." He raised his camo pants to show a prosthetic. "That's how I was identified as dead. Nothing left of me but my foot."

"But you didn't die."

"I'm not allowed to die until Ranger and Kinsey die. Only part of me burned in the explosion. The rest of my mortal body is waiting."

"Why weren't you found with the rest of the men in the truck?"

"I was captured and caged. After years of imprisonment, when I realized my purpose for living, I escaped. I inched my way out of the Middle East, to Europe, to rehabilitate myself enough to complete my mission. And here I am." He said this very matter of fact, his hands folded in his lap. "Imagine how saddened I was to learn that Ranger and Kinsey had infected two women with their evil. Although in a way it enhances the process for them. They'll have the additional agony of knowing someone they loved had a painful and early death. Perhaps it will save them from eternal hell. So you see I'm not actually a zombie. I'm an angel."

I was sure he believed it. He believed everything he said. The whole crazy jumble of devil and divine intervention and abandonment.

"I've brought this fire starter," he said. "I thought I would burn you a little at a time. Let you enjoy the pain. Allow you to see your flesh blister and melt away. I don't want to go too fast and rob you of the experience."

"I could help you," I said. "Counseling, drugs, a religious advisor, a girlfriend."

"I don't need help. I'm in a good place. I just need to finish my task. It's taken me years to get to this point. It's all I've worked for."

He grabbed my ponytail and set fire to it.

I shrieked and tried to jerk away but he held fast. I smelled my hair burning, felt the fire burning my neck. And over my shrieking I heard someone pounding on my door, ringing my doorbell.

"I hate this sort of distraction," Orin said.

He yanked me up by my hair, shoved my head under the faucet, and turned the water on to put the fire out. He went to the door and looked through the security peephole.

"It's a man," he said. "Tell him to go away."

I went to the peephole and looked out. I'd

expected to see Hal but it was Brody Logan. "Go away," I said.

"I want Tiki. I got a bad feeling. Tiki's sending out weird vibes. I want to see him to make sure he's okay."

Orin had me by the arm, squeezing hard enough to bruise.

"Go home," I said to Logan.

"I don't have a home."

"Then go to your tent."

"No way. I want to see Tiki."

"Help!" I yelled at the door. "*Get HELP! Call the police! Get the Rangeman guy!*"

Orin grabbed me by my bound wrists and threw me across the room. He opened the door, yanked Logan inside, closed and relocked the door, and drew his gun.

"Dude!" Logan said, eyes wide.

I struggled to my feet, got a running start, and head-butted Orin, knocking him to his knees.

"Do something," I shrieked at Logan. "*Do something!*"

Logan went spastic, arms flailing, feet not knowing which way to move. He spotted Tiki in the kitchen and lunged for him, lifting him off the counter, wrapping him in his arms.

Orin stood and pointed his gun at Logan. I knocked into Orin again, jostling the gun, and Orin drilled two rounds into Tiki.

Logan let out a roar and charged Orin, bashing

him in the face, using Tiki like a battering ram. Blood gushed from Orin's nose, and Logan immediately rammed Orin again, catching him square in the chest. I heard something go *plink* onto my tile floor. I looked down and saw that it was a pin to one of the grenades. Time stood still for a moment while we all stared at the pin.

Orin grabbed at the live grenade still taped to his gun belt, and I kicked him hard in his prosthetic. The prosthetic flew off and Orin lost his balance, wheeling around on one leg. Logan and I dove into the kitchen, and Orin fell facedown and blew up in the foyer.

I was stunned, sitting on the kitchen floor with my ears ringing. Logan was next to me hugging Tiki.

"He shouldn't have shot Tiki," Logan said. "Hawaiian gods get even. Did you see what Tiki did to his foot? It flew right off his leg when you kicked it!"

"It was a prosthetic," I said to Logan.

"I guess that would make it easier," Logan said.

I have a metal fire door with four deadbolts, but Orin had only thrown one of the locks when he closed the door. I heard someone put his foot to the door from the other side, and on the second attempt the door crashed open against the wall. It was Hal. He took a couple steps in, gun drawn, avoiding what was left of Orin, and looked in the kitchen at me.

"I'm okay," I said.

I thought there were sounds of elephants running in the hall, dimly heard over the ringing in my ears. It was Ranger and two more Rangeman guys. Not as big as elephants, but the two men with Ranger could easily have made the NFL playing defense.

Ranger moved around Orin, stepped into the kitchen, and lifted me to my feet. He took a knife off his gun belt and cut my tape away.

"I was on Hamilton when the alarm went off," Ranger said. "I listened to you all the way, and got here just as the explosion occurred. Hal was already at your door by then."

I looked down at the plus sign on the watch face. Hard to read because I was shaking.

"I wasn't fast enough to hit the button when he first appeared," I said. "And then my wrists were taped. He must have accidentally pushed the button when he grabbed me."

People were accumulating in the hall. Ranger told one of the men to close the door and stand guard outside. Some of Orin was facedown on the tile. Some of him was on my foyer wall. What was on the floor was charred and smoking. Only the prosthetic foot was still intact, halfway across the room.

"What happened here?" Ranger asked me.

"He had what I thought might be explosives and a couple grenades taped to the ammo belts across his chest. There was a scuffle and one of the grenades lost a pin. Logan and I dove for the kitchen and Orin exploded."

Ranger squatted beside the body. "The most common grenade sends fragments over a wide radius. Orin was a munitions genius, and I'm guessing this was some sort of designer incendiary device. We need to clear this area and bring in a bomb expert to make sure there aren't any more live explosives on him."

"Is he dead?" Logan asked.

This was a no-brainer question considering what was left of Orin.

"He's been dead for years," Ranger said.

TWENTY-FOUR

LOGAN CARRIED TIKI INTO the hall, I grabbed my messenger bag, and Ranger carried Rex's hamster tank. By the time we reached the parking lot, emergency vehicles were rumbling in. A fire truck, an EMT truck, two police cars. Morelli in the Buick.

Morelli parked and jogged over to us. He stood hands on hips, his expression grim.

"Are you okay?" he asked me.

"Except for my ponytail," I said. "And some minor burns on my neck."

He looked up at my apartment windows. "What's going on?"

"The rocket guy blew himself up," I said. "He needs to be checked out to make sure he's not still booby-trapped."

"Are you on the job?" Ranger asked Morelli.

"No," Morelli said. "I'm off today. Jean Matson was working dispatch and called me when Rangeman asked for police assistance."

"I'm going to see this through," Ranger said.

"It's not necessary for anyone else to stay. I'm sure Stephanie will have to give a statement, but she can do that downtown some other time. I have the explosion and events immediately preceding it recorded."

Morelli took Rex from Ranger. "Where do you want to go first, my house or a hair salon?"

I gave up a sigh. "Your house," I said. I glanced at Logan, and thought he looked lost, cradling Tiki, unsure of his place. "Can we take Logan with us?"

"Sure," Morelli said, slinging an arm around me. "Let's go home."

We piled into the Buick and chugged out of the lot. Minutes later we were in Morelli's nice normal neighborhood, and the explosion seemed far away.

"I thought you were taking me to jail," Logan said when we parked.

"It's not at the top of my list," I told him. "I want to change out of this wet shirt, zone out on Morelli's couch, and let it sink in that the nightmare is over."

I went upstairs, swapped my shirt for one of Morelli's T-shirts, trudged into the bathroom, and looked at my hair. Any other time I would have burst into tears, but right now I was happy just to be alive. It's hair, I told myself. It'll grow. I crawled into Morelli's bed and woke up hours later in a panic. The wedding! I'd forgotten all about the wedding.

I ran downstairs and found Morelli, Logan, Tiki, and Bob on the couch watching television.

"Did Ranger call? Did I miss anything?" I asked.

"We got the bullets out of Tiki, filled him in with wood putty, and colored it with a brown Magic Marker," Logan said. "He's feeling a lot better."

Morelli had his hand in a bag of chips. "Ranger called and I told him you were sleeping. He's coming by at two o'clock with the dress. Since the original maid of honor didn't think she could lose thirty pounds in time to fit the altered dress she relinquished the gig to you. And apparently Amanda really wanted you to still be in the wedding. Ranger said if you needed anything from your apartment you should call him."

"It's almost two now," I said. "Why didn't you wake me?"

"I went up to look in on you and you were out like a light. I thought you needed the sleep."

I felt around the back of my head for the burned-off ponytail. "I need to do something with my hair."

"Cupcake, that's a lost cause. I can cut the singed ends off if you want."

The doorbell rang and Ranger walked in, carrying the plastic-bagged dress. He was in his tux, with a five o'clock shadow and dark circles under his eyes.

"You look like you could use a beer," Morelli said, getting to his feet.

"It's been a long day," Ranger said, handing the dress over to me.

I carried the dress upstairs, took a fast shower, and pulled what was left of my hair into a ponytail again. I searched in Morelli's medicine chest for aloe ointment and smeared some on my blistered neck. I slipped the acres of pink taffeta over my head and struggled to get it zipped. What had originally been a dress from the Little House on the Prairie collection was now straight out of the Little Whorehouse on the Prairie collection. It was so tight and cut so low in the bodice that my boobs were all popped out. If the material hadn't snagged on my nipples they'd have been popped out too. I smashed myself in as best I could and went downstairs.

I marched into the living room in my dress and sneakers. "Do not say *one word*," I said. "I will personally make a eunuch out of anyone who makes a crack about this dress or my hair."

"I like it," Morelli said.

"You're skating on thin ice, mister," I told him.

Ranger set his empty beer bottle on the coffee table and stood. "Let's get this done."

I followed him out and stood looking at the 911 Turbo. "I'm not going to fit," I said. "How am I going to get all of this dress into this little car?"

"Get in and I'll do the rest," Ranger said.

I swiveled around, dropped into the seat, and Ranger beat the dress into submission and stuffed it in. He was laughing when he got behind the wheel.

"Now what?" I asked.

"You're wearing sneakers. I hope the bridal shop lady never finds out."

"You didn't notice in the house?"

"My eyes never got lower than your nipples. If it wasn't for the fact that Morelli would shoot me I would have taken you on his front lawn."

Perfect, I thought. I have half my hair burned off, I'm wearing the dress from hell, and all I have to do is show a little nipple and I'm a sex goddess. Something to remember.

Ranger rolled out of the lot and headed for Hamilton Avenue. "Your apartment is relatively clean and your door is fixed. I have another cleaning crew coming in the morning. I wouldn't advise going back there tonight. It'll be fine after tomorrow."

"Orin?"

"Defused and taken away."

"Do you want to talk about it?"

"No," Ranger said. "I want to let it rest."

"When you're ready to talk about it I'll tell you what he told me before he set my hair on fire. He was very, very sick."

"I know he was sick. And maybe someday I'll want to know his reasoning and his inner demons, but right now I'm moving on."

He parked in the church lot and we walked to the side door. We were originally supposed to be with Kinsey and Amanda prior to the wedding, but circumstances had of course changed that. The other ushers were already collected in the vestibule. Guests were beginning to arrive. A room had been reserved for the bride and her bridesmaids. Ranger dropped me there and went to wait for Kinsey.

Everyone was there but Amanda. She was coming with her parents. None of the other women were popping out of their dresses and no one else had hair styled by a Bic lighter. They were relatives of the bride, college roommates, and best friends. They were all good people, including me in their pre-wedding excitement. No one mentioned my hair, but it was the elephant in the room.

"It was set on fire," I finally said. "I had an episode with a crazy person, and he set my hair on fire."

Everyone went bug-eyed.

"What happened to the crazy person?" one of the women asked.

"He blew himself up."

"Get out! You mean like guts all over the place?"

"Not *all* over the place," I said. "He was pretty well contained, all things considered."

Ranger called on my phone and asked me to come into the hall. I went out and found him smiling.

"They eloped," he said.

"Seriously?"

"Kinsey just called. They're on a plane for Paris."

"Gee," I said. "I'm all dressed up. I was looking forward to walking down the aisle in my sneakers."

"You can wear your sneakers to the reception. They're going ahead with it."

"I'll pass on the reception."

Ranger kissed me on the top of the head. "Good choice."

• • •

Morelli, Logan, Tiki, and Bob were still in front of the television when I returned. Logan and Bob were asleep. Tiki was ever vigilant. Morelli looked bored.

"Short wedding," Morelli said.

"They eloped at the last minute."

Morelli looked at Logan. "What am I supposed to do with him? Are we adopting him?"

"No. Give me a minute to get out of this monstrosity and I'll take him off your hands."

I ran upstairs, shucked the dress, and got back into my jeans and Morelli's T-shirt. I went into Morelli's upstairs office and sat at his desk. I pulled up an online travel site on his computer, searched for tickets to Hawaii, and booked Logan and Tiki on a red-eye leaving from Newark. I returned to the living room and grabbed my messenger bag.

"I need the keys to the Buick," I said to Morelli. "I'm taking Logan for a ride."

"You're not going to drop him off in a field like a stray cat, are you?"

"No. And I wouldn't do that to a stray cat either."

I woke Logan, gave him a granola bar, and told him we were heading out.

"Are we going to jail?" he asked.

"No," I told him. "I'm going to get you and Tiki back to Hawaii."

"I haven't got the moola," Logan said. "I only saved up enough for half a ticket."

"My treat," I said.

"This could be construed as helping a fugitive to flee," Morelli said.

I rolled my eyes at Morelli. "He bashed in a police car. That's everyone's fantasy."

Morelli turned back to the television. "I didn't hear anything. This conversation never took place. Do you want me to ride along with you?"

"Not necessary," I said, "but thanks."

I got Logan and Tiki buckled into the Buick and I made my way to the highway. Route 1 wasn't bad at this time of evening on a Saturday, and once I got on the Turnpike I flew. I pulled into short-term parking and walked Logan to the terminal. I waited while he and Tiki sailed through check-in with their e-tickets for two seats and went through security without a hitch. I walked back to the Buick feeling good. It had been a really weird day, but it was ending happy.

I got a mental message from Tiki a few minutes before seven that they were about to take off, and he wanted to thank me. Minutes later I got a text message from Morelli telling me to pick up a pizza on my way home.

TWENTY-FIVE

MORELLI AND I WERE halfway through the large pizza, extra cheese, extra pepperoni, when Grandma called me.

"I cracked the case," she said. "I got it all figured out. Millie Debrowski and I went to the diner on Livingston for dinner tonight because Millie was hankering for their rice pudding. That's the diner the old coots went to when it turned out they couldn't rough up Geoffrey Cubbin. Well, we're walking in and I notice they got business hours on the door and it says they close at one o'clock. That means the nurse fibbed about seeing Cubbin in his bed at two o'clock. Cubbin went missing a lot earlier."

I was gobstruck. It was suddenly so clear why we didn't see Cubbin leave. We were watching the wrong segment of video.

"You're a genius," I said to Grandma.

"Yep, I'm a regular Sherlock."

I hung up with Grandma and told Morelli about the diner hours. "We watched the wrong part of the video," I said. "We need to go back and watch from the beginning of the shift."

I called Briggs and told him we'd meet him in his office in a half hour, and that we wanted to see earlier video. He said he'd have everything ready to roll by the time we got there. Morelli gave the last piece of pizza to Bob, I gave a small chunk to Rex, and we took off for the hospital.

"I was going to ask for twenty-four hours of video to begin with," Morelli said, "but I have a monster caseload, and after reviewing the nurses' statements I was hoping it wasn't necessary."

My excuse wasn't that legitimate. I hadn't wanted to spend that much time with Randy Briggs.

We parked and walked through the lobby together. Visiting hours were coming to a close and Morelli badged his way past the reception desk. I'm used to working with Ranger but not so much with Morelli. I always feel like an illegitimate stepchild when I work with Morelli. He's a Trenton cop and I'm someone with a badge I bought on the Internet.

Briggs was waiting in his office. Mickey Zigler was patrolling the floors.

"Holy crap," Briggs said when he saw me. "What happened to your hair? It looks like you got too close to a barbecue."

"Pretty close to the truth," I said. "Are you set to go?"

"Yeah. I have all the cameras on the screen and backed up to eleven o'clock."

Morelli and I pulled chairs around to face the monitor and Briggs got the video rolling at fast-forward. The time ticked off on the bottom of the picture. At 11:45 the Yeti stepped out of the service elevator, pushing a large laundry hamper.

"Stop!" I said. "It's the Yeti."

The picture was grainy and the light was low, but I was sure it was him. He was dressed in scrubs, like an orderly. He kept his head down and quickly moved down the hall and off camera.

"Are you sure?" Briggs asked. "How could it be the Yeti?"

"Pull just that camera up," I said. "I want to see it again."

Briggs went back to 11:45, the elevator doors opened, and the Yeti came on screen. We watched him disappear down the hall and we let the video keep running. At 11:53 the Yeti appeared again, pushing the laundry hamper. It was clear from the way he was pushing that the hamper was heavier than before. He rolled the hamper back to the service elevator and disappeared into it.

"That's how Cubbin got off the floor," I said. "In the laundry hamper."

"There's laundry pickups like that all day long," Briggs said. "Nobody would even notice this guy."

Morelli leaned forward. "Run the camera on the loading dock."

"Give me a minute to find it," Briggs said.

He scrolled through a series of cameras. He

locked onto the loading dock and reset the time for 11:55. A white panel van was already backed up to the platform. At 11:59 the Yeti rolled the laundry hamper into the van, the van doors closed, and the van drove away.

"Damn," Briggs said. "That's how they did it."

We looked at the video several more times. There was no writing on the side of the van and the license was obscured. The driver wasn't visible.

"Dollars to donuts that van went to The Clinic," Briggs said.

I looked over at Morelli. "Do you want to take another look?"

"At The Clinic?"

"Yep."

"Now?"

"Yep."

He slouched back in his chair and looked at me. "I shouldn't do this. This could get me in a lot of trouble."

"If you get kicked off the force you can always get a job here," I said. "Briggs would hire you."

"Not funny," Morelli said.

I stood and returned my chair to the front of Briggs's desk. "I'm going to The Clinic with or without you, and I'm going to find out what happens to these guys after they leave the hospital."

"I'm with you," Briggs said. "Count me in."

Morelli scraped his chair back. "Me too."

I went in the Buick with Morelli, and Briggs

followed in his car. We turned onto Route 1, drove a couple miles, and turned off into the light industrial complex. We drove to the end of the cul-de-sac and idled in front of The Clinic. Lights shone on the second floor.

"I'm pretty sure that's the area they're using for a surgical suite," I said to Morelli. "The dayroom and the lab are in the back of the building. The operating room and patient rooms are in the front. When I was here last time I parked in the lot next to The Clinic."

Morelli drove to the Myron Cryo lot and cut the engine. "Do you have a plan?" he asked.

"No. Do you?"

"Nope. I assumed we'd play it by ear. If we attempt entry into The Clinic and an alarm goes off and the police show up, I'm running into the woods and hanging you out to dry."

"Been there, done that," I said.

"Thought I should get it out in the open," Morelli said.

"No problem."

Fact is, if the police showed up I'd be in the woods before Morelli.

We got out of our cars, stumbled through the patch of woods, and stood looking at the back of The Clinic.

"How do we get in?" Morelli asked.

"Briggs lets us in."

"Then what?"

I didn't know *then what*.

"Suppose we send Briggs in and he snoops around and comes back with a report," Morelli said.

"I guess I could do that," Briggs said.

"Shouldn't he have a wire or something?" I said. "What if he gets caught?"

Morelli looked at me like I was from Mars. "It's my day off," he said. "I don't have any wires in my back pocket."

"Hey," I said. "I'm just saying."

"Do you have a gun?" Morelli asked Briggs.

"Yeah, I have a gun," Briggs said.

"Well, if you get caught you can shoot someone," Morelli said. "If we hear shooting we'll call the police."

"Don't pay attention to him," I said to Briggs. "Just be careful and you'll be fine."

I went to the drop box and opened it. "Okay," I said to Morelli, "pick him up and stuff him in."

Morelli looked at the drop box and looked at Briggs. "You're not going to tell anyone I did this, right? Blood oath. Sworn to secrecy."

"Just stuff him in," I said.

Morelli picked Briggs up and slid him into the drop box. I closed the box, there was some banging, and then there was quiet. I opened the box and looked in. Empty.

"He's inside," I said to Morelli.

"This is freaky," Morelli said. "What do we do now?"

"We wait."

Morelli wrapped an arm around me. "Want to make out?"

"No! Suppose something goes wrong and the Yeti comes out after us. If we're making out you might not be able to run."

"Why not?"

"You know . . . "

"I can run like that," Morelli said. "I can jump out of second-story windows like that. I had a lot of experience when I was in high school."

We waited for five minutes but didn't see any sign of Briggs. Ten minutes. No Briggs.

"I'm worried," I said to Morelli.

"Do you want me to try to stuff *you* into the drop box?"

"Try the door. Maybe he opened it before he wandered away."

Morelli tried the door and it opened.

"This is illegal entry," Morelli said.

"Only for you," I told him. "I have rights."

I stepped inside the dimly lit garage and let my eyes adjust. There were four cars parked. White panel van, black Escalade, silver Lexus, red Jaguar.

"Something's going down," I said to Morelli. "All the players are here. Maybe we should call the police."

"I'm the police."

"I was thinking it might be better to have guys in uniform."

"What are you going to say to the guys in uniform? Are you going to tell them I shoved Briggs into the drop box and he didn't come out so you want them to bust the door down?"

"Of course not. I'll think up a fib."

"I can do better than that."

He climbed onto the hood of the Escalade and then onto the roof. He reached overhead, punched the smoke detector that was attached to the ceiling, and the fire alarm went off. He jumped down, and we ran out of the garage and hid in the wooded area.

Lights went on all over the building and after a minute the alarm went silent. Ten minutes later the lights began blinking out and there was no sign of police or a fire truck.

"They must not be hooked into an alarm company," Morelli said.

My cellphone rang. It was Briggs, whispering so low I could barely hear him.

"You gotta get me out of here," he said. "I saw feet. Big naked feet. I think they might have been dead but I don't know for sure."

"Were they attached to something . . . like a body?"

"They were sticking out from under a sheet."

"Where are you?"

"I'm on the second floor, under a desk, and there's a guy sitting in that little lobby area reading a paper. I can't get past him."

"Hang tight," I said. "We're on it."

I disconnected and looked at Morelli. "He's

under a desk on the second floor and can't get past some guy in the lobby."

"Call him back and tell him to make more of an effort. I'm missing a really good ball game."

"He said he saw naked feet sticking out from under a sheet. He sounded a little freaked."

"Were they live naked feet or dead naked feet?"

"He said they might have been dead but he couldn't be sure."

"So much for the ball game," Morelli said.

We went to the door beside the drop box and found it locked.

"They must have noticed the door was unlocked when they went around checking smoke detectors," Morelli said. "This makes things more complicated."

We were standing there hoping for a brilliant idea when the garage door rolled up. We flattened ourselves against the building, the door went totally open, and Kruger's red Jaguar glided out of the garage and down the driveway.

"She's going to work," I said.

The door started to roll down, and Morelli and I slipped under it and into the garage before it closed completely. A moment later we saw the light go on over the elevator, indicating it was in motion.

"Someone else is coming down," Morelli said.

We scrambled into a dark corner behind some packing crates and watched the elevator doors open and the Yeti come out carrying two insulated chests. He loaded the chests into the van, got behind the wheel, pressed the remote for the door, and drove out of the garage.

Morelli grabbed my hand, yanked me across the garage at a full run, and we slid under the door just as it closed. He was instantly on his feet and sprinting across the lot, through the small patch of woods. He had the Buick cranked over by the time my hand touched the door handle.

"Briggs can wait," he said, peeling out of the lot. "I want to see where the van is going."

We caught sight of the van just as it left the park and headed south on Route 1. It got off at Spruce and fifteen minutes later it turned in to a private fixed base operations facility at Mercer Airport. The van pulled up to the FBO gate, was admitted onto the tarmac, and drove up to a midsize business jet. The two insulated chests were handed over to the captain, and the Yeti drove the van off the field and back to the access road.

Morelli called the plane's tail number in to one of his contacts and asked for owner information. He listened to the answer, thanked the person at the other end, and put the Buick in gear.

"The plane is owned by Franz Sunshine Enterprises," Morelli said. "And it's filed a flight plan for a Nevada destination."

"I guess it's not a big surprise that Sunshine owns the plane, since the chests came from his clinic."

"I wouldn't mind knowing what was in those chests," Morelli said.

"Drugs? Body parts? Lunch?"

Morelli made another phone call and suggested that the chests be checked out on arrival in Nevada.

"I suppose we should try to rescue Briggs," I said when Morelli finished his call.

"He's not my favorite person," Morelli said.

"He's not *anyone's* favorite person."

We turned onto Route 1 and my phone rang.

It was Briggs. "Where the hell are you? I finally was able to get out by the skin of my teeth and you're not here!"

"We're ten minutes away," I said. "We followed the white van to the airport, but we're on our way back."

"This clinic is creep central. I don't know what the heck they do here but it involves dead people, and it smells bad."

"How many dead people did you see?"

"Just the one. Isn't that enough?"

"Is that what smells bad?"

"If the stiff smelled bad I wouldn't know over the stench coming from the lounge. There's some guy cooking something in the microwave that's stinking up the whole floor. I heard someone call him Abu."

"Abu Darhmal," I said.

Morelli looked over at me when I hung up. "He saw dead people?"

"One. And he managed to get out. He's waiting for us in the lot."

TWENTY-SIX

"I WAS GETTING LONELY here," Briggs said when we parked and got out of the car.

"We followed the Yeti to the airport and watched him hand over two insulated chests and leave. I imagine he came back here."

Briggs shook his head. "He didn't come back here. Nobody's here. The doctor and the Abu guy just left. The only one who didn't leave is the dead guy. Except I guess he could be in someone's trunk since he isn't in the hall anymore."

Morelli looked at The Clinic. "It's empty?"

"Yeah," Briggs said. "The party's over."

Morelli got a flashlight from the Buick. "Let's take a tour."

There were no cars in the garage, just as Briggs had said. We entered the stairwell and climbed to the first floor in darkness. Morelli opened the door and we moved into the first-floor hall. Also dark. We walked the length of it, returned to the stairwell, and went up another flight. The second-floor hall had path lighting. Not so much that you could read by it, but enough that Morelli didn't need his flashlight.

We did a quick check of the empty offices, crossed the lobby past the elevator bank and reception desk, and aimed light into the first patient room. It was just as I remembered it. Bed made. No sign of occupancy. En suite bathroom unused.

Morelli flashed light into the second patient room, and I saw that the bed was stripped bare. Somebody had been in the bed and now they were gone, I thought. The guy with the feet.

"This is different from when I was here," I said. "This bed was made up when I was here."

We looked through the room and the bathroom, but found no left-behind personal effects. There was a lingering smell of antiseptic. The room had recently been cleaned.

"Where did you see the feet?" I asked Briggs.

"In the hall here, outside this room."

Morelli looked over at me. Probably checking to make sure I wasn't going to faint.

We left the room and went across the hall to the lab. A half-filled coffee cup had been left on a counter, so the lab was clearly being used, but there were no obvious science experiments going on. No slides under the microscope. No petri dishes growing the unthinkable. No beakers of urine.

Morelli went through drawers. He found nicotine gum, Rolaids, sticky pads, and pens, but no notes. No computer.

"It used to be you could always look for a phone book," Morelli said. "Now they're obsolete. Everyone carries their phone book in their phone. Same with computers. They're portable and almost never left behind."

We moved from the lab to the lounge. It was furnished in standard hospital lounge furniture. Inexpensive. Easy to clean. Beige and orange. Two round tables with four chairs each. Small kitchen area with a fridge, microwave, and sink. Large flat-screen television. Couch and two club chairs in front of the television. There were dishes in the sink. They'd been rinsed and left to dry.

The surgery was the only room left to investigate. We all took a deep breath before pushing the door open. Not sure what we expected to find, but we were all reluctant to enter.

The room had no windows, so Morelli flipped the light switch and we were blinded by brightness. I'd seen it before and there were no surprises. No body on the table. No blood spatters. No gallon jugs for cellulite collection.

Morelli looked around. "This is a really well equipped room. You don't spend this kind of money if you aren't going to use the equipment. So what do they do here? My first thought would be very private cosmetic surgery, but the patient rooms weren't luxurious. What else could they use this for?"

I had an idea but I didn't want to say it out loud. It was too gruesome. I looked at Morelli, and I knew he had the same idea. Body parts.

I heard the scuff of footsteps in the hall behind us and turned to see the Yeti and Franz Sunshine.

"Organ harvest," Sunshine said. "Very lucrative. The donor never complains because he's dead. And the recipient is happy to pay an astronomical amount of money to live. It's a win-win deal. We only harvest from losers who have a reason to disappear, and we were doing well until Ms. Plum came along. Now as it turns out we have three new donors."

"I'm a dwarf," Briggs said. "Nobody's gonna want my organs. You might as well let me go. I won't tell anyone. I swear."

The Yeti was holding an assault rifle. "Don't anyone get frisky," he said. "I have real good aim with this. I go for knees since they don't bring much money on the black market."

"Why were you in Cubbin's house?" I asked him.

"Looking for his money. He said he had money hid there but I couldn't find it."

"He was trying to buy his way out of donating his heart?"

"Something like that," the Yeti said.

"Let's move this along," Sunshine said. "We're all going down to the garage now. Hands on your heads. Single file. If anything bothersome happens John will shoot you."

So the Yeti's name was John.

We followed instructions and walked down the hall to the lobby. We shuffled into the elevator and lined up against the wall. The Yeti was steely-eyed with the assault rifle trained on us. Morelli was wearing his cop face. No emotion. Watching the Yeti. Waiting for his moment.

I was still wearing Ranger's GPS watch. I had my hands on my head, one hand over my wrist, and I pushed the audio button. No one seemed to notice. I couldn't see the watch face, but I hoped I was sending.

The elevator doors opened onto the garage and we exited, hands still on our heads. The white van and a black Mercedes were parked side by side, noses to the wall.

"You're going to turn and walk to the far side of the garage," Sunshine said. "Walk very carefully. John is known to have a short fuse when he feels threatened."

I knew this to be true. He'd zapped me with the stun gun, and I hadn't seen it coming.

We got to the end of the garage, and I realized there was a door that I hadn't noticed before. It had another of the number-sequenced locks on it, and it looked like a door to a vault.

Sunshine punched in six numbers, the door released, he pulled it open, and cold air rushed out at us. I sensed Morelli shift foot to foot. He wasn't liking what he saw.

"What is this?" I asked, hoping Ranger was listening.

"It's a freezer," Sunshine said. "Convenient for storing bodies until we can arrange disposal. Because we're short-staffed right now and can't sedate the three of you, we'll slow your respiration for a few hours. When Dr. Fish returns you'll be barely alive, but hopefully some of your organs will be usable."

He flipped a switch and a light went on in the freezer. It was commercial grade. Possibly originally designed as a morgue or maybe a walk-in for Shop n Bag. Sunshine took the rifle from the Yeti and motioned for him to go into the freezer.

"Haul them out," Sunshine said.

The Yeti went in and came out with a black plastic body bag. Whatever was in it was frozen solid and about 5'10". The Yeti lifted the bag and carried it to the van. He got a second frozen bag, struggled a little under the weight, and shoved it into the back of the van as well.

"Pitch and Cubbin?" Morelli asked.

Sunshine didn't answer. He handed the rifle over to the Yeti. "In you go," Sunshine said to Morelli.

Morelli lunged for the rifle, and the Yeti shot him in the leg.

I screamed, the Yeti hit me in the stomach with

the rifle butt, and I crumpled to the ground unable to breathe.

"I don't want to go in there," Briggs said. "I'm too young. I'm not ready. I'm diseased. I've got everything. Herpes and warts. My liver's crap."

The Yeti herded Morelli and Briggs in and slammed the door shut. I was still lying on the cement floor.

"Get up," Sunshine said. "You're going with us in case we need a hostage."

"Why would you need a hostage?" I asked.

"Your boyfriend is a cop. I don't know if he was stupidly acting alone or if this was a planned operation."

The Yeti dragged me up to my feet and prodded me with the rifle. "Move."

We reached the van and Sunshine bound my hands at the wrist with electrician's tape. I couldn't stop from rolling my eyes. Jeez Louise, I thought, how many times in one day can this happen?

We all got into the van, Sunshine driving and the Yeti holding the gun on me. We motored out of the garage and down the driveway. I didn't see any Rangeman cars.

"Where are we going?" I asked.

"The cemetery, of course," the Yeti said. "It's not like we're animals. We give everyone a decent burial."

Sunshine went north on Route 1 for about a mile and then turned in to what I saw from a sign was the Sunshine Memorial Park. The cemetery gate opened, Sunshine drove through, and the gate closed behind us.

"One of my many holdings," Sunshine said. "This used to be farmland but I got it for taxes. Turns out there's more money in death than in cows."

I'd had a chance to look at my watch before my wrists were taped and I knew the audio was active. The plus sign was visible in the watch face. My hope was that Ranger had rescued Morelli and Briggs by now and gotten help for Morelli before he lost too much blood. I was trying to stay calm. This was helped by the fact that I was exhausted.

The cemetery was dark, lit only by a sliver of moon. We drove through acres of headstones. All uniform. The Levittown of cemeteries. Sunshine took a road that went off into a raw field. No headstones here. I was in the back of the van with the body bags but I could see through the windshield. Sunshine pulled to the side and stopped.

The Yeti hauled me out of the van and went back for the body bags. He dragged them to a big hole in the ground and pitched them in.

"God bless," the Yeti said.

"Now you," Sunshine said. "Get into the pit."

"I thought I was a hostage."

"Only for this far. The facility can't handle more than two patients at a time. The process becomes too complicated. We have to hold the donor and keep him healthy until all the recipients are in place. It's most lucrative when you can harvest multiple organs, but that requires precision timing."

The Yeti shoved me to the edge of the grave. "Get in," he said. "Jump."

"Are you going to bury me alive?"

"No. I'm going to shoot you," the Yeti said, "but it's neater if you're already in the hole."

He shoved me again, I lost my balance and fell into the grave, on top of the body bags. I saw the Yeti raise the rifle to shoot me, I opened my mouth to scream, but before I could make a sound I heard *Crack, crack!* The Yeti and Sunshine went down. I was on my back on the frozen corpses, numb not just from the cold seeping up into me but from the horror of the day.

I struggled to my feet and stood on one of the body bags to look over the edge of the hole. The Yeti and Sunshine were sprawled on the ground, not moving. I tried to climb out, but the dirt gave way under me. A car drove up in the dark, no headlights but I could make out the outline. The car parked and Ranger and two of his men got out.

Ranger walked to the edge of the grave and jumped in. He lifted me up into the arms of one of his men, and I was back on solid ground. The man gave Ranger a hand up, and Ranger was next to me, cutting the tape off my wrists.

"This is getting to be a bad habit," Ranger said.

"This is the second time I've had to cut you out of tape today."

"Morelli?" I asked him.

"He's fine. Getting locked in a freezer is a good way to stop bleeding from gunshot. Tank and Eugene got him out and took him to St. Francis."

"I love this watch," I told him.

"Remember to shut it off when you go into the bathroom. I don't want my men in the control room getting distracted."

A second car drove up, and Hal got out.

"I'm going to have Hal take you home," Ranger said. "I have some cleanup to do here."

"Are you just going to shovel dirt on them?"

"I'd like to. That would be much easier. Unfortunately the police will have to get involved."

• • •

Morelli, I found out, was still in surgery when we got to Trenton, so Hal dropped me off at St. Francis. I thanked him and told him it wasn't necessary for him to wait. He said the Buick was parked in the garage, and Morelli had the key.

I waved Hal away and walked into the ER reception area. Briggs was there huddled in a blanket, looking tired. He jumped to his feet the instant he saw me and rushed over, suddenly all smiles.

"We heard you were okay! What happened?" he asked.

"I got pushed into an open grave. It was awful."
I felt myself choke up and I swiped at tears. "Sorry,"
I said. "It's been a long day."

"Tell me about it. I was bawling like a baby in
the meat locker. The tears were all frozen on my
face when the Rangeman guy broke in."

"How'd they get the door open?"

"The little guy, Eugene, had an electronic gizmo
that figured out the combination. The whole operation was freakin' impressive. Rangeman had an
EMT truck and medics waiting for us when we got
out."

"Thanks for staying with Morelli."

"No problem. I guess you'll take over now."

I nodded. "I'll wait here."

"That would be great. I think I pissed my pants
when I got shoved into the freezer. I wouldn't mind
going home and throwing these clothes away. I
don't want anything that reminds me of tonight."

It was a couple more hours before I got to take
Morelli home. We went to his house because Rex
and Bob were there and so I didn't have to worry
about finding leftover pieces of Orin. Morelli was
zonked out on painkillers, and I was so fatigued I
was vibrating.

TWENTY-SEVEN

LULA AND CONNIE WERE already at the office when I rolled in Monday morning. Connie had a birthday cake on her desk.

"Whose birthday?" I asked.

"No one's," Connie said. "We're celebrating that you're not dead."

"It was touch and go," I said. "Saturday isn't going down as one of my better days."

"Yeah, but you got a lot accomplished," Lula said. "You got a whole shitload of bad guys killed."

I scooped some icing off with my finger and ate it. "True. And I found Cubbin and Pitch."

Connie and Lula exchanged glances.

"What?" I asked.

"Turned out when they unzipped those bags one of them was Pitch but the other one was some homeless guy."

"That's impossible. What happened to Cubbin?"

Lula and Connie did shoulder shrugs. They didn't know what happened to Cubbin.

I called Morelli. "I just got in to work and I'm hearing it wasn't Cubbin in the body bag."

"I was briefed on it two minutes ago," Morelli said. "It was Pitch and a John Doe."

"So where's Cubbin?"

"Don't know. Right now we can't confirm that he's dead."

"What did Nurse Kruger and Craig Fish have to say?"

"Kruger was found on the floor in her apartment, foaming at the mouth from an overdose. She's locked down at St. Francis. She's expected to live, but we haven't been able to question her yet. Craig Fish is in custody but he isn't saying anything on advice of his lawyer."

"How's your leg?"

"It hurts like a bitch."

"I'll kiss it and make it better tonight."

"It's going to take more than a kiss, Cupcake."

Lula and Connie were watching me as I disconnected.

"So?" Lula said.

"Kruger and the doctor aren't talking. That means they can't confirm that Cubbin is dead. That means we don't get our bond back."

"I was counting on a bonus from that bond," Lula said. "I need new tires on the Firebird."

"Good thing Vinnie isn't here," Connie said. "He'll be doubling up on his blood pressure medication. That was a huge bond."

I sliced off a piece of the birthday cake and sat down to eat it. "Let's think about this. We're pretty sure they had Cubbin. We saw the Yeti push something out in the laundry hamper. And the Yeti said he was looking for Cubbin's money, so obviously Cubbin talked to him. If Cubbin escaped he would have gone to the police. At the very least he would have tried to access some of his money. If he didn't escape, he's dead. He wasn't in the freezer. And he wasn't in the rest of The Clinic. So he must be . . ."

Lula and Connie stared at me.

"In the cemetery," I said. "That's where they disposed of the bodies."

"Uh-oh," Lula said. "I'm not liking this turn of events. I like cemeteries even less than I like hospitals."

I finished my cake and thought about taking a second piece. Not a good idea, I told myself. I'd go into a sugar-and-lard-induced coma.

"I'm going to the cemetery to take a look around," I said. "Anyone want to come with me?"

"I guess I need to make sure you don't get into more trouble," Lula said. "The one day I'm not with you all hell breaks loose what with crazy people getting exploded in your foyer."

A half hour later I turned off Route 1 into Sunshine Memorial Park. It looked a lot less sinister during the day, but it would never win any awards for beauty. The first couple acres were flat. No trees. No shrubs. No flowers. Just small headstones sunk into the ground. I followed the road to the part of the park that was undeveloped. There were some hills there and an occasional tree. The grass was scrubby. I drove past the large excavated pit that Sunshine and the Yeti had tried to bury me in. The grass around it was trampled from police and emergency vehicles. The pit was still open. Yellow crime scene tape fluttered on stakes in the ground.

I parked and Lula and I got out and walked to the hole in the ground.

"This had to be scary as snot," Lula said. "It's creepin' me out and it's not even nighttime."

"I was okay until I got pushed into the hole." I left the grave site and returned to the road. "Cubbin hasn't been missing all that long. If they buried him here the ground would still be freshly disturbed. You look on one side and I'll look on the other."

After a couple minutes Lula called out that she'd found some freshly dug dirt.

"Me too," I said. "I have two potential grave sites here."

"How're we going to know which one of these is Cubbin?" Lula asked.

"I guess we have to dig them all up."

"Nuh-uh. Lula doesn't dig up dead people. You get cooties like that. And they don't like being disturbed. They get pissy and put the whammy on you. You don't want to do it either. You get in enough trouble all on your own. You can't afford to have the whammy."

"If I go to the police it'll take forever. They'll have to get special permission and court orders and grave diggers. And I need the money. I just ran my credit card over my limit sending Tiki back to Hawaii."

"What we need is our own grave digger," Lula said.

"And I know just such a person."

"You're thinking about Simon Diggery," Lula said. "I'd rather dig the grave myself than have dealings with Diggery. Last time we went to his crap-ass trailer you opened a closet door and a twenty-foot snake fell out."

Simon Diggery was a wiry little guy in his fifties. His brown hair was shot with gray and usually tied back in a ponytail. His skin was like old cracked leather and he had arms like Popeye's. He lived in a raggedy double-wide in Bordentown with his wife, his six kids, his brother Melvin, Melvin's pet python, and their Uncle Bill. They were like a bunch of feral cats living in the woods, and Simon Diggery was Trenton's premier grave robber.

"I have a shovel in the trunk," I said. "We could start digging."

"Okay," Lula said. "I was bluffing. Let's go talk to Diggery."

I was bluffing too. I didn't have a shovel in the trunk.

It took almost forty minutes to find Diggery's trailer. It was off Route 206, down a winding two-lane road filled with potholes. The rusted-out cankerous trailer was up on cinderblocks and held together with duct tape.

I knocked on the door and Lula stayed about ten feet behind me with her gun drawn.

"Put the gun away," I said. "You'll scare him."

"What if the snake attacks us? That snake could eat you in one gulp. I saw it with my own eyes. It's the King Kong of snakes."

Diggery opened the door and squinted out at me. "I didn't do it," he said.

"What didn't you do?" I asked him.

"Whatever it is you're gonna arrest me for."

"I'm not going to arrest you. I want to hire you."

"You mean a job?"

"Yes."

"I don't need a job. I get food stamps."

"What about the snake? Can you get snake food with food stamps?"

"We just let him loose under the trailer to catch rats. We got enough rats to feed a whole pack of pythons."

"I'm outta here," Lula said. "I heard that and I'm not staying around with no snakes and rats. I got peep-toed shoes on and my big toe could look like a snack."

"It could be fun," I said to Diggery. "I know where there are some unrecorded graves."

"Unrecorded graves? It's hard to find them these days. Mostly you have to go to the landfill in Camden. I might be interested in some unrecorded graves."

"Terrific. Grab a shovel and let's go."

"Hey, Melvin," Simon Diggery yelled into the dark trailer. "We got some unrecorded graves to dig. Put your pants on and let's go."

Simon and Melvin followed us in a pickup that was in worse shape than their trailer. It was eaten up with cancerous rot, spewing black smoke, its tailgate held on with clothesline.

"It's never gonna make Route 1," Lula said. "I think I just saw the muffler fall off."

I was praying that the truck would hold together long enough to get to the cemetery because I *really* didn't want to put Melvin and Simon in the Buick.

We turned in to Sunshine Memorial Park and the truck was down to fifteen miles per hour, lurching and belching fire from the undercarriage. We made it to the unmarked graves, the truck gasped to a shuddering stop, and Simon and Melvin jumped out and got shovels. All excited. Ready to go.

"Jeez," I said. "Sorry about your truck."

"What about it?" Simon said.

"It sounded like there might be a mechanical problem."

"It's just temperamental," Simon said. "It gets ornery when we go a distance. Where's these graves you were talking about?"

"There are three of them in this area. Two on this side of the road and one on the other." I showed him my file picture of Geoffrey Cubbin. "I'm looking for this guy. If you find him he's mine, but I'll give you his jewelry if he has any. The others are all yours."

"Sounds fair," Simon said. "Let's get to work."

"We're going to hell for this," Lula said. "This here's sacrilegious or something. I'm pretty sure it's a sin."

Thirty minutes into the dig Simon yelled out that he'd found something.

"I think this might be your man," he said. "Come take a look."

"I'm not looking," Lula said. "I get nightmares about these things. I get chased by boogeymen all the time. Sometimes they look like people I know."

I walked over and forced myself to look beyond the pile of dirt Simon had accumulated. I caught a glimpse of a black body bag partially unzipped, and what was in the bag wasn't in perfect shape.

"He's still pretty good," Simon said. "I've seen a lot worse. Sure he's a little wormy and all, but you could see he's got the right color hair. Some of that's left. And I took a ring off him that had his initials on."

"Good enough for me," I said. "Zip him up and get him in my car."

Simon and Melvin lugged the body bag to the Buick and shoved it into the trunk.

"He don't all fit," Simon said. "He's not at that stage yet where he bends easy. Problem is as you can see he's a little gassed up."

"Maybe I could borrow your clothesline to hold the lid down," I said to Simon.

Simon took the clothesline off his tailgate, the tailgate fell onto the road, and he picked it up and tossed it into the back of his truck.

Simon and Melvin tied the lid of my trunk to the bumper so Geoffrey Cubbin wouldn't slide out onto the highway, and we were good to go. I gave Simon and Melvin each a twenty and they thanked me profusely and went back to digging.

"I have to say I admire your determination to get the job done," Lula said when we were back on Route 1. "I'm freaked out about it all, but I gotta hand it to you, you got guts."

"Hey," I said. "No guts, no glory."

"That's so true," Lula said. "I say that all the time. That's practically my motto."

I turned off Route 1 onto Olden and slowed down. "Keep your eye on Geoffrey in case he bounces out when we go over the railway tracks," I said to Lula.

"He seems like he's okay," Lula said. "I think a lady just run her car up on a curb looking at him, but he's holding tight."

I swung into the police lot and parked near the back entrance. Lula and I ran around to the back of the Buick, untied the clothesline, and lugged Cubbin in to the docket lieutenant.

"Geoffrey Cubbin," I said, setting him on the floor. I pulled my documentation out of my messenger bag and presented it. "I need a body receipt."

There were a bunch of cops, keeping their distance, gawking at us.

"Lady, that smells really bad," one of them said.

"He's a little gassy," I told him.

"Yeah, and we can all relate to that," Lula said.

"How am I supposed to know it's Cubbin?" the lieutenant at the desk asked.

"Some of his hair is left," I said. "And he's got most of his teeth. You can identify him by his teeth."

Clumps of dirt were still clinging to the body bag, falling off onto the floor.

The lieutenant grimaced. "What did you do, dig him up?"

"Of course not," I said. "That would be illegal, right?"

"Right," the lieutenant said.

"We found him on the side of the road," Lula said. "We was driving along and we saw this body bag and stopped to investigate and lo and behold we realized it was Geoffrey Cubbin. He must have fallen off a truck or something."

The lieutenant looked down at Cubbin. "I can't give you a receipt until we identify him."

"That could take weeks," I said. "Maybe months."

"I can't wait months," Lula said. "Somebody's gonna have to step up to the plate and make an executive decision here. And in fact this is making me all upset and I'm gonna be sick. I have a delicate constitution and I feel my lunch coming up. It was cabbage leaves stuffed with rice and pork. It's not gonna be good. Cabbage throw-up is the worst. Oh Lord, I'm sweatin' now. It's coming up any time."

"Get her out of here!" the lieutenant said.

"No way," Lula said. "Even though I'm sick I can't leave until she gets the body receipt. Maybe if I stick my finger down my throat it would come up faster and I'd feel better."

"That's disgusting," he said.

"It's just nature taking its course," Lula said. "I might even be getting diarrhea too!"

He grimaced and scribbled out a receipt. "Take it! *Go!* Take her with you."

Lula and I hustled out of the station, jumped into the Buick, and took off.

"That went well," Lula said. "I'm hungry. All that talk about cabbage and pork got me thinking about one of them Taylor Pork Roll sandwiches."

• • •

I had one loose end to tie up. I had Susan Cubbin drinking coffee in a kitchen filled with gold bars, not knowing what to do with them. I parked and followed Lula into the office. I gave Connie my body receipt and took a chair by her desk.

"What do you know about gold?" I asked her.

"Not a whole lot. What do you want to know?"

"How much a bar is worth."

Connie surfed around on her computer. "Gold is up today. A kilo bar would be around fifty thousand dollars."

I was pretty sure Susan had kilo bars. I punched some numbers into the calculator on my phone and gasped at the result. Over the course of Geoffrey's career at Cranberry Manor he'd embezzled five million dollars, converted it to gold, and the gold was now worth $6,650,000. Turned out Geoffrey Cubbin was the best thing that ever happened to the folks at Cranberry Manor.

"Gotta go," I said to Connie and Lula.

"Are you buying gold?" Connie asked.

"No. I'm helping Susan Cubbin clean house. I'll tell you all the details tomorrow."

Forty minutes later I was in Susan's kitchen.

"It's worth more than he stole," I told her. "Gold has risen in value since Geoffrey bought it. All you have to do is take the gold to Cranberry Manor and tell the residents it was a misunderstanding, that Geoffrey was actually making smart investments on their behalf. They'll probably name a wing after him."

I wasn't a hundred percent sure it would go down like that but it was the best I could do.

Susan had sheets draped over the stacks of gold. "How am I going to get this moved? Do I need to hire an armored truck?"

"I have a friend," I said.

I called Ranger and told him I needed to transport 133 kilos of gold.

"Now?"

"Now would be good."

"I'll send Tank with a couple cars. I have a client meeting in five minutes. I assume I'm not necessary."

"You're desirable, but in this case not necessary," I told him.

"Babe," Ranger said. And he disconnected.

Two Rangeman SUVs arrived, we loaded the SUVs and headed out. I led the parade in the Buick, and Susan brought up the tail in her van. We parked in front of Cranberry Manor and I told Tank to stack the gold up in the lobby.

"This is from Geoffrey," Susan Cubbin said to the room filled with gawkers. "It was all a misunderstanding. I found a note from him, and it turns out he was investing your money in gold and now you're all rich."

There was stunned silence and then a cheer went up.

"It worked," Susan said to me. "Let's get out of here before they start asking questions."

"We'll need a receipt," I said to Carol, the facility's tour guide.

She counted the bars and wrote out a receipt. "One hundred and thirty-two bars," she said.

I looked at Susan.

"I might have left one in the kitchen," Susan said.

"One hundred and thirty-two bars is correct," I said to Carol.

• • •

I stopped at Pino's, got lasagna with meat sauce, extra bread, and tiramisu for dessert, and took it to Morelli's house. He was on the couch, watching television with his leg propped up on the coffee table. Bob was by his side, offering sympathy, standing guard.

"How's it going?" I asked.

"It's going good. And it's even better now that I have you here with dinner."

I went to the kitchen and got knives and forks and napkins and beer and brought it all back to Morelli.

"I hear Cranberry Manor had some good fortune today," Morelli said. "Apparently a photographer and a news guy arrived shortly after you left."

"Geoffrey had the bars buried in his backyard. Susan found a landscape plan and dug them up. When I got there she had them stacked up in her kitchen."

"Why did she give them back?"

I shrugged. "I guess she felt bad. I think she might not have had a storybook marriage, but she cared for him. Probably she still loved him. She didn't want to be the one to rat on him."

"Suppose it was me," Morelli said. "And I had gold buried in my backyard . . ."

"I'd love you even more."

Morelli grinned. "So are you telling me that you love me? Just not as much as if I were rich?"

"Yep. That's what I'm telling you."

"Good to know," Morelli said.

We ate dinner and watched television and Morelli was asleep on the couch by nine o'clock. I got him upstairs, gave him a pill, and tucked him in.

I carted Rex out to the Buick and drove to my apartment. Stars were out and the air felt warm and gentle. My apartment building looked benign and safe, dark against the night sky, lights shining from my neighbors' windows.

I took the elevator, walked the length of the hall, and balanced the hamster tank on one knee while I opened my front door. I stepped inside and flipped on the light. Everything looked perfect. No Orin splattered on the wall. No broken window. Clean floor.

There was a bottle of champagne on my kitchen counter plus a check and a note from Ranger.

For a job well done, the note said. *I'll be around later. I need a date.*

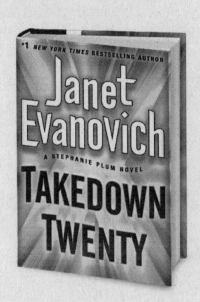

IT WAS LATE AT night and Lula and I were hunting down Salvatore Sunucchi, better known as Uncle Sunny, when Lula spotted Jimmy Spit. Spit had his prehistoric Cadillac Eldorado parked on the fringe of the Trenton public housing projects, half a block from Sunucchi's apartment, and he had the trunk lid up.

"Hold on here," Lula said. "Jimmy's open for business, and it looks to me like he got a trunk full of handbags. I might need one of them. A girl can never have too many handbags."

Five minutes later, Lula was examining a purple Brahmin bag studded with what Spit claimed were Swarovski crystals. "Are you sure this is a authentic Brahmin bag?" Lula asked Spit. "I don't want no cheap-ass imitation."

"I have it on good authority these are the real deal," Spit said. "And just for you I'm only charging ten bucks. How could you go wrong?"

Lula put the bag on her shoulder to take it for a

test drive, and a giraffe loped past us and continued on down the road, turning left at Sixteenth Street and disappearing into the darkness.

"I didn't see that," Lula said.

"I didn't see that neither," Spit said. "You want to buy this handbag or what?"

"That was a giraffe," I said. "It turned the corner at Sixteenth Street."

"Probably goin' the 7-Eleven," Spit said. "Get a Slurpee."

A black Cadillac Escalade with tinted windows and a satellite dish attached to the roof sped past us and hooked a left at Sixteenth. There was the sound of tires screeching to a stop, then gunfire and an ungodly shriek.

"Not only didn't I see that giraffe, but I also didn't see that car or hear that shit happening," Spit said.

He grabbed the ten dollars from Lula, slammed the trunk lid shut, and took off.

"They better not have hurt that giraffe," Lula said. "I don't go with that stuff."

I looked over at her. "I thought you didn't see the giraffe."

"I was afraid it might have been the 'shrooms on my pizza last night what was making me see things. I mean it's not every day you see a giraffe running down the street."

My name is Stephanie Plum, and I work as a bond enforcement officer for Vincent Plum Bail Bonds. Lula is the office file clerk, but more often than not she's my wheelman. Lula is a couple inches shorter than I am, a bunch of pounds bigger, and her skin is a lot darker. She's a former streetwalker who gave up her corner but kept her wardrobe. She favors neon colors and animal prints, and she fearlessly tests the limits of spandex. Today her brown hair was streaked with shocking pink to match a tank top that barely contained the bounty God had bestowed on her. The tank top stopped a couple inches above her skintight, stretchy black skirt, and the skirt ended a couple inches below her ass. I'd look like an idiot if I dressed like Lula, but the whole neon pink and spandex thing worked for her.

"I gotta go see if the giraffe's okay," Lula said. "Those guys in the Escalade might have been big game poachers."

"This is Trenton, New Jersey!"

Lula was hands on hips. "So was that a giraffe, or what? You don't think it's big game?"

Since Lula was driving we pretty much went where Lula wanted to go, so we jumped into her red Firebird and followed the giraffe.

There was no Escalade or giraffe in sight when we turned the corner at Sixteenth, but a guy was lying facedown in the middle of the road, and he wasn't moving.

"That don't look good," Lula said, "but at least it's not the giraffe."

Lula stopped just short of the guy in the road, and we got out and took a look.

"I don't see no blood," Lula said. "Maybe he's just takin' a nap."

"Yeah, or maybe that thing implanted in his butt is a tranquilizer dart."

"I didn't see that at first, but you're right. That thing's big enough to take down an elephant." Lula toed the guy, but he still didn't move. "What do you suppose we should do with him?"

I punched 911 into my phone and told them about the guy in the road. They suggested I drag him to the curb so he wouldn't get run over, and said they'd send someone out to scoop him up.

While we waited for the EMS to show I rifled the guy's pockets and learned that his name was Ralph Rogers. He had a Hamilton Township address, and he was fifty-four years old. He had a MasterCard and seven dollars.

The EMS truck slid in without a lot of fanfare. Two guys got out and looked at Ralph, who was still on his stomach with the dart stuck in him.

"That's not something you see every day," the taller of the two guys said.

"The dart might have been meant for the giraffe," Lula told them. "Or maybe he's one of them shape-shifters, and he used to be the giraffe."

The two men went silent for a beat, probably trying to decide if they should get the butterfly net out for Lula.

"It's a full moon," the shorter one finally said.

The other guy nodded, and they loaded Ralph into the truck and drove off.

"Now what?" Lula asked me. "We going to look some more for Uncle Sunny, or we going to have a different activity, like getting a pizza at Pino's?"

"I'm done. I'm going home. We'll pick up Sunny's trail tomorrow."

Truth is, I was going home to a bottle of champagne that I had chilling in my fridge. It had been dropped off as partial payment for a job I did for my friend and sometimes employer Ranger. The champagne had come with a note suggesting that Ranger needed a date. Okay, so Ranger is hot, and luscious, and magic in bed, but that doesn't totally compensate for the fact that the last time I was Ranger's date I was poisoned.

The champagne had been left on my kitchen counter yesterday, and I was saving it for a special occasion. Seemed like seeing a giraffe running down the street qualified.

Lula drove me back to the bonds office, where I picked up my car, and twenty minutes later I was in my apartment, leaning against the kitchen counter, guzzling champagne. I was watching my hamster, Rex, run on his wheel when Ranger walked in.

Ranger doesn't bother with trivial matters like knocking, and he isn't slowed down by a locked door. He owns an elite security firm that operates out of a seven-story stealth office building located in the center of Trenton. His body is perfect, his moral code is unique, his thoughts aren't usually shared. He's in his early thirties, like me, but his life experience adds up to way beyond his years. He's of Latino heritage. He's former Special Forces. He's sexy, smart, sometimes scary, and frequently overly protective of me. He was currently armed and wearing black fatigues with the Rangeman logo on his sleeve. That meant he was most likely filling in for one of the men on patrol.

"Working tonight?" I asked him.

"Taking the night shift for Hal." He looked at my glass. "Are you drinking champagne out of a beer mug?"

"I don't have any champagne glasses."

"Babe."

"Babe" covers a lot of ground for Ranger. It could be the prelude to getting naked. It could be total exasperation. It could be a simple greeting. Or, as in this case, I'd amused him.

Ranger smiled ever so slightly and took a step closer to me.

"Stop," I said. "Don't come any closer. The answer is no."

His brown eyes locked onto me. "I didn't ask a question."

"You were going to."

"True."

"Well, don't even think about it, because I'm not going to do it."

"I could change your mind," he said.

"I don't think so."

Okay, truth is Ranger *could* change my mind. Ranger can be very persuasive.

Ranger's cellphone buzzed, he checked the message and moved to the door. "I have to go. Give me a call if you change your mind."

"About what?"

"About anything," Ranger said.

"Okay, wait a minute. I want to know the question."

"No time to explain it," Ranger said. "I'll pick you up tomorrow at seven o'clock. A little black dress would be good. Something moderately sexy."

And he was gone.

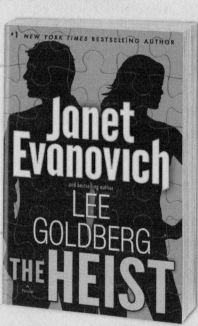